GRIM RIDERS

Tim Curran

GRIM RIDERS

1

It was flat country. Flat, dry, and dead. The ground was hard-packed, blown by rivers of sand, loose stones jutting everywhere as if at one time long past a great and rushing stream had wound through there and these were its bones.

Beneath that merciless, hazy Arizona sky, Nathan Partridge came riding on a dappled mare, his narrow face a study in shadow beneath the brim of a flat-crowned hat. He was long and lean, raw-boned, wiry as a bundle of compacted springs.

There was death in his eye and ice in his heart.

He kept going, pushing on, because he knew no other way.

The mare was thirsty and nickered for water.

But there would be none; not until Partridge got where he was going and if the horse collapsed from exhaustion and dehydration before that, then he'd leave it to die. To broil under that furnace sun which rode the western sky like a shimmering pearl. Maybe the nag wasn't used to laboring in the afternoon heat. Maybe it had never known the sort of desperation and inhumanity that had driven Partridge himself for these past five years behind the walls.

After all, it was just an animal.

And Partridge was a man...or nearly. And a man could take things that would make an animal lay down and die. A man could subsist through sheer force of will and steel himself on nothing but hatred and anger. This was beyond an animal. In prison, Partridge had taken punishment and deprivation that would've killed ten other men. His mind was a relentless machine, turning, moving, plotting.

He had been riding through the burning Arizona desert all day and had yet to take a drink of water. In prison, he had gone days. Suffering was his specialty.

But he knew that without rest, the horse would not make it much more than another mile at best. It needed rest. Feed. Water. Because if Partridge himself could sup full on suffering, the horse could not.

He ran a leathery tongue over his flaking lips, his eyes forever fixed on the horizon, unblinking colored glass. In prison, he had gone as much as fifteen minutes without blinking his eyes. An exercise in mind over body, nothing more. After five minutes, your eyes felt like they'd been rubbed full of sand; after ten, rubbed with salt, tears coursing down your cheeks; and after fifteen, agony like razors were being scraped over your eyeballs. It was then you shut them until the red-hot aching ceased. But you did it to prove that your mind was the master of the flesh that housed it. You did it to prove to yourself that there was nothing you couldn't take. That your will was iron and immovable once its path was set.

Partridge's will was like that.

And, if in a day or a month, he fell to earth and died as all men must, then it would be because his body was weak. But never his will, his spirit. He figured that even when his body was nothing but an envelope of buzzard-picked skin, his will would still exist— immortal, indestructible, a force of nature like blowing wind or lightning cutting a dark sky.

All day long, the landscape had been a monotonous, flat waste. A tedious and repetitive expanse of emptiness that was maddening in its redundancy. Partridge had heard tell that this unvarying desert uniformity had driven men insane. And he did not doubt it.

Just ahead, the land began to dip and climb, the foothills of the Gila Bend Mountains beginning to make themselves known (though, in reality, they were a dozen miles away yet). He saw outcroppings of rocks ahead, pools of shadow and withered stands of vegetation, knew that while water was not near, there would be a place to rest for a time. The mare desperately needed it. And it would give him time to think before he reached Chimney Flats.

Because that's where it would begin…and maybe end.

2

He was making his way down a shallow, dry wash when he heard gunfire.

The mare became skittish and Partridge pulled on the cinch, at the same time stroking her mane and whispering softly to her. He led her down into the wash, behind a shadowed bank of stone. He tethered her to a slab of granite and made his way up a bluff of crumbling rocks and wind-sculpted sand. At the top, he crawled on his belly through a parched stand of greasewood.

In a small valley just below, he saw a wagon and team. A man and woman huddled together. A trio of bandits ringing them in. There was no doubt in Partridge's mind that they were drunk, hopping and weaving about carelessly. The three of them wore Confederate hats, stained cotton shirts wet with spreading patches of sweat. Just a couple more Johnny Rebs having trouble facing the fact that they'd gotten their asses sorely whipped. Ridge runners. From his position atop the rise, Partridge was less than two hundred feet away. Much less. Close enough to smell the stink of them. Soundlessly, he moved back down the bluff. He slid his 1873 Winchester from the saddle boot and crab-crawled back. He could hear the Rebs insulting the man and his wife.

Give 'em ten more minutes, Partridge figured, and the whiskey in their bellies'll give em the courage to kill him and rape her.

Getting the drop on them was child's play. He already had a bead drawn on the fat one with the long, greasy hair. He looked like a bowling pin dipped in wet bacon lard. Partridge teased the trigger with his finger. He was going to kill them. He knew that much. It was only a matter of when.

None of your business, he told himself and kept telling himself, but he just wouldn't listen. None of your damn business. You should ride out, save yourself. Because you know there's men after you, that there's a bounty on you.

But he had no intention of riding off.

Greaseballs like that, common bandits. If he didn't drop them today, then maybe tomorrow it would be him they gunned down. So, he would help the man and woman. Do his heroic bit and save their fool hides. But his reasons weren't entirely altruistic...his mare was done in and, way he was figuring it, after he did his manly, neighborly duty, he'd take the bandits' horses, money, guns, whatever else they had.

Hell, yes.

Soon they would start. He needed to get a clean shot. Or shots. What he wanted was for the Johnny Rebs to get clear of the man and woman...and the horses, of course. Didn't want to do them any damage. In this hard and brutal country, horses were worth a hell of a lot more than men. Particularly former Confederates turned outlaw. They were a dime a dozen and the countryside was peppered with their bones.

There. The three of them were away from the couple.

Now was the time.

Partridge followed the drunken stagger of the fat man with the sight of his Winchester. One eye squeezed shut, the other staring and unblinking, he aimed for the center of the fat man's back. Drawing in a shallow breath through tightly clenched teeth, he squeezed off a single shot. It struck the fat man directly between the shoulder blades, the impact throwing him forward face-first into the dirt. The slug pulverized his spine and ejected vertebrae right through the front of his chest. The two others went for their pieces, but it did them no good. Partridge levered and fired two more times. Before the fat man had even kissed the desert floor, he shot the second one through the throat and third one in the side of the head, his skull coming apart in a bloody mist.

The woman and man were crouched by a wagon wheel, holding each other. The woman was shrieking out what almost sounded like passages from the good book in her hysteria.

Partridge went down to his mare and mounted again, keeping the Winchester in his grip. He took the reins and led the tired horse up the bluff and down into the little valley. He took his time, the horse's shoes ringing out over flat stones. In the desert, you didn't hurry, you didn't push things. Everything came about in its own way.

Ten feet from the wagon, he watched the wide-eyed faces of the man and woman just as they watched him—a tall man astride a dappled mare in dusty, dark trail clothes. They watched his long, narrow face, the grim set of his mouth.

"You folks unharmed?" he asked them, his voice even.

The woman was crying, nodding, shaking her head and trembling. The man held her tight, stroked her auburn hair. "Easy, Gwen," he told her. "It's all over now. All over." He looked up at Partridge, managed to smile. "Yes, sir. We're fine now." He looked at the bodies lying in the dirt. "Did you…"

"Yes. From up there."

The man sighed. "Thank you."

The woman got hold of herself. "God bless you. Are you...you the law?"

"No, not the law. Just a traveler like yourself. One that's always willing to help those in need."

"Bless you," the woman said.

Partridge waited there on the mare, his shoulder-length raven hair stirring in the dry wind. He sported a drooping black mustache which hung to his sharp jawline like stalactites, his eyes black and shining like those of a hunting cat seen from the depths of a cave.

He studied his new friends.

They were a young couple, couldn't have been anywhere near thirty. It was a rough sort of life for them he bet. The country was harsh and unforgiving.

Partridge dismounted, his stovepipe boots and army spurs kicking up clouds of dust as they struck the earth. He tethered his horse to the wagon—an old mud wagon that had seen far too much use, heaped with crates and bundles and sacks, everything the couple owned.

"Name's Davy Wilson. This is Gwen, my wife." He offered his hand.

Partridge gave it a limp shake, but did not offer his own name. He touched the brim of his hat to the lady, pulled off his canteen, deciding maybe it was time before he dried out like a prune in the sun.

There came a groaning from the far side of the wagon. Partridge looked at them and they looked at him. Gwen seemed almost apologetic. "Mr. Styles," she said. "Dear God...it slipped my mind with everything...oh dear..."

Partridge followed them around the side. There was a man lying in the dirt, his eyes barely focusing. He seemed to see them and not see them. He was painted up red, more holes in him than a colander. Partridge squatted next to him, looked him over. It was maybe another five miles or so to Chimney Flats. There was no way in hell this man would make it that far. And even if he did, no surgeon could hope to plug him up.

Partridge stood up, shook his head. "Won't be long. If there's something you want to say," he said to Gwen, "then you'd better say it now."

Styles was looking up at something in the sky, something none of them could see. Partridge had seen it before—dying men staring intently at some invisible horizon. Heaven? The Holy Ghost? Partridge didn't discount it nor did he accept it.

Styles' lips trembled. There was a ragged, whistling sound as he breathed. A bubble of blood expanded and deflated with each breath.

"We hired him on as sort of a guide," Wilson said. "He was a good man. Good with a gun. He'd been in the Army years back. Fought the Arapaho and Cheyenne in the sixties…"

He waxed on about the virtues and skills of Mr. Styles. Partridge did not listen. It was a eulogy and nothing more. If he was as smart as Wilson claimed, the Rebs would never have gotten the drop on him.

"…seemed all right. Came right up to us, friendly like, told us they'd ride into Chimney Flats with us. Sounded all fine and proper. Then they opened up on Styles…well, shit, you know the rest."

"I know the rest," Partridge said and stalked off amongst the bodies of the bandits. He flipped the fat one over with the scuffed tip of his boot. The man's chest was a bloody crater. His eyes were wide open and staring. The other shot in the head was equally as dead, flies blanketing his face, investigating the crevice of his skull. But the third one Patridge'd popped in the throat…he was still among the living. Barely, but still there. He was drawing in raw, bloody breaths, foamy slime running from his mouth. He glared up with feral hatred.

Partridge brought the barrel of the Winchester inches from his left eye socket.

"Dear God," Gwen said. "You can't…I mean, you can't…"

"Turn away, ma'am, if it offends you," was all he would say on the matter. He pulled the trigger and the man's brains exploded into the hot sand, ropy bits of them glistening like maggots in a dead cat's belly. Partridge studied his death, then turned away. "Better this way, you see. Even a bandit like this deserves better than to be left to the buzzards."

"But they feed on the dead," Gwen said.

"They'll feed on anything that don't have the good sense to swat them away or don't have the strength," he explained. "It's better this way. Believe me."

Partridge turned back to them, but his real attention was focused on the bandits' horses picketed off yonder in the rocks. "Tell me, Davy," he said. "Where were you headed?"

"Coming from Mohawk. Making for Chimney Flats. Got me work there."

Partridge nodded. "Don't say?" He went over to his mare and slid the Winchester back into its scabbard. He looked up at the cloudless sky. "Hell of a time of year to make such a crossing."

"Don't I know it," Wilson said. "If you hadn't come along…"

There was an ancient flintlock lying in the dirt. Partridge stooped over and picked it up. He handed it to Wilson. "Yours?" Wilson nodded and Partridge said, "Not much of a weapon for this country."

"Best I could do."

A head popped out of the wagon. A boy in a drooping sodbuster hat much like Wilson's. His face was muddled with grime, giving it a dark cast like maybe the boy was part Apache, spent his life in the wind and sun. There were two clean trails down his cheeks, the paths of tears.

"It's okay now, Louis," Gwen said.

She made to pull him out of the wagon. He shrugged her hands aside defiantly, every bit the little man. He hopped off on his own. He stood in Partridge's shadow, studying him as if he were a new species of bug, not entirely sure what to make of his family's savior.

He took off his hat, aired his head. "You a desperado, mister?"

Partridge said, "No, son."

"You a lawman?"

"No, son."

"Indian fighter?"

"No, son."

"Road agent?"

"No, son, just a man like your father. No better, no worse."

Louis walked around Partridge in a tight circle, hands on hips. He saw the bodies sprawled around them, but had seen such things before. Not frequently, but enough so that the novelty had long since vanished.

"You killed 'em all?" he said.

Wilson took him by the arm, dragged him over to his mother. "You leave mister…ah…*mister…"* He chuckled. "Never did catch your name, stranger."

Partridge looked away. "Smith. Call me Smith."

He helped Wilson load Styles into the wagon, placing him unceremoniously atop tarp-covered crates. Gwen and the boy brought the outlaws' horses over. Three fine animals. But the best was a taut-muscled gelding with a double-rig saddle and a coat like polished black glass. Partridge had found his new ride. As a bonus there was a Greener in the saddle boot—a sawed-off, double-barrel shotgun. He had always favored such weapons. There was also money in the saddlebag…something else he had always favored.

"I'll help myself to this one if you don't mind," he told Wilson as he transferred his saddlebags to the gelding. "I'll ride with you folks far as Chimney Flats. See that you make town all right, then I have business elsewhere."

"We'd appreciate that, Mr. Smith," Gwen said.

3

They tethered the leads of the other two horses and Partridge's mare to the back of the wagon. Then Wilson and he began collecting up the dead men's weapons. Partridge found a .38 Colt Lightning and a Shofield .45. He kept these, too, as well as the belts and cartridges for each. He buckled the Colt on. It was in a cross-draw scabbard that rode his left hip. He hadn't worn such a fine weapon in five years.

"You folks can keep everything else. Horses, too, including my own. Worth a bit of money when you get into town. Help you get started." He studied the mountains in the distance, the desert behind them winding out flat and lifeless as a washboard. "We'd best get going. We're in Coyotero territory here. Out here like this, we'd be easy marks."

"Haven't seen any injuns whatsoever," Gwen said.

"And you won't," Partridge told her. "But I'm willing to bet they've seen you. Might be watching us all right now."

They all looked around nervously.

But it was just bullshit intended to get them moving. Apaches these days were a lean and starved lot languishing in reservations like San Carlos. There were still a few renegade bands out raiding in the mountains, but their world was one of the past now. Word had it even Geronimo, last of a fearless breed, was holed up in the Sierra Madres. His days were numbered.

Partridge knew very well the way of the Apache. He'd fought them more than once. He had no real love for them…nor did he hate them. Like rattlesnakes or tornadoes, they just were: a force of nature. But he did respect them and their ways. In a fight, few white men were their match. Very few. They were experts at stealth and concealment. They could go to ground where a white man could see no cover. You could practically step right on them without knowing they were there. They'd lived in the deserts and mountains for hundreds of years and they swam in them like fish in a stream. Shadows, ghosts. There one minute and gone the next. And they were raiders, for pleasure and profit. He didn't hold this against them. It was their life and they knew no other.

And now that was at an end.

For some reason, this saddened him. Too much of the old world was dying now and year by year by year, there was less of a place in it for people like the Apache or men like Nathan Partridge.

Riding towards Chimney Flats with the Wilsons was not entirely altruistic, again, on his part. Maybe he thought they were nice people—he did—and maybe he didn't want anything more to happen to them—he didn't—but his real reason was that, if anyone was looking for him, they wouldn't be expecting him to be riding with a family. It had been over ten days now since—

"Hey, mister," the boy said to him. "You got a fast draw?"

Partridge found that for the first time in these five years he had a desire to smile. But the muscles in his mouth didn't seem to work. His face had been drawn hard and etched firm like an epitaph cut into marble for so long that a smile just wouldn't come.

"No, son," he said. "Speed is of little virtue, I'm afraid, only accuracy counts."

Wilson laughed as he settled into the wagon and took the reigns from his wife. "You'll have to forgive him, Mr. Smith. He's been reading them dime novels and such. Got his head full of frontier dreams."

"And who is it he gets them from?" Gwen chided him.

Wilson only smiled conspiratorially.

They rode out with Partridge in the lead. The land became fertile as the Gila Bend Mountains reared up. It was still desert for the most part, but jutting now with outcroppings of rocks and sudden dips. Great flat tables of sandstone were piled atop each other like poorly-shuffled cards. There were clumps of prickly pear and the shaggy tops of mesquites.

The pounding of the horses' hoofs and the creak of the wagon wheels disrupted the midday ruminations of a big sidewinder rattlesnake and it slid away over the sand and stones. An eagle flew high above, screeching.

And was that a good sign or a bad one?

Partridge rode on wondering and wondering who would hunt him. There had to be a bounty on him. He was certain of it. The law would be looking—federal marshals and local sheriffs and their deputies—but he knew from experience that bounties and the lure of easy cash would bring killers and manhunters of every conceivable stripe—outlaws, renegades, bounty hunters, soldiers, out of work hands. They were always around looking to fill their pokes. Even the local Indians would be keeping an eye out. Not all of them, but many. For a man in his position, death came in many forms, necktie parties and cold steel around every corner.

But they wouldn't take him.

They'd never take him back. He was getting what he'd come for and God help any dumb sonofabitch that got in the way of that. Whether they wore a badge or not, they'd die all the same. This was his mantra. He lived by it, died by it. It was better to die free, he figured, gun in hand, blood in your mouth, than to live as a caged animal, full belly, head packed with impossible dreams. No, death was sometimes better. Sometimes the only real choice.

They navigated a dipping hollow clogged with chollo and greasewood and clawed their way up a steep shale-littered slope. Partridge's heart began to pound. He couldn't honestly say the last time he'd felt his heart in his chest, alive and virile. Now it had woken up, was beginning to stretch and yawn, filling itself with hot life. It had been so long, so very long…

Chimney Flats was nestled below, shaded by scrawny pines. It lived and breathed in the ominous shadows of the Gila Bend Mountains, which looked as if they might topple over at any moment and crush the little hamlet. He studied the crags and peaks, billowy white clouds like wads of fluffed cotton passing just over their tips. The motion of the clouds made the mountain seem to move, to tip forward.

It was beautiful country. As dry as the desert was, the mountains were equally as lush. Carpeted in green from spruce and fir trees, capped in white where the snow-belt began. It positively sucked the wind from his lungs. He had forgotten just how breathtaking it all was. He could almost taste that high alpine air dispelling the furnace kiss of the desert.

Chimney Flats occupied a great and level slab of real estate in a countryside that was all peaks and bluffs. To all sides were pines and towers of volcanic rock that, yes, looked oddly like brick chimneys thrusting from the earth. Hence the name. But to Partridge those towers had always reminded him of withered and worn fingers reaching skyward, as if they were biding their time, awaiting the proper moment to clasp into a fist and crush the defiant little town of his childhood.

"By God, there she is," Wilson said.

He and his son took off their hats and simultaneously hooted and hollered.

Partridge, despite himself, was happy for them. Happy in the black and cold clot of his heart. Maybe like dark ashes in a firepit, there was still some warmth beneath, it just needed a little stirring was all. He was happy for them, but envious as well. He would never know such peace and contentment as they enjoyed on a daily basis. His would always be a hard life awaiting a hard death.

Chimney Flats looked like a cluster of toadstools from where they were—homes, stables, barns, and pastures, all cut through by a main road upon which brooded churches and saloons and liveries and mercantiles and, yes, brothels. All the things which made life possible and pleasurable. All the structures were bleached colorless by the winds and weather like bones on a hillside. Off to the right was a graveyard riding a hill and beyond, in the distance, farms and log houses.

He had arrived after so long.

"This is where I leave you folks," he said. "You may want to mention those bandits to the sheriff, though I'll doubt he'll want to bother with the bodies. Buzzards'll strip 'em soon enough."

"Seems we owe you a great deal…" Gwen started to say, but he was already riding off, hand raised in good-bye.

"Good luck, desperado," the boy called after him.

Partridge rode off and was soon just a shadow topping a rise and then was nothing. The Wilsons sat there silently for a time, just watching the landscape where it had swallowed up their savior.

"We can thank the good Lord this day that he still feels fit to put men like our Mr. Smith on this earth," Gwen said, adjusting her bonnet.

"I've been doing just that," her husband said.

"Bet he's a bankrobber or a killer," Louis said. "Wanted all over the Territories. You think?"

"Shush with that," Gwen said, ruffling his hair which was like cornsilk in the breeze blowing down from the mountains. "He's no such thing."

But the truth was that the boy was right and they were wrong. What they knew of "Mr. Smith" would have filled a thimble and what they didn't know would have overflowed oceans. For he *was* a killer and bank robber and many things they would never know of. Couldn't know of.

But right then he was a wanted man.

Nearly two weeks earlier he'd escaped from Yuma Prison.

4

Partridge stopped in the cemetery which had no name.

Born in Wichita, Kansas, but raised in Chimney Flats, he'd never known it to be called anything other than "the cemetery on the hill" or "the old boneyard up yonder". He tethered his gelding to a stunted, dead oak and walked amongst the graves. There were a few marble slabs and stones belonging to the more prosperous members of the community, but most were simple affairs—

wooden crosses and plaques. Rough-hewn for the most part, they were bleached by the sun and weather. His mother was here, dead some seventeen years now. As was his kid brother and baby sister, both of whom had expired of the grippe one long, harsh winter when Partridge was but seven.

He found their crosses.

His throat felt suddenly tight. They were faded, kissed by mildew, ravaged by the harsh climate, but he found them, all right. Mother. Sister. Brother. Side by side. All dead and buried these many years. Partridge missed them. He hadn't thought much about them in some time…but now that he did, he missed them.

So long ago. So very long ago.

Jesus.

And as he missed them, he also envied them, by God. Dead. Gone. Why did that seem almost *preferable* now? Was it because life had become an endless series of hardships piled one atop another and when he looked towards the future all he saw was pain and despair and violent death? Maybe. But as he thought of them lying in the grave, some part of him wanted to curl up tight with them and sleep, just sleep. It would have been so much easier that way.

But he hadn't come here for that. Maybe he shouldn't have come here at all.

He plugged a black cheroot into the corner of his mouth, lit it and drew off it slowly. A wind coursed down from the mountains, cool as frozen bones. It blew among the pines behind him, howling through lonesome places. He swallowed down his misery, his longing for those long dead. It went down uneasily like warm grease in his throat.

But he felt better.

He moved amongst the graves, searching, searching.

She was here somewhere. She had to be.

He kept at it, hunting through the tangled grasses, grasshoppers launching themselves away at his approach. Somewhere a cicada buzzed. He kept looking, but also listened for the approach of riders. What he was expecting could come at any time and he had to be ready. His fingers brushed the Colt .38. He could hear his gelding pawing at the earth, pulling at its lead.

He found what he was looking for in a shady spot hidden by clumps of juniper.

A simple wooden cross. On it was written:

ANNA MARIE PARTRIDGE 1861-1885

That was it then.

She was dead.

Partridge took off his hat and sat cross-legged over her grave. He thought of the last time he'd seen her. It was at the trial, just after they'd sentenced him to ten years for train robbery. She'd been young and pretty and full of life, crying that they were carting her man away to the Arizona Territorial Prison at Yuma. He licked his lips, unable to shed a tear. They'd only been married a year. He'd been so busy in that time riding and robbing that he hadn't seen a lot of her. He wasn't even sure that he'd ever even truly loved her. He tried to picture himself with her...but it all seemed blurry in his head.

He stood up, blew smoke into the wind.

At least he knew it was true now. That was the important thing. The superintendent at Yuma Prison had called Partridge into his office last October, some eight months earlier now, and told him his wife had died in a fire. That his home had burned down, too. Everything he had, that he might return to someday, was all gone. Ashes.

Partridge hadn't truly believed it.

But now he had no choice.

He crushed his cheroot out under his boot and mounted his horse. He had to see the ruins of the house. That was what he needed now. And when he got there, he'd start digging. Start sifting through the old cinders and older memories. Because what he'd come for would still be there, he figured. Buried in the cold earth beneath the root cellar.

And he wasn't leaving without it.

5

Growing up in Chimney Flats, Partridge couldn't honestly remember seeing his father more than three or four times, if that.

Like a bad storm, from time to time he'd blow into town and make folks cover their heads, then move on. On these rare occasions he would hang around the farmhouse, mostly sleeping or drinking out in the barn. A week or two later, he'd disappear again. And the crazy thing was Partridge couldn't honestly remember his mother and father saying more than "Good morning" or "Good afternoon" to one another. It was a strange relationship and even a child could see that. If there was love burning between them (or even barely flickering), it seemed you would have needed an awfully big shovel to dig deep enough to find it.

His father, Jake Partridge, was a man of few words. When he was home, he entertained his friends out in the barn where they would talk into the wee hours of the morning. Drinking, always drinking. But to his children? Rarely a word was ever said. In Partridge's mind, the man was always an enigma. A stranger who visited now and then, a shadow of fleeting substance. Partridge could remember going deer hunting with him once when he was eight. Up in the Gilas. He rather doubted more than a dozen or two sentences ever passed between them.

His mother told him his father was always running off to one business venture or another, always trying to make something of himself. She would tell Nathan this like maybe she wanted to believe it herself. Maybe she *needed* to believe it. He knew his father brought back money for them because he'd seen him hand his mother a wad of folded bills. And although they were never rich or even remotely well-to-do, there always seemed to be money for food and clothes, the few scant items that were needed around the farm.

His father was too busy trying to support them to ever stay long. He had business to attend to. Important business.

And Partridge believed this. Then when he was fourteen years old something happened to change all that.

Somebody told him the truth.

He'd gotten himself a job at the Four Points Saloon as a swamper. After school he'd spend six, sometimes seven hours a day mopping up urine and blood, vomit and spilled beer. He dragged drunks outside and helped the bartender carry a bullet-ridden body out to the undertaker's wagon more than once.

Chimney Flats was and would always be a violent little town. It had its share of miners and hunters and gunmen. Shootings were commonplace.

Then one day a drunken deputy sheriff from Phoenix was in the Four Points. He'd picked up a prisoner at the jail. Said prisoner was chained outside the bar to the hitching post, a crazy-eyed Tonto Apache that was wanted for murder in Phoenix. Every time Partridge peered through the batwings, the Apache was watching him. If he stayed there long enough, the Indian would start singing some high, shrieking dirge.

The deputy sheriff was a grotesque, obese man name of Stannard. He had a tumorous cluster on his nose that looked like a mouse giving birth. Twice in as many hours, he'd staggered outside and vomited, only to drag himself back in and start drinking again…after pistol-whipping his prisoner or urinating on him. Whichever struck his fancy.

Partridge was wiping down the bar when Stannard said to him, "Boy? Yeah, I'm goddamned well talking to *you,* boy. Get your miserable ass over here."

Partridge did. He wasn't exactly afraid being that he dealt with drunks and desperados on a daily basis. Yet, as he strolled over there, his heart began to thud like a war drum. Again, not out of fear really, but caution and anger that slowly began to boil in him like a vat of tar. All night long he'd been cleaning up after this bastard. The tobacco juice spit on the floor. The piss on the batwings when Stannard couldn't quite make it outside. It was starting to get under his skin like ringworm. His mother had told him he had inherited his father's temper, for good or bad. But he kept it in check. A few fights at school, but other than that he kept it tied up in a bag like a rattlesnake.

"Yes, sir?" he said, staring into that face like oiled mahogany, counting the black stubs of teeth, and steeling himself against that wet-dog stink that clung to the lawman in a noxious mist. "Yes, sir?"

"How old you, boy?"

"Fourteen, sir."

Stannard laughed at that, hawked up a wad of phlegm and spit it at Partridge's feet. "Know what they do with boys your age up in the mining camps?"

"No, sir."

"All right," the bartender, Mick, said. "Let's keep things clean here."

Stannard's face seemed to melt like lard on a hot stove lid, reconfiguring itself into something evil and violent. "You shut the fuck up, you worthless bag of goatshit or I'll bury you right now!" he snapped. His right hand went for the gun at his hip, but the holster was empty. He didn't seem to notice.

Partridge took a step back. He knew where the gun was; he'd seen the blowhard sonofabitch drop it out front. He was thinking he might go sneak it over to the Tonto. See what transpired on the road to Phoenix.

"What's your name, boy?" Stannard asked, turning back to him.

"Partridge. Nathan Partridge."

"Partridge?" he said like he'd bit into rotten meat. "Partridge? Your old man...he ain't...he ain't old Jake, is he?"

Partridge just nodded. "Yes, sir."

Stannard's eyes went wide with astonishment. Had someone slid an oiled thumb up his ass he couldn't have looked more shocked. *"Black Jake?* Your old man is *Black Jake Partridge?"* He burst into a fit of ugly laughter. "Well, I'll be goddamned. Black fucking Jake. You know what he does for a living, boy?"

Partridge looked over at Mick who looked away. "He's...he's a businessman."

Stannard barked out that ugly, harsh laughter once again. "Businessman? Well, ain't you the one! Ain't you just the mother-loving one! Sure, boy, old Jake is a businessman and his business is killing and robbing! He ain't nothing but a white trash Confederate murderer that spent the war raping and looting because he didn't have the balls to fight like a real man!"

Partridge just stood there, impotent.

It wasn't true.

It couldn't be true.

Stannard lapsed into silence and passed out shortly afterwards, still laughing from time to time. But the truth had come out. And once it was out, like a bad stink, there was no containing it. His mother burst into tears that night when he asked her. Nobody—not friends or neighbors—would tell him a thing. But they all got that same peculiar look on their faces when he asked—like maybe they'd just seen the Grim Reaper galloping in their direction and had to get away real fast.

The sheriff of Chimney Flats back then was a huge and deadly man name of Rafe Short. He was brutal to his enemies and only passably social to everyone else. He wore a sharp pirate's mustache that curled from his upper lip like a serpent. But he liked children and went out of his way to be kind to them, to protect them from vice. It was he who'd gotten Partridge the job at the Four Points.

"You seen your daddy lately, son?" he asked when the question was put to him.

"No. Not in four years," Partridge told him. "He used to stop by…but…"

"You don't see him because he's on the dodge, Nate. Your father is an outlaw." Saddened, it seemed, that any of this had come out into the open, the sheriff dug through his desk and brought out a sheaf of dodgers. The wanted fliers told the story, all right. "I'm sorry you had to find out."

And so was he.

It took him some years to put together the truth about "Black Jake" Partridge, but put it together he did. And like a corpse on a slab, when his father's life was laid open raw, the story it told was not very pleasant.

With Black Jake's genes bubbling in him, what he became was really no mystery. It was in the blood and blood, as they say, will always tell.

6

Partridge rode through a stand of spruce, following the winding road which led to the old farmhouse. He took the path slowly, liking the fresh green smell of the pines. He had traveled the road hundreds of times. Each step the gelding took, each turn of the trail, each cluster of rock, every deadfall and dip filled him with memories. Of being a boy and running these woods. Of being a man and wondering how his childhood disappeared so quickly. A thousand other things. The road was sadly overgrown now. You could still see the ruts made by wagon wheels, but a single season of spring growth had pocketed them with weeds. A few more summers and there would be no road.

After a time, the trees parted and he saw his home.

The home he had inherited from his mother, the family farm as it were. He drank it all in—the overgrown fields, the barn worn gray from the sun and wind, the windmill tank looking ready to collapse. It filled him with a longing for years past.

But there was no time for that.

If they were looking for him—and he knew they were—this was a good place to start.

He sat there on his horse, listening, *feeling,* waiting for some sign that he was being watched and waited for. He got none. After five minutes or so he kneed his mount and made his way to the house. It hadn't been much of a house, really. Just a log structure with a sod roof, but damn, it had been home. Now, of course, it wasn't much more than a jackstraw tumble of blackened timbers carpeted in dead leaves and needles from the previous Autumn. It looked, if anything, like a heap of scorched bones.

Partridge tethered his gelding to the hitching post out front.

He wanted nothing better than to sit down in the grass, maybe lay there in the sun and let the memories wash over him like some tideless, eternal sea. It didn't seem that much to ask for, but under the present set of circumstances, he knew it was like asking to draw down the moon. Time was precious and every moment hesitated or lost was deadly.

He left the Greener and .45, but strapped on the .38 Colt and took the Winchester with him. He went into the barn, praying there would still be tools left. There was. An old wooden plowing rig going to rot and rust. A few shovels, rakes, hoes, an axe. Lots of dead leaves which had blown in through the open door. The hay was dark and dry and smelled of organic decay. He could hear pigeons and sparrows nesting up in the rafters. A squirrel chirped from the loft.

He took a rake and a shovel, figuring (hoping) they would be enough for the job at hand. A three-foot rat snake slid out of the leaves and over the tip of his boot. He knew it was harmless. He had kept a few in the barn to keep down the mice. Better than a cat any day.

A few minutes later, he was navigating the sooty remains of the log house. Rough-hewn beams were balanced against one another precariously. It wouldn't pay to have one come down on him, trapping him there. He moved amongst them carefully and ducked beneath them. He'd gotten lucky there: if he'd had to actually move any of the big timbers, he would've needed more than one horse. But the big ones had fallen away. Pawing through the soot and ash and leaves, he kept trying to figure out where he was in the cabin, but it was impossible. The fire had been too thorough. Only the blackened mast of the chimney guided him.

After fifteen, twenty minutes of searching and shoveling and raking and sweating and cursing, he found what he was looking for: the iron ringbolt. Rusted and seized-up, it jutted from a bed of cinders. Pushing aside a tumble of planks, he was able to uncover the trapdoor itself. By this time, he was covered in black soot and powdered with gray ash. Using his hands, he dug the trapdoor free and then forced it open and over with everything he had.

The root cellar was untouched.

It was about four, maybe five feet in depth, squared-off earthen walls jutting with dry tree roots like the skeletal fingers of a cadaver. He threw the shovel and rake down there and jumped in after them. There was a ladder against one wall, but he didn't trust it anymore. Low shelves crowded one wall. The dirt floor was blanketed with shattered glass. The shelves had held canned pickles, beans, and onions. The heat from the fire had burst them. He remembered putting up the pickles himself. *Him.* Nathan Partridge, hardened outlaw as it were. But it was a task he'd relished as a boy and then later as a man. It was funny the things you took with you.

He raked away the glass. Then he started digging.

He'd buried the strongbox down three feet. He knew that to be a fact. He thought about it continually in prison, that box of dreams. After the Gila River Gang, as they'd come to be known, was massacred save Partridge himself, he'd gathered up all their booty and put it in the strongbox. More than $80,000. Only he and Anna Marie had known about it. He buried it and shortly afterwards, they'd come for him. Taking him down to Chimney Flats in chains. He hadn't resisted.

He dug down three feet. Then four.

It had to be here.

He kept digging until the floor was a cavern. But there was no box, no money, no evidence of the same. Exhausted, panting, his face and hands dark with dirt, he finally gave up. It just wasn't there.

Maybe the law had come and found it. Possible, but unlikely. The prison had a grapevine and if they had found it, he was sure he would've heard about it. Anna Marie had not mentioned them searching the house in her letters. He had strictly forbade her (as they chatted in his jail cell in Phoenix) from ever mentioning the loot to anyone or even making casual reference to it in the letters she wrote him. But he was certain that if the house had been turned upside down, she would've made mention of the fact.

So if the law didn't get it...

Partridge sat there on a heap of damp, rich earth, thinking and thinking. The prison superintendent told him she had perished in the fire. If that was true, then she hadn't absconded with it. Maybe she dug it up and hid it somewhere else. If she had, then his dreams of getting the money and riding down into Mexico a rich man had gone up in smoke.

Only Anna Marie would know what happened.

And she was dead...wasn't she?

He intended to find out.

7

He needed darkness for what had to be done.

He led his gelding off into the woods, through the foothills and thickets until he found the stream he was looking for. In early summer, it was still deep from winter run-off. He had fished trout here as a boy. He knew every stone, every bend, ever deep pool. Stripping away his soilcd clothes, he dipped himself in and scrubbed himself clean with a cake of soap. His gelding, picketed beneath the spreading branches of a big willow, nibbled grass and swatted flies with his tail.

When Partridge was clean, he dressed in brown cord pants and pulled on a gray army shirt, looping the suspenders over his shoulders. The clothes were a little baggy on him, but when they were leant to you by a dead man, you couldn't be too choosy.

He sat down by the bank and chewed jerky, sipped from his canteen.

He was trying to sort it all out in his mind, make some sense of it. Anna Marie and he had only been married a year when he went off to prison. And all that time he'd been riding with the Gila River Gang. He hadn't seen much of her. He had planned on that last heist, that last job. It would've set them up good. With the money they could've went anywhere. He had been thinking about a ranch up in Montana Territory. Never been there, but he liked what he heard. Mountains, lush forest. But no goddamn desert. These had been his plans. Then he was arrested and given ten years.

But what of Anna Marie?

What did he really know about her?

It pained him some thinking ill of the dead...but the truth was he hadn't really known her. He fell in love with that beautiful face of hers, those auburn tresses, that body standing full and hard beneath her dress. But beyond that, he knew very little. The wedding had been a quick affair. And when it was over, he was out with the gang. A few days home from time to time. That was it.

Jesus, he started thinking, what if—

But then a rider was coming in and there was no time to think.

8

"Way we're figuring it," the bounty hunter said, "our boy must've gone to ground around here somewhere."

"That so?" Partridge said.

It was an unreal scenario, that's what it was. Kress was a bounty hunter and he was hunting Partridge. He had started in Yuma and canvassed the desert and hills for these past two weeks before arriving here. He had no idea who it was he was sitting with.

"If I was him," Partridge said, "I reckon I'd be down in Mexico about now."

Kress laughed with a dry, knowing chuckle. "You'd think so, wouldn't you? But this Partridge, he's got loot hidden hereabouts somewhere. Law never did find where. If I get him—" he laughed that low chuckle again "—maybe I'll make that robbing, murdering sonofabitch tell me where he's hid it. Right before I give him a load of buckshot to the belly."

Partridge only nodded.

The law *hadn't* gotten the money then. Which laid the burden right back on Anna Marie. Partridge kept watching the Kress over the low cookfire they'd built. He drank the bounty hunter's coffee, ever aware of the Colt at his hip. Kress had a double-barrel Remington scattergun sitting next to him in the grass. There was no way the man recognized him as Nathan Partridge. Had prison changed him that much? He knew he was thinner, more wiry and muscular. His face had narrowed, sharpened with age. He supposed he did look like a different man.

Kress waxed on about other outlaws he'd run to ground. He was dressed in worn, threadbare buckskin. They were dark with sweat and dirt. He smelled of filth and urine, too many nights spent sleeping in leave piles and ditches. His face was a mass of pockmarks, a greasy beard hung from his chin.

"I was just over to his house," Kress said. "What there is of it after the fire and all. Thought maybe I'd get lucky. My guess is he's hiding up in the hills. But I'll sniff him out. I always do."

Sighing, Partridge took another look at the wanted flier Kress had. He remembered the photograph well. It had been taken in Chimney Flats shortly after his arrest. What bothered him was that there was a more recent photo out there somewhere. One they had taken for his files at Yuma Prison. Thankfully, this guy didn't have it. Not yet, anyway.

The question here was: what to do?

Kress was a threat to him. Men like him came and went regularly. If he dropped off the face of the earth, no one would suspect anything. At least not for a time. Yet, Partridge had had a belly full of killing. He was dog-tired of it. The benchmarks of his life were best described by men he'd gunned down. But he didn't see where he had a choice.

His hand slid down onto his lap, inching towards the Colt.

Kress sipped from his coffee, made a face and emptied out the tin cup, set it aside. He sat there staring at Partridge, like maybe he'd really just seen him for the first time, even though they'd been chewing the shit for the better part of an hour.

"You sure we never run across each other?" he asked, eyes narrowing in that face like desert stone. "Something about your eyes is familiar."

And maybe he was good at hunting men, but he wasn't very smart.

Partridge pulled the Colt in one swift motion.

Kress started, glanced sidelong at his shotgun. He attempted a smile, more of an upturned frown than anything. Partridge had seen wolves smile like that in the mountains. Kress licked his lips. His teeth were angled like headstones, the color of yellow snow…what there were of them. "Is there a problem, friend?" he said in a low voice.

Partridge stared at him. He did not blink. "Just one," he said, dropping the wanted flier into the flames, watching it burn. "Name's Partridge."

Kress's eyes went wide, rising like full moons in his sallow, pitted face. "Damn…goddamn." He quickly recovered himself. Sighing, he carefully stuffed a plug of chew in his cheek. "Best thing for you, Mr. Partridge, is to simply surrender. See, I'm hooked up with two other men. One of em's an Injun. Commanche. Something happens to me, they'll hound you till your dying day."

"No shit?" Partridge said.

Kress glared at him. "I'm telling the truth…"

"Are you? I got the strangest feeling, mister, that you're blowing smoke up my ass and expecting me to dance."

The bounty hunter's face hitched in a snarl, he darted his head forward and spat a stream of tobacco juice at Partridge's eyes. Partridge let it fly over his left shoulder and shot Kress directly in the face. The slug erased his nose and Kress fell back, arms whipping, his face a red ruin. He writhed and gagged on the ground and Partridge put another in the back of his head. Then he was quiet.

Well, you're just a real terror, ain't you? a voice in his head said to him. *You killed four men today and, hell, the day's not even over yet.*

But that was guilt talking. Self-recrimination. And he wasn't biting. Those were things a law-abiding man might feel, a man spoon-fed on morality and personal ethics. Human things and Partridge didn't exactly feel human any longer. He saw only the money and freedom and God help any self-righteous, self-deluding bastard who got in the way of that. Mercy? Hell, he was leagues beyond that now. If it took blood to get the money and what came with it, he'd spill gallons of the stuff. It would always wash off.

Besides, *who* was it he'd killed? Three robbing and murdering Johnny Rebs? And Kress, a lowlife saddletramp bounty hunter? He was willing to bet they'd never shown mercy to a soul. In his shoes they'd have done the same and probably worse.

Thinking it over as he dragged the bounty hunter's corpse into the brush, he realized he didn't truly blame those men. Any of them. He knew their kind. War veterans to the man. Men who, when the hostilities ended, found themselves out of work, their only skills being killing and hunting. The war had made them. Union and Confederate alike, take away the uniform and they were all the same.

He buried Kress in a shallow grave and searched his saddlebags. He found some chew and jerky, a nice Bowie knife, and about forty dollars in folding money. He took these and stripped Kress's mount of saddle, bags, and assorted equipment. He buried them with the bounty hunter. Only decent weapon he had was the Remington and that had to go being that the stock was customized. Too easily recognizable.

He fired a round next to Kress's horse, sending the animal fleeing up the mountain trails.

And that was that.

He waited for sunset. Because what he had to do required darkness.

9

Described by thin moonlight, the cemetery squatted on the hill, a shadowy expanse of crosses, markers, and craggy trees. Partridge tethered his horse down below in a thicket and went up on foot. A strong breeze blew, cool and insistent. Leaves scattered underfoot. An owl hooted in the distance. A scythe of a moon drifted in the sky, a narrow bank of clouds brushing it like fingertips. He could see Chimney Flats spread out on the flatlands beneath him, lit up for the most part, still bustling with wagons and horse traffic. He could hear the occasional shout or a tinny strain of music from one of the saloons.

He was by himself. Alone with the dead.

Striking a match off his heel, he lit up the lantern he'd taken from his barn. He kept it glowing at a low ebb. Just enough light to see by so he could do what had to be done. When he found Anna Marie's grave, he set the lantern down and dropped the shovel. What he was doing was unthinkable, ghoulish. But desperation knew no bounds, he supposed.

Wetting his lips, he brushed away leaves from the grave, a branch that had fallen from a nearby tree. Rubbing his hands together to warm them, his duster whipping around his legs in a sudden gust, he picked up the shovel and sank it into the cool earth. And that's how it was for him: the moon, the wind, the thud of the shovel biting into moist earth, black dirt dumped into a heap. A coyote howling in the hills.

It pained him some to lower himself to this.

To become a common grave-robber of sorts.

But he had to know. He just had to know. It took him about twenty minutes to make it three feet. It was not easy going. She'd only been in the ground seven, eight months, but already the soil was hard. It was stony. It smelled rank and dark like the underside of a rotting log. The duster hung from a nearby tree now, his shirt open to the waist, his face beaded with sweat. He kept going. Wondering, thinking, *imagining* what it was going to be like when he hit that simple pine box, when he broke the hasps and threw it open. The stink of decay. The sight of his wife's face collapsing into dank mold and jutting bone—

And he was so lost in morbid worlds and the rhythmic sound of the spade eating into the ground, he never heard the sound of someone approach. He didn't even know they were there until a deep, resonant voice said, *"What in the name of Christ do you think you're doing?"*

10

John Pepper said: "The reason I'm going after him is because it's my job. That's why I'm doing it, understand? I've been deputized by these United States of America and I'll be goddamned if I'll take that lightly. If there's a job to do, I'll do it. And it won't be because I've got any personal stake in it. But because it's my job."

And that seemed clear enough, but Terrel Hobbs, sheriff of Yuma, didn't look entirely convinced. When you got to know someone the way he knew Pepper, sometimes it took a little more than a pat explanation of duty. Sometimes it took a lot more.

Feet up on his desk, Hobbs sipped coffee from a tin cup. "I'm not trying to tell you your job, John. God knows I'd never do that. I just can't help wondering if you should pass on this one. Let someone else handle it."

Pepper looked at him hard for a time, then turned away. Everything but Hobb's face seemed interesting—the gun case on the wall, the calendar next to it, the activity out on the street, even the deputy taking out the piss pots from the cells to be emptied into the privy in the alley.

Pepper rolled a cigarette. Gave it some flame. "I'm going to bring Partridge in," he said, exhaling a stream of smoke. "And that's that."

"Alive or dead?"

"Depends entirely on him."

"Yes," Hobbs said. "I suppose it does at that."

Pepper sipped his coffee and suddenly, as he made to set the tin cup back down, his hand began to shake. With great effort he placed it on the desk without spilling any.

"You okay, John?"

Pepper massaged his temples vigorously. "Headache," he said. "Get 'em now and then."

Hobbs looked at him and found it hard to look away. He had a nasty feeling there was more to it than that...but he didn't push, knowing the marshal wouldn't confide that which he deemed a private matter.

Pepper's face was weathered like old steerhide, burnished from too many hard years on too many hard trails, a maze of intersecting lines and draws that hung slack on the bone beneath. His beard was closely-trimmed and his pale blue eyes were always watching. It was not an unfriendly face, but it was stern, determined.

Hobbs set his cup down. "You know me, John. We've been friends for going on twenty years and you know my way. I speak my mind. And what I'm saying to you is that I think this business is simply too personal."

"I guess I'll have to keep my feelings in check."

"Can you?"

Pepper just looked at him.

Hobbs shrugged. Yes, of course he could. If there was any man who kept his emotions in check it was John Pepper. He was always the same. Never angry or excited, happy nor sad. His face was carved from wood and his eyes shining flat stones. But Hobbs worried. Worried because the man had seen a lot and rarely spoke of any of it. He was not a young man anymore. Fifty-four was not old certainly, but it was definitely not young.

"All I'm saying, John, is that Partridge being married to your niece—"

"My niece is dead. We both know that." He dragged off his cigarette. "I don't blame Partridge for her death. He was in prison. The fire was accidental. I'm going to run him down because it's my job. That's all."

Hobbs' eyes narrowed. "As I recall, you were opposed to the marriage."

"Certainly I was. Wouldn't you have been?"

"I reckon."

"I don't blame Partridge for the way he turned out. He's got Black Jake's blood in his veins. I don't necessarily dislike the man, but I don't approve of his sort and neither do you."

And that was a fact.

Nothing good could come of Black Jake Partridge.

Black Jake was a thief, a gambler, a road agent, and a murderer. He had developed something of a specialty through his years of robbing and looting: when he took down a stage, for example, he killed everyone on board. He wasn't a man who believed in allowing witnesses to live. Witnesses that might later testify against him. Long before the War Between the States, Black Jake had a bloodied career behind him. When the Territory of Arizona was created and then seceded from the Union, Jake joined Confederate guerrilla forces and rode with the infamous Bloody Bill Anderson in Missouri and then, along with Anderson, joined Quantrill's Raiders in the atrocities at Lawrence, Kansas. Later, again with Anderson's gang of cutthroats and bushwhackers, Black Jake was involved in the Centralia Massacre along with the James brothers. There was no amnesty for guerrillas and murderers after the war, however, and Black Jake Partridge spent the rest of his life as a wanted man. In Arizona, he assembled a gang of Confederate veterans and, much like the James gang he was earlier involved with, began raiding and robbing and killing. In 1874 his gang was gunned down by federal troops during an abortive train robbery in New Mexico. Black Jake himself survived, only to be arrested by Pinkerton agents a year later. He was hanged at Wickenburg, Arizona in 1876.

Hobbs had been there. It was a great day in his memory.

The war was over and the sooner the country was scoured of murdering bandits the better. And nobody was more effective at hunting the vermin down than John Pepper. Though a Confederate veteran himself, he served the Union faithfully as he had before the war. He gave no quarter to Johnny Reb guerrilla bands that were little more than common outlaws (both during and after the war). He'd brought in many for trial and many others for burial.

But that was his job.

John Pepper was the deputy U.S. Marshal for the southwest district of Arizona. He was a career lawman. He'd been born on a longhorn ranch in Texas. Cattle had been his life until a range war ensued and gunmen were brought in by rival ranchers. His parents were both killed, the ranch house burned to the ground. The local sheriff (who was firmly in the pockets of the rich ranchers) refused to hunt down the men responsible. So at sixteen, Pepper did it himself. It took him four years, but he brought the gunmen in—three living and two dead. If nothing else, he developed a certain reputation among lawmen. After that, there was always plenty of work for a hunter of men: railroad detective, soldier, Indian fighter. In 1875, he'd been one of 200 Deputy U.S. Marshals hired by Judge Issac C. Parker to track down outlaws in western Arkansas and Indian Territory. It was a lawless, untamed region and the perfect sanctuary for criminals and outlaw gangs on the lam. There were very few towns in the Territory, a scarcity of any true law, only great numbers of Indians who only had jurisdiction over their own kind.

It became a learning ground for John Pepper.

A great schoolhouse which occupied some 75,000 square miles of hard country. What he had been good at before, he became expert at now.

Like the other deputies, he rode out of Fort Smith in Arkansas to Forts Reno, Sill, and Anadarko, a round trip of some 800 miles...if you were counting. Often he rode alone, but just as often with a posseman or two and a cook. He tracked gangs, murderers, whiskey bootleggers, horse thieves, and rustlers. The Indian Territory was a hotbed of vice. In those years, Pepper rubbed shoulders with legendary lawmen such as Bill Tilgman, Heck Thomas, Bass Reeves. Men who were expert at their craft.

After Indian Country, he rode with the Texas Rangers for a few years hunting down Commancheros, renegade Commaches, and even chasing wanted men deep into Mexico. Shortly afterwards, following a brief stint with Wells Fargo, he was appointed deputy U.S. Marshal for the southwest district. His predecessor had been murdered by vicious scalp hunters from south of the border looking for Maricopa scalps.

So, Pepper had done little else but hunt men.

He was good at it. Effective. In a line of work where most men were dead long before they saw forty, Pepper kept going and going. He'd been shot three times, stabbed twice, been blown off his horse when a stick of dynamite turned his mount to raw meat, been tortured by the Kiowa...but he kept going and going. As a Chiricahua raider had once told him, he was possessed of powerful medicine. And maybe that was true. And maybe he was just really goddamn lucky and really goddamn stubborn. Regardless, he was an almost mythical figure amongst lawmen and outlaws alike.

But for all of it, he was just a man. Maybe luckier, maybe tougher than most, but still a man. And after thirty odd years of locking horns with the worse trash of the west, his number had to be coming up. And this, more than anything, is what worried Hobbs. Pepper couldn't last forever.

"You gonna at least wait until morning?" Hobbs said, hopefully.

"No. Make better time at night." He crushed out his cigarette. "In fact, I better get moving."

"Wish I could go with you."

Pepper shrugged. "No need. I'll be back soon enough with Partridge. One way or another."

Hobbs watched him go. "Good luck," he said, but Pepper was already gone.

11

The desert was cool by night.

Cool, dark, and flat like some winding black sea. Some men were afraid to travel it after sundown, but Pepper was not among them. In his career of hunting men, he found that desert travel was swiftest once that unforgiving sun had slipped beneath the horizon. Some, he supposed, were just superstitious, but there was nothing in the night that wasn't there in the daytime. And if renegade Apaches or highwaymen were looking to kill and rob a man, they'd be looking to do the same in broad daylight.

The sky was the color of fireplace ash, parting occasionally to let the eye of the moon glare down and wash all and everything with an eerie, surreal glow. Pepper kept to the hard-packed trail, his mount moving slowly and carefully, meandering through flat wastelands and finally into the alien landscape of giant saguaro country. It was somehow threatening, haunted. Full of pocketed shadows and reaching fingers of darkness created by those odd-looking cacti. Good places for bandits and renegades to hide. It was easy to draw a bead on a lone rider in the dark. But that was nerves talking and Pepper was surprised that by this point he still had any left. It was just another trail he was on. Another trail, another night. And, truth be told, it seemed that there had been little else through the years.

It's what I do, he told himself. It's all I know.

Trails, nights, camps. Always hunting one man or another. Very little else between assignments. Definitely never enough time to get married, to raise a family. He had a son somewhere...a son he'd conceived out of wedlock with a farm girl in Alabama during the war. He'd never seen the child. Countless times he'd thought of finding him (he would have been near on twenty-two by now) and each time he'd backed down. Cowardice? Maybe. But who was he to suddenly barge himself in on the boy's life? He'd been no father when the boy needed one and now it was simply too late. Or at least that's what Pepper kept telling himself.

More often than not these days when he was humping the lonely trail, his mind had a tendency to turn in upon itself and minutely examine his life. It wasn't a good thing. A man needed clarity when he was hunting down the desperate and the criminal. He did not need emotions and memories and guilt blurring the fine edges of reason.

In his line of work everything had to be very black and white. He was kind man, he thought. And a caring one when circumstances permitted it. Problem was, in his job, a man had to turn a blind eye to suffering, had to ignore things like compassion and mercy if he wanted to get the job done. And these things bothered him more lately than ever before. Maybe it was old age creeping stealthily in. Maybe he was just getting soft. Regardless, he kept seeing his life spread out before him and countless opportunities missed, choices never made. And when he thought back of the men he'd killed and taken in...he couldn't seem to clearly picture their faces any longer. They all looked the same. And this bothered him greatly, because once he'd had a photographic memory, a personal rogue's gallery of his achievements. Now that gallery was all yellowed and faded like old photographs tacked to a wall. And he wondered if it was age...or something worse.

Because there was no getting around certain facts. The headaches which had been plaguing him on and off for the past year or so were getting more numerous. The fits of shaking that were once rare were now commonplace, occurring several times a day. And when they struck, his vision darkened, dimmed really as if the lights were being turned down. Things grew fuzzy, lost any true clarity.

Maybe he'd see a doctor when this was done.

Maybe.

Atop a rocky bluff, he paused. Squinting his eyes in the grainy darkness, he scanned the terrain behind him. Yes, *they* were back there. He'd felt them at his back since leaving Yuma. A wagon and team, he thought, with another rider out front. They were hanging back, trying to move with stealth, but there were few men who could trail John Pepper without him knowing about it. He knew it would've been easy enough to break from the trail and confuse them, lead them off into the wrong direction and ride off, leaving them circling.

But he had no intention of that.

So, scarcely three hours out of Yuma, he picketed his horse at the lip of a dry streambed and gathered wood from a mesquite patch. The fire he built was small, but functional. Enough to get a pot of coffee going. As it brewed, he waited for the riders to come in because he knew they would.

About twenty minutes later, they did.

12

The fire was going good and the coffee was hot when the lone rider came up a nearby ridge and, remaining mounted, looked down at John Pepper and his little camp. Pepper was ready for him. He had his Colts waiting if the need arose. A few minutes later, the wagon rolled up, stopping behind the rider. Pepper could hear the horses snorting up there. It was an old medicine wagon by the looks of it. But it was hard to be sure, though, in the darkness.

He didn't care for any of it, but if they were willing to be peaceful and law-abiding, then he would welcome them. And if they wanted a fight...well, either way, he would not disappoint them.

"Come on in then," Pepper called out.

After a moment, the rider picketed his horse. Joined by the driver of the wagon, he came on down. Pepper knew they were bounty hunters without getting too much of a look at them. They'd been trailing him since Yuma. It wasn't unusual for these manhunters to follow lawmen about at a discreet distance, hoping they'd be led to a rich payday. He figured these two knew who he was and who he was going after. Probably waited across the street from the jail while he'd visited with Hobbs.

Again, no surprise.

"May we share your fire, friend?" the first said. He was small and lithe, wore a tattered bowler hat and dusty broadcloth coat, both ragged and threadbare as old throw rugs. The coat hung open, greasy buckskins beneath and the butt of an old Remington Army .44 jutting from a homemade holster. His face was unshaven, teeth yellow as piss in the snow. "Name's Farren. Coy Farren. This here is my brother, John Lyle. And we surely do appreciate your hospitality, Marshal," he said, his Virginia accent rich as French chocolate.

He looked at the star pinned to Pepper's sheepskin coat as he said that, though there was no doubt he knew who and what Pepper was the moment he left Yuma.

"Don't have any spare cups, I'm afraid," Pepper told them. "Traveling light."

But that proved to be no problem. The Farren brothers had their own and duly filled them. Pepper decided they were even, he and the bounty hunters. For just as they knew who he was, he now knew who *they* were. The Farren brothers were bounty hunters with an alarming record of bringing in men dead more often than alive and very often only the heads, which they severed from the bodies and carried in leather sacks tied to their saddles. They were the sort of men that operated right on the bare periphery of the law…and often, he suspected, on the wrong side of it.

"Yes, it certainly is a cold night in the desert," Coy said, his face like that of a weasel, always grinning, full of too many sharp edges and contours. His eyes were beady as marbles in a can. "What brings the law out here on such a night, Marshal? That is, of course, if you don't mind me inquiring."

"Business," Pepper said, sipping from his coffee. "I'm tracking an escaped convict."

"Don't say?" John Lyle muttered.

He was much larger than his brother. Well over six feet, huge and brawny, put together like a concrete pillar. He wore a filthy beaver coat, sleeveless, his heavy arms outfitted in a deerskin shirt mottled with stains. He sported a thick and shaggy beard that could have been stripped off the skull of a buffalo. His face was oily and wide, eyes dark as pitch glaring from fleshy-rimmed hollows. He carried no weapons that Pepper could see and didn't seem to be a man that would need any.

Coy said, "An escaped convict?" He clucked his tongue. "Why, how exciting. Ain't that exciting, Lyle?"

"Yessum," John Lyle said in a voice rough as sandpaper, "that it is."

Pepper just watched them over the smoke rising from the fire. They both carried a stink of old blood and rancid body odor about them. But there was something else coming from them, a black and unwholesome smell. He wasn't sure whether he smelled it with his nose or merely in his head. Regardless, it left him cold. He cleared his throat. "What business are you fellas in?" he asked.

Coy smiled. "Oh, just about anything that comes our way. Entrepreneurs is what we are. I do believe that would be the correct word. Is that the correct word, Lyle?"

"Yessum," John Lyle said. "That would be, yes."

Coy produced a cheroot that had already been half-smoked. "Out here in these terrible lands where life is just as cheap as loose women, a man has to maintain a certain vigil, I would say, in order to be ready when opportunity knocks. Lyle and I...why, we just go whichever way the wind doth blow. Hands out and pockets empty. Am I right in this, Lyle?"

John Lyle nodded his assent. "Yes, what you said."

Pepper knew they weren't about to admit their business. Maybe they didn't know that he already had them pegged. Maybe they did and were just enjoying this little game. He doubted that John Lyle was capable of anything more strategic or surreptitious than eating and shitting and belching, but Coy...yeah, he was the one to watch. He was the deadlier of the two. By far.

Pepper knew their type and what they were capable of. They would follow him until he located Nathan Partridge and then they'd kill the both of them and collect the bounty with no surviving witnesses to muddle their plans. Chances were, most men they brought in (or parts there of) were merely taken from the clutches of other bounty hunters and lawmen. They were creatures of opportunity. Like vultures circling a meaty, maggoty kill. If it was near and it was free, then they ate.

Pepper said, "Just the two of you? Or are there others in that wagon up yonder?"

"Well, to be honest, sir, there *are* others," Coy told him, almost apologetically. "But, trust me, they are of no possible consequence. Just Mother and Father, the right honorable Major Farren that being and Mother Farren. Both aged and infirm. As good sons, we provide their every need."

Pepper didn't believe this either.

"Anyway," Coy continued, sighing dramatically, blowing out a puff of smoke. "You see, after the war and all, didn't seem to be much point for Lyle and I to be staying in Virginia. Yankees done ran roughshod all over the family holdings and what not. Weren't much left there. So, with Mother and the Major, we came out here for greener pastures, or the promise of them. Would you say that's the truth, Lyle?"

"Truth, yes," John Lyle said, grinning now, his mouth filled with angular, discolored teeth which looked oddly sharp in the flickering firelight.

"That war was a bad thing for all concerned," Pepper said to them in all sincerity.

"Did you serve, sir?" Coy asked. "I mean, if you'll excuse me for being somewhat brash and inquisitive as it were. Curiosity has always been my downfall, yes sir. And before you answer—even though Lyle and I are born and bred sons of the Confederacy and proud veterans of the Twenty-Second Virginia Infantry—understand that we hold no animosity towards the Union nor its glorious forces."

Like hell you don't, Pepper thought.

"I served with the Confederacy," he told them. "Thirty-Seventh Alabama. Regardless, those were evil times for our land. Bad things were done on both sides."

"Amen to that," Coy said.

"Amen," said John Lyle, brushing ash from his scuffed stovepipe boots.

Coy drew slowly from his cheroot. "Bad things, bad times. Evil doings and evil men. I believe it has been said that war brings out the best and worst in people. With this I rightly agree. You agree with that statement, Lyle?"

"Yessum," John Lyle said, his face orange in the firelight. "I agree."

"Course, some of us saw more horrendous things than others. You see, Marshal, Lyle and I had the unfortunate luck of being captured in Loundon County, Virginny, by Yankees. We were packed into a train car like so much Texas beef and sent north to the Elmira Prison." Coy stared into the fire. "Yes, sir. I wouldn't wish that abominable place on Mister Lincoln hisself. Ain't that so, Lyle?"

"Yessum. What you said. Hellmira."

Pepper knew of it. Knew of the starvation and disease and brutalities inflicted upon Confederate POWs at that awful place. There was nothing he could really say to them about it. Nothing they probably hadn't already heard a hundred times.

Coy continued: "Disgusting really, sir, the things a man of even the most gentile upbringing will do to stay alive. I did things that were…shall we say, unpleasant and unmentionable in civilized company." His face went dark at the thought of it, then immediately brightened as if hit by a ray of sunlight. He smiled. "Course, I don't hold no grudges whatsoever towards the North for such things. To the victors go the spoils and all. No, Marshal, my brother and I are firmly entrenched in the new order. There is not a single shred of malice nor hostility in these meek and mild forms you see before you. Humble we are and humble we shall remain, God bless the Union."

Jesus H. Christ, Pepper thought. This fella's got more shit coming out of his mouth than his ass.

Coy threw his cheroot into the fire. "But if I may be so brash once again, could you tell me, dear sir, all about this escaped prisoner of yours. Entertainment being lacking this night, a fine and suspenseful tale would be highly appreciated."

Pepper sighed. He produced a hand-rolled and lit it with a burning stick. "Name's Nathan Partridge. Escaped from Yuma Prison. He's desperate and dangerous. I hope to take him alive, if possible. If not..." he blew out a column of smoke, dismissing that. "You may have heard of the Gila River Gang? Bank robbers, train robbers. Partridge was one of their member."

Coy clutched his hand to his chest in an almost feminine gesture. "Why, it's positively blood-curdling. Raises my hackles, I must say. Does it raise your hackles, Lyle?"

"I believe it does, yessum." But if the big man was truly frightened, you wouldn't have known it. His face was impassive as always, as though it were quarried from granite. He smiled from time to time—that is, the corners of his lips curled upwards—but it never touched those cold and predacious eyes.

Coy shook his head and sucked in a sharp breath. "Why, I pity the man that runs afoul of such a vile and despicable individual as our Mister Partridge. I must confess in all due honesty, Marshal, that such types fill me with a certain loathing, a certain inbred terror. Do they fill you with terror, Lyle?"

"Fill me with it," Lyle said. "For certain."

Coy wrapped his arms around himself as if to keep warm. "I think we can thank the good Lord this day that such valiant and honest men such as yourself are protecting us, Marshal. Makes me feel cozy, snug and sheltered as if I were at my mama's breast. Lyle? Does it make you feel all—"

"All right! That's enough," Pepper snapped. "I been feeding off your bullshit train long enough, Farren. It's time to get off. Are you going to sit there all night and cornhole me with this Southern gentility nonsense or are you going to get to the point?"

John Lyle suddenly slid a hand into his beaver coat. Tried to move it slow and natural like a slug inching across a stone.

But Pepper brought one of his ivory-handled Colts out smooth and easy, cocking it, all in one graceful, well-practiced motion. "You tell your brother, Coy, that if his hand don't return to his goddamn lap and return right now, I'm going to splatter what brains he has across the desert sand."

John Lyle's hand retreated, but his eyes, unblinking, stayed on the marshal. And those eyes were smoldering pyres of hatred.

Coy sighed. "I can see, sir, you are not a man of breeding. Your social skills are atrocious. I've seen monkeys in a New Orleans zoo who chewed their own waste that had more self-control than you. You all sure you're not a Yankee?"

"Shut that pisshole you call a mouth, Farren. You and this walking heap of buffalo shit you call a brother have been trailing me since I left Yuma and only a sun-stroked blind idiot wouldn't have known it." Pepper kept the gun on both of them. The slightest wrong move and they'd be buzzard bait. "Now, here's how it works. I'll make it real simple so even the lowest Virginny trash like yourselves can understand. I'm going after Partridge. You will keep away from me. You will not get in the way or try to take him yourself. If you do, I will kill you. Just like that. No questions asked, I'll just kill you and free the world of a couple more parasites."

Coy wasn't smiling anymore. His eyes had gone hard. "I declare, Marshal, it's a sad day for the race when two men can't engage in a civil conversation. Your manners leave me cold. Positively cold. Do they leave you leave you leave cold, Lyle?"

But John Lyle wanted blood now and he merely nodded.

"Ride out while you still can," Pepper warned them.

"There's a bounty on Partridge's head, Marshal, and we plan on having it. One way or another."

Pepper gave him back his icy stare. "Are you threatening the life and well-being of a federal officer? Are you planning on interfering with a federal marshal in the performance of his duty? Because if you are, I can take you both in right now. Alive or dead."

Coy gave his brother a look and the latter moved slowly away the fire and back up to his team on the ridge, where he waited, huge and hulking and as dangerous as a sack of cobras.

"I'll bid you good evening, Marshal," Coy said. He took off his hat and bowed with great exaggeration. He climbed up on his mount. "But be rest assured, you *will* see us again. And at that time, you would be best on your guard."

They rode off into the night and Pepper didn't put his gun away until they were long gone. He sat there thinking about it.

Partridge in front of him and these Virginia crazies behind. It wasn't exactly a promising situation.

Things were about to get interesting.

13

As soon as he heard the voice, Nathan Partridge dropped the shovel and cleared leather in one quick, decisive motion. He held the Colt .38 in one hard fist, ready and willing to add more customers to the boneyard if need be. "State your business," he said in a low and angry voice, "before I put holes in your hide."

"Easy, easy, easy," the voice said. "I'm unarmed."

Partridge stared at the dark figure. Never taking his eyes off him, he scooped up the lantern and turned it up a notch. First thing he saw was a tin star pinned to a leather vest and the second thing he saw was a face he'd known many years before. Maybe fatter, maybe older, but the same damn face. It swam up at him from his childhood.

"Kreger?" he said. "Joshua Kreger?"

The man nodded. "Yes, Nate, it's me."

So he'd been recognized, too. "You're the sheriff of the Chimney Flats?"

"The same."

"But you don't carry a gun?"

"Not unless necessary."

Partridge was amazed. Unless Chimney Flats had undergone some biblical transformation from snake den to preacher's pulpit, then only a real fool of a lawman prowled its streets without iron strapped to his side. But what was even more amazing, astounding even, was that Kreger would end up as sheriff. He simply wasn't the right sort for the job. Unless he, too, had undergone some incredible transformation. School days, Kreger had been bullied and picked on by the other boys and had taken it all, mind you, without so much as batting an eye.

"You here to do your duty and take me in?"

Kreger shook his head. "Hell no, Nate. We were friends when we were kids, weren't we? I wouldn't do that. Maybe I'm disgracing the badge, but I'm not about to turn in an old friend."

And that bullshit was so ripe it stank like a manure pile in July. Partridge had had few friends in school and Joshua Kreger was not among them. The only friend he really ever had was Davy Tomlinson and he'd been thrown from a horse and killed when Partridge was but ten years old.

Partridge pulled himself up and out of the hole and Kreger gave him a wide berth like you might a cougar coming out of its den.

"Okay, Josh, okay," he said. "What then? I can't believe you're just passing by. You're telling me you're not here to talk me into surrendering?"

The sheriff shrugged. "I'd like you to consider it."

"Ain't gonna happen. I'd rather be in a hole out here than in one in prison. And I'll gladly take any man with me what don't believe such."

"I believe it." A match was struck and a clay pipe lit, shadows dancing over Kreger's face. "When I heard you'd broke out—they wired us immediately, of course—I knew you'd be coming this way. I knew you'd be coming to this very spot, in fact. And here you are."

"And here I am." Partridge motioned towards the dark, encroaching forest. "Josh, you sure you don't have a posse hiding out in those trees yonder?"

Kreger took his pipe out of his mouth. "C'mon, Nate. You got my word. I'm not about to turn you in. Believe me, if and when you get taken down, it won't be because of me." He puffed away. "But you best be careful. There's bounty hunters creeping about all hungry for that price on your head."

Partridge just nodded, thinking of Kress moldering in his shallow grave. "I don't plan on staying too long."

"Good. I was kind of hoping I could talk you into moving along tonight."

"Nope."

"Tomorrow?"

"Maybe."

Kreger sighed, spreading his hands apart, indicating that it was simply out of his control. "I can't guarantee your safety, Nate. That money—"

"How much?"

"A thousand. For now, anyway. Longer you're loose, more it's bound to go up."

Partridge considered it. The authorities were probably smarting that he'd slipped out of their cage. More than anything, he figured, they probably wanted him back so they could grill him and get him talking. Get him to tell them *how* he'd made his run without being picked up somewhere. But he'd never confess to that. Because if they hadn't figured it out, maybe someone else would try it again and be successful. There was a certain satisfaction in that.

"And it's gonna get worse, Nate. Give it another month and there'll be two grand on you. Six months and it'll be five easy. There's nowhere you can hide with money like that on you. They'll hound you until your dying day." Kreger shrugged. "And it won't be just amateurs either. The pros'll be sniffing after you. I got word this afternoon that they're assigning a deputy U.S. Marshal to bringing you in."

None of this moved Partridge. His face was flat and unreadable as hieroglyphics. "I suspected as much, so I don't plan on being around long. I've come for something that belongs to me and I'm not leaving until I'm sure it's out of my reach."

Kreger just nodded. He didn't seem to be surprised by any of it.

Partridge didn't like it.

Sure, it only made sense that Kreger would figure that he would show eventually for the money. Any sane man would. It was never as much as reported in the newspapers, but it was still a lot. What bothered him was that Kreger was a sheriff and yet, he wasn't trying to take an escaped convict in. Partridge was willing to bet that the man was lying, that he did indeed carry a gun. But tonight he hadn't strapped it on. And hadn't with the hopes of running into a certain escaped convict. Maybe it was the money. Maybe he was hoping to be lead to a stash of greenbacks.

"You can take that gun off me, Nate," he said. "It's unnecessary."

Partridge kept it on him. "Is it?"

"C'mon, Nate."

"C'mon, my ass. What gives here, Josh? Tell me what this is all about. If you do, I'll trust you...or as much as I would any man with a tin star." He waited and Kreger said nothing. "Okay. I guess either I shoot you now and dump you in this grave or let you walk away. If I do the latter, I'd have to be pretty stupid because, chances are, in an hour or two you'd be after me with a posse."

"I wouldn't do that."

"You wouldn't, eh?" Partridge just glared at him. "Tell me something, Josh. How'd you know I'd be up here? You see the lantern light and guess? Or are you just really lucky?"

Kreger smiled thinly. "Lucky I guess. I figured you'd come to see the grave of your wife. Figured it was only a matter of time. What I didn't figure is that I'd find you trying to dig her up. And we have ourselves a problem there, Nate. I might be turning my back on my duty as a lawman by not taking you in...but I ain't about to let you rob a grave."

Partridge still had the gun on him. His eyes were narrow slits in the shifting lantern light. "Don't see where you have much of a choice. In fact, don't see why I should do anymore digging at all. Not with you here, old friend."

"Nate..."

"Get down in the hole," Partridge said. "Start digging. Or just stand there and start dying."

Kreger calmly emptied his pipe against his knee. "Ain't no need for that, Nate."

Partridge said, "No? And why's that, Josh?"

"Because she ain't in there."

14

Nathan Partridge killed his first man when he was sixteen.

It was at the Four Points Saloon. Same place he'd learned about his father. Looking back, the Four Points always seemed pivotal in the man he became. He'd been working there nearly five years by then. As a swamper, fill-in bartender, and cook. There wasn't much he didn't know about running such an establishment by that point. He even knew what went on upstairs with the women imported from New Orleans. And by the time he'd turned sixteen, he'd been up there more than once himself. But always with the same girl.

And that was what led him to leaving Chimney Flats.

That and a young prostitute named Cora May Shields. She had affected a French accent like many of the other girls in order to lure in more business and it always worked. She was a petite thing, barely twenty, with hair the color of blowing wheat and eyes bluer than a July sky. The first time Partridge saw her, he couldn't stop staring. At her hourglass figure. At her breasts straining at the velvet fabric of her dress. At her huge eyes and pouting lips. She moved with such confidence and ease, breathing life into any room she entered. The first time he only looked. The second time he watched her through the keyhole with a customer. The third time he was in her bedroom.

Though he was not naïve, really, in the ways of men and women, and surely not naïve in the ways of violence and human evil, in her presence he was just a kid. Green as desert cactus. She filled his belly with fluttering moths. Made his skin feel too tight on his bones. Made everything inside run like pine sap. She made the wrong words come out at the wrong times and very often no words at all but a mindless mumbling that embarrassed him to no earthly end.

"You ever been with a woman, Nathan?" she asked. Her voice was a storied coo, very sweet and understanding.

You couldn't lie to such a voice. No more than you could stand before the Virgin Mother and fondle yourself. It just wasn't possible. Oh, he had tales of sexual adventure all spun and ready in his head. Ones oft-told to boyhood chums. But when she plied him with that question, they fell to rot at his feet. They had no more substance than smoke ghosts. They scattered in the high winds of his mind like the pages of a shredded book in a tempest.

"No, ma'am," he confessed. "I have not."

"Don't have a girlfriend?"

"No, ma'am."

"Would you like me to be your girlfriend tonight?"

"Well, I…"

"Are you scared? It's okay to be scared," she soothed him. "Everyone's scared at first."

"No, I'm not...*yes,* ma'am. I reckon I am."

"Come to me."

She was sitting on the edge of the bed. Her hair was down, laying over her bare left shoulder like gold. It caught the sputtering light of the oil lamp, held it, made it its own. Her eyes were clear and sparkling. She opened her bodice and freed her breasts. She took one of Partridge's trembling hands and placed it on one firm cone. "There," she said. "That feels nice, doesn't it? Nothing to be afraid of."

Partridge was hard. It felt like he had a railroad spike in his pants. She freed him and stroked his length. "That's not so bad either, is it?"

"No...no, ma'am...*Cora*...Jesus..."

"What we're going to do is surely the finest thing in God's creation, Nathan. It's what men and women were made to do," she promised him and he did not doubt her fine words or her fine touch. "Does that feel good?"

Her nipple hardened under his fingertips. "What..." he managed. "What will it be like?"

She smiled and in that smile was a world of seduction, a garden of delight. "It will be like heaven. It will be like drawing down the stars into your palm and holding them there. Just for an instant," she told him, working him faster now, expertly.

"Oh...God...that's what it's like..."

"No," she said, "this is what it's like." And took him then, in her mouth. And as she did so, Partridge had what he then considered to be the closest thing to a religious experience he'd ever known in his young life. He was certain that when he was in her mouth and then later slid in between her thighs that he saw the face of the Almighty.

As the weeks passed he spent more and more time with Cora. He fell in love with her even as she warned him against it. Pleasure and lust and momentary happiness were all part of what she was, what she did, and who she could be, but love was not. But despite what she said, their couplings were more frequent and she brought him gifts and he was certain that she was falling in love with him, too.

But it was never easy.

Love at any age is like fire in the belly, but love at sixteen is like a gutful of acid and burning sulfur; it smolders and consumes completely. Each night as Cora took men upstairs, Partridge died inside. He raged and boiled like an angry sea, one whose waters were white-hot liquid steel. And in the coming weeks he died dozens and dozens of times.

Something had to come to a head and it did.

A miner by the name of Tom Horsely came into town from a silver camp up in the Gila's. He came for his Friday night steak. His Friday night drunk. His Friday night fuck. And, maybe most important of all, his Friday night fight. Sober, Horsely was a shy and retiring man. But with a belly full of whiskey, he was the devil's own. Violent, abusive. He would take offense at the most minor of transgressions. Many, imagined. In fact, *most* imagined. Friday nights he either gave a good beating or received one and many was the night he spent in the Chimney Flats lock-up...after the doc had stitched him back up, that was.

The night in question, Partridge was mopping up the floor and on Friday nights this was no simple matter that could be completed and dispensed with—it was something that had to be done hourly. The floors were thick with mud and dirt in the summer and in the winter, melted snow and ice. All year round (and doubly so on Friday nights) there was spilled beer and whiskey, blood, vomit, and urine...a foul and reeking miasma of things. Because on Friday nights the ranch hands got paid and so did the miners.

Partridge was making the rounds, trading jibes and jokes with the regulars, mopping his way across the hardwood floor...and suddenly he made the mistake of drawing his mop right over the toe of Horsely's square-toed boot.

Horsely set down his drink. He was a small man, angular and swarthy, but put together like a brick shitter. And right then, he was ten feet tall and weighed 600 pounds. And every inch and pound of that girth was rage and attitude and intolerance. "Made a mistake there, didn't you, boy?" he said and his tone, while raw and piercing, was not especially menacing. But neither is a Gila Monster until it chomps down on your hand. And Horsely had only begun to bare his toxic fangs as it were. He butted his cigarette, a knife-edged grin slashed across his face. "Yup, helluva mistake, I'd say."

Partridge knew he'd fucked up in a big way. "Sorry, Mister Horsely. Here, let me polish that boot clean for you."

But as he made to wipe down the tip of that black snakeskin boot with the fine toolwork on it, Horsely grabbed him by the back of the neck and shoved him back, making him stumble over his bucket of water.

"Yes sir," Horsely said. "I'd say you certainly stepped in the shit this night."

Another miner, name of Cosling, a big fellow with a gut on him like a sack of feed, said, "Easy, Tom. Kid didn't mean nothing by it. Here, let me buy you a drink."

Horsely turned on him. "Stay out of this, George, or I'll bust my fucking hands on that fat head of yours."

Cosling stepped back.

He outweighed Horsely by more than a hundred pounds. Towered over him by more than a foot. Had arms on him like the carnival strongman, yet he wanted no part of Tom Horsely. And that was a good indication of the crazy sonofabitch Horsely indeed was.

Ass on the floor, centered perfectly in a pool of spilled beer (or maybe piss or both), Partridge felt his blood bubble and burn like oil spilled on a hot skillet. The heat went right through him. He thought steam would rise from him when Horsely picked up his bucket and dumped it on him. He was certain his skin would blister and pop open. And if it did, if it did, what was waiting beneath would be something so dark and pissed-off that even Horsely would have soiled his drawers.

But the skin held intact.

Partridge tried to get up, but Horsely kicked the legs out from under him. But it all wasn't quite humiliating enough, so he kicked Partridge with three, four hard shots from the tip of his boot. In the ribs, each and every one. Ten minutes before, the barroom was louder than an artillery barrage. But now? So quiet all you could hear was the snap of Horsely's pantleg and the thud of that polished leather kissing flesh.

And the truly sad part of it was, in that crowded saloon, not a soul offered to help Partridge...so he helped himself. His ribs threaded with pain, he came up off the floor like a ball from a cannon mouth, so fast and furious that even old tough guy Tom Horsely didn't see the shit flying until it spattered across the front of his shirt. Partridge hit him hard in the face with three solid right jabs. Then a roundhouse left followed by another that Horsely wisely ducked away from. He ducked and kicked Partridge in the belly and that was all she wrote. He folded up like an umbrella, deflated like a balloon with a pinhole in it. And Horsely, his face smeared with blood from the rivers that ran from his busted nose and split lips, kicked Partridge unconscious.

And would have kicked him right into the promised land if a group of burly ranchers hadn't took hold of him and ejected him through the batwings.

But it didn't end there.

The next night, bruised and swollen and hurting something awful, Partridge found Horsely staggering drunkenly from a rival saloon. When he made to relieve himself in an alley, Partridge came up quick and kneed him in the crotch, slammed him back against the façade of a dry goods store and gave him exactly what he deserved.

Which was six inches of steel in the belly.

Cora had given him a hunting knife as a gift and now he gave it to Horsely. He drove the blade into the drunken man's belly and kept driving it until Horsely stopped shrieking and his face went white as spilled flour. Until he pissed and shit himself and fell to his knees and Partridge's arm was red and glistening right up to the elbow.

He left town the next day.

For the next four years, he took whatever came along. He worked in cow camps in New Mexico and Texas. Laid track side by side with tough Irish immigrants for the Union Pacific Railroad in Wyoming. Worked as a nightherder and line rider in northern California. Cut timber. Broke horses. And finally, in Utah Territory, began to steal them. He threw in with a gang of misfits who all seemed to have one thing in common—they had no pasts. If they did, it was never spoken about. They rustled horses and cattle and made a lot of money. Eventually, they were broken up and arrested. Partridge managed to escape before trial and after that, he kept clear of Utah...except to rob and pillage. Nobody ever learned his real name, not his partners in crime nor the sheriff and his posse. Still, he kept clear. He often wondered if they hung the others as was the custom.

Somewhere during this period, he heard his mother had died. She had a stroke and perished shortly afterwards. There didn't seem to be much reason to go back to Chimney Flats then.

So he worked the plains, tried the straight and narrow again as a buffalo hunter. He worked as part of a team. Skinner, hideman, and shooter. The hours were long and hard. The work back-breaking. When the herds were thick, there was very little rest. And there were always marauding Indians and rival hunting teams to deal with. But it was a good living. Problem was, by that point, Partridge had tasted the fruits of ill-gotten gains. A good criminal could make in a few hours what it took an honest man months or even years to earn. And maybe it was in his blood, but he lusted for the fast and hard lifestyle. The dirty company and dirty money.

And when the herds began to thin, he was already gone.

Then came the Gila River Gang.

15

Josh Kreger had a cabin not too far away and Partridge spent the next few hours there. The sheriff lived alone and that was a good thing. He fed the outlaw a good meal of fried beans, sowbelly, and biscuits. Even some canned peaches. After it was done, there were cigars and a good bottle of Scotch whiskey.

"We searched those ashes best we could," Kreger told him. "Believe me, we did. We could find no trace of Anna Marie. My guess is she was burned to ashes herself."

Partridge had considered that...yet, it just didn't wash in his mind. He'd seen bodies pulled out of fires before. He'd seen them reduced to shrunken, blackened things. Seen them reduced to nothing but charred bone. But in his experience there was always *something.* It took a hell of a lot of heat to reduced bone to powder. Much more heat, he figured, than you found in your average house fire. It was possible, of course, that Kreger's men had simply missed her. The cabin was such a mess of cinders and stone and blasted timbers it would have been easy to overlook something like a few blackened scraps of bone. Unless the remains of the cabin were systematically pulled apart and sifted, she might never be found.

But why did he have that nagging feeling she wasn't there at all?

Kreger poured him more Scotch. "Course, she still might be out there…such a goddamn mess. Well, regardless, there's nothing more I can tell you really."

Partridge thought it over. His mind wrapped around it all and it still didn't work for him. "While I was away, did you see much of her?"

Kreger shook his head. "Very little. I believe she came to town from time to time, provisioned, but other than that, no. Can't say I ever knew her very well, Nate. A year after you were gone I became sheriff and she never had any business with me in that regard."

"Did you ever speak with her?"

"No. Never anything more than a quick hello when she passed me by." Kreger butted his cigar. "Nate? You're thinking she's alive, aren't you?"

"I'm thinking a lot of things."

Kreger's brown eyes swam in a face just as soft as butter. "She had the money, didn't she?"

Blue smoke drifted from Partridge's mouth. "What makes you think that, Josh? My wife is dead. Maybe I need certain particulars in order to be satisfied."

"Maybe. But between you and me and that stove over there, I don't believe it."

"Don't? Or don't want to?"

Kreger drank his whiskey, studying the unreadable face of the man seated across from him. "You had a lot of money, Nate. You and them Gila River boys. Least that's what they're saying. The rest of the gang is dead. Rumor has it you came into possession of the collected loot. My guess is you buried it around these parts somewhere. Put it in a hole or down some old mine shaft or well. I'm also guessing Anna Marie knew where."

"Maybe I'm just concerned over my loss. That ever occur to you?" Partridge said, trying to sound offended but failing miserably. "Maybe I loved that woman."

"Did you?"

"None of your goddamned business." He threw his cigar into the fireplace. "Know what, Josh? I'm willing to bet that two-thirds of the men coming after me are doing it not for the bounty but in hopes I'll lead them to the stash of money. In fact, I'm figuring you might be one of them."

"Listen, Nate—"

"Don't feed me that shit, Josh. I don't accept it and I don't wanna hear it. If you weren't interested in that money, you'd be stupider than I already think you are." Partridge threw back the rest of his whiskey. "But it don't matter much. Don't really matter at all. Because you're right: Anna Marie *did* know where that loot was. And now she's dead and the money's gone."

"Well, we never did find a body…"

No, they didn't. And until that happened, Partridge couldn't see himself resting easy. That money was all that kept his sanity from falling to pieces like fragile crockery the entire time he was in the hole. For he knew if and when he managed to get out, it was waiting for him out there. That the hard years, the desperate years would be done with. That money would allow him an easy life.

But now he didn't even have that.

"What will you do?" Kreger asked.

He shrugged. "At this point, I don't have a clue."

Kreger thought about that, drew into himself for a moment or two. "The money, Nate, is secondary to me. First, I want you out of my town. That's the bottom line. I just want you gone."

"And I told you I can't go just yet."

"What if…" He stared hard at Partridge. "What if I told you about a rumor I heard about?"

"Concerning Anna Marie?" Partridge said, interested now.

"Yeah. Just a bit of gossip I picked up about her spending time in a place called Dead Creek at the foot of the Superstitions. Gossip is all it is. Just a rumor about her buying a saloon up there."

"Is that all?"

"That's all I ever heard. And that in passing. That was a few years back and it didn't mean much to me at the time."

"Any other dirty little secrets you wanna pass on?"

"Not a one."

Partridge didn't believe that for a minute, but he let it pass. "Then I'll ride out, Josh." He pulled on his hat and duster. "One thing, though, Josh. I'm gonna make myself scarce around here. But if I hear you sent men after me...if I survive, then I'll be coming back for you. You understand what I'm saying?"

Kreger swallowed dryly. "Yes," he said. "I believe I do."

16

When John Pepper arrived in Chimney Flats the first thing he did after stabling his horse was to see the sheriff. He found Josh Kreger in his office, feet up on a battered desk that had been old twenty years before and was now merely ramshackle. Kreger was much like the town he ran—dirty, overfed, seedy. There was something sordid about the man and Pepper wasn't sure what it was, but he didn't like the smell of it whatsoever.

"Sheriff," Pepper said, helping himself to a cup of the man's coffee and instantly wishing he hadn't, "I'm here on the trail of a man who escaped from Yuma Prison."

"Nathan Partridge," Kreger said.

"Then you were expecting me, maybe."

Kreger smiled broadly, almost too broadly. "I was wired that a deputy U.S. Marshal would be coming through here. But, hell, lately everyone's been asking about Partridge. You asking about him is business as usual these days."

Pepper sipped his coffee which tasted like it had been drank before, passed through someone's bladder, then reheated. He winced. "Then you haven't seen him, I take it?"

Kreger motioned behind him. "Well, if I had, he'd be locked up tight and pretty in one of those cells. He's a wanted man, Marshal. Don't have to tell you that, but, shit, if he shows around here I'm taking him in. End of story."

"Haven't heard any rumors or such?"

"Nothing yet. Give it time, though. My guess is that the more the bounty increases, the more folks'll be seeing him just about everywhere. You know how that goes."

Pepper did, all right. If the price was high enough, people would be seeing him everywhere and anywhere. Things like that had a way of getting out of hand. Before long, greenhorn bounty hunters, miners, self-styled vigilantes, just about every sort of drifter and tramp you could imagine would be hauling in innocent men they were sure were Nathan Partridge. Kreger would have his work cut out. That was for sure.

"You plan on staying long, Marshal?"

"A day or two. Hard to say. I'll poke around a bit, see what I see."

Kreger grinned broadly again. "Well, I sure hope you bring him in."

"I'll do my best."

Pepper got out of there then. There was something about Kreger he simply couldn't stomach. There was a smell about the man. A smell that had nothing whatsoever to do with his bathing habits. It was a bad, corrupt smell and Pepper had smelled it enough to know that nothing good could come of it.

With that in mind, he decided he'd hang around a spell. Something was going on here and he intended to find out what. Maybe he was crazy and maybe he was too damn old for the job, but he had a strong suspicion that Kreger was lying to him.

17

It was just after sunset when Kreger got a visitor.

He was a tall man dressed in a khaki duster and a dark Stetson. His hair was shoulder-length and white as bleached bone. His face was hard and just about as ugly as festering sin, the left eye sitting in a pocket of ancient mangled flesh that feathered out into a series of deep-hewn scars which pulled the corner of his mouth into a perpetual grimace.

Kreger saw him and felt his guts go to sauce.

"Evening," he managed, quickly shutting the door to his office, after scanning the streets to make sure no one had seen his visitor.

Although Kreger knew his name and knew it well, he never spoke it. It wasn't healthy to do so. He found that sometimes he was simply too unnerved to even think it, as if maybe the scar-faced man could read his mind. So, he called the man Jones. Just Jones. The Apaches had another name for him: Devil-Face. "Tell me," Jones said in his low, evil voice. "Tell me of it."

Kreger poured himself a cup of tepid coffee with a trembling hand. "I found him just as you said I would. He was up in the cemetery, digging."

"He opened the grave all the way?"

"No, I stopped him. Not that it matters, I guess."

The scar-faced man lit a hand-rolled. Smoke encircled his head like a noose. And for a moment, Kreger thought, he looked pretty much like old Satan himself.

"And how did you do that?"

Kreger cleared his throat of lint. "Did exactly as we said: I told him the truth. Told him his wife wasn't in the ground, that we never found her."

Mr. Jones nodded, his black eyes glistened in the glow of his cigarette. "What was his reaction to that?" he wanted to know.

"Like you said. It seemed to be exactly what he wanted to hear." Kreger went on about how he'd managed to gain Partridge's confidence—or nearly—and had brought the outlaw up to his cabin, fed him, talked with him. "I worked him pretty damn easy, I must say."

The scar-faced man was not impressed. "But it wasn't you, was it? You were just telling him what he wanted to hear, what he suspected all along."

"I suppose that's true."

"Did you steer him towards Dead Creek as we said?"

"Yes. I just gave him the rumor and his mind did the rest."

The scar-faced man's lips attempted a smile, but fell miles short of the mark. His lips wriggled on his face like worms caught in the sunlight. That was as close as it came with him. "You did good," he said. "If I get that money, you'll get your cut."

"There's a federal marshal after him. He was in here today," Kreger said, not sure whether it was something he needed to be concerned about or not. As with most things, he let Mr. Jones decide for him how he should feel about things. "He's pretty good, I hear. Name's—"

"Pepper?" the scar-faced man said as if he'd just bitten into something rancid. "John Pepper?"

"That's him, all right. And he's good, real good. Some say the very best," Kreger told him, turning it up a notch or two simply because the idea of John Pepper being thrown into the mix seemed to be bothering his guest like salt bothered a slug. This brought Kreger a certain satisfaction. "Heard when he goes after a man, he hunts him down like a bloodhound. Won't give up until they're worn right out or dead. Either way, he gets 'em. They say he could track a fly through a sandstorm."

If Mr. Jones seemed concerned before, you couldn't tell it now. "Don't be such a goddamned fool, Kreger. That's just talk. Pepper's good, but he's just a man. If he gets in the way, I'll put him down. Things are starting to fall into place and I won't allow anyone to bugger that up. Not Pepper, not you."

Those last words seemed to echo in the air with a savage finality. Like the sound of an iron door slamming closed...on a cell or a burial vault. Kreger found that his throat was suddenly too tight to swallow with.

The scar-faced man stepped closer to him, that horrible face inches from his own. His breath smelled of steel and blood. "Hear me good, Sheriff. I'm too close to that money now. I can smell it. I can taste it." He grinned at the idea of it, his teeth narrow and yellow like those of a rodent. "You or anyone else messes this up and I'll bury their sorry fucking asses. That's my promise to you."

With that, he let himself back out.

Kreger just stood there after he was gone, his face locked tight with an idiot's grin.

18

John Pepper wasn't sure what he was feeling at that moment.

He stood in the shadows of the livery barn across the road from the sheriff's office. Painted in darkness, only the tip of his cigarette glowing, he stood stock still, confused, curious, and concerned. He'd seen the tall man arrive and then leave Kreger's office. And that walk, the way the stranger carried himself...Jesus, it was familiar. Too familiar. It made him start thinking things. Crazy, impossible things that just couldn't be. It filled him with a gnawing apprehension, a gnawing dread.

He waited until the man had climbed onto leather and was gone up the rutted dirt street. Then he crushed his cigarette under boot and crossed over to the plank boardwalk outside the sheriff's office.

When he opened the door, Kreger was sitting at his desk. He looked tired. "Marshal," he sighed, as if relieved.

Pepper didn't waste time with pleasantries. "That man who just left," he said, "who was he? He's familiar to me."

Kreger's face was just as white as fresh cream. "Him? Oh, no one. Just some—"

"Tell me the truth."

Kreger fought hard to maintain his composure. "His name is Jones. That's all I know. That's all he told me. He's just passing through. He's after the same man you are."

And that seemed reasonable enough to Pepper. And it would have satisfied him under any other circumstances, but not today. Not this night. Not after what he'd seen...or thought he'd seen. Particularly when he knew Kreger was lying to him. Lying big and bold and that lie, it stank like fresh horseshit.

Pepper pulled up a chair, set his hat on the desk. "This is your town, Sheriff. I would never consider stepping on your toes. I would never consider throwing my weight around or getting involved in matters that don't concern me. But right now—" he slapped his hand flat on the desk "—right now, you are lying to me. And I don't think it's the first time. Now maybe out of professional courtesy you would consider being truthful with me."

But Kreger had it in check now. "Marshal, I hear tell you're a good man. I accept that. And I accept that you've got a job to do. But don't come in here and call me a liar. I'm not about to stand for it."

Pepper just stared at him. But Kreger met his eyes and would not look away.

"I want to know who that man was," Pepper said flatly.

"His name's Jones. Why in hell isn't that enough for you?" Kreger said, allowing his words to be touched, just touched, by anger. "Who in Christ's name do you think it was? Nathan Partridge? Is that what you think?"

But Pepper only looked at him coldly. "No, that's not who I think it was. That man who just left here, I think, was his father, Black Jake."

19

It was an October morning in 1876 when they hanged Black Jake Partridge in Wickenburg, Arizona Territory. The air was chill, the sun still attempting to burn away the tapestry of clouds overhead. Overcast, dismal, a cool dampness twisted in the air.

John Pepper was there as were maybe two-hundred other people.

It was a carnival atmosphere with beer wagons, vendors selling everything from lemonade to roast pork sandwiches. Men were drinking and gambling. Prostitutes were openly hawking their wares and seeing record profits. Women were clustered in great groups, talking and shouting and enjoying themselves, glad for this day of days. Men—settlers, miners, soldiers, ranch hands—had been drinking since early that morning and by 9:30 a.m. many were drunk and boisterous, others were passed out in the back of wagons or right on the boardwalks. There were fights, there were bets, and more than one woman became pregnant that dark day. Children ran through the streets, hollering and singing and carrying on, grateful to be free from chores and school. A brass band had set up directly across from the gallows beneath a spreading oak and were attempting, poorly, to bang out "Shall We Gather at the River". No easy feat considering most of their members had been pulling off bottles of corn liquor all morning.

It was a great gathering of country folk and townspeople alike.

By dawn, they had started to assemble, wagonloads of settlers and their families all jostling for space. They rubbed shoulders with lawmen and whores and gunmen and hunters and landbarons and pickpockets and half-breeds alike. The only ones not in attendance, Pepper heard, were Partridge's wife and son.

By ten—the scheduled hour of execution—the crowd was getting restless. They thronged as close to the gallows as the sheriff's deputies would allow. The best spots, of course, were taken by the city fathers, their minions, and journalists, of which there were many.

Assembled from huge oak timbers and posts, the gallows was weathered gray and had already been standing for some time, having helped more than one outlaw into the promised land.

Pepper had passed on the liquor that flowed as easily as the waters of the Atlantic, but he had been seduced by the lure of roast corn and pig. By the time ten had rolled around, his belly was full.

It never occurred to him that day that it was all very ghoulish, turning a man's death into a circus. No more than it occurred to anyone else. Those were hard and desperate times and the measures the law took were often extreme, but necessary.

Just after ten, a hush fell over the crowd as the doomed man was led from the jail. He was escorted by no less than four armed guards and the county sheriff himself. Black Jake Partridge had a black hood over his head. Pepper thought it unusual, being that most weren't hooded until they reached the platform itself.

But he didn't pay much mind to that.

Perhaps it was Partridge's final wish.

Pepper watched the outlaw and noticed with some curiosity that the guards were half-dragging him towards the gallows platform. And that surprised him because Black Jake was nothing if not confident and capable, arrogant and defiant. He wasn't the sort of man who cringed from death being that he'd faced it down so many times.

As the crowd called out obscenities and the newspapermen scribbled frantically in their notebooks, the condemned man was ushered to the scaffolding steps that led to the platform and the short drop waiting there. Up on the platform, Partridge's death sentence was read loudly and clearly so all could hear. The clergy said a few prayers and a throng of the faithful broke into a few hymns…but half-heartedly, for Jake Partridge, among other things, was a blooded killer. His hands were secured behind his back, his ankles tied together.

Many men did not choose to speak at the hour of their death, but Pepper had known others to wax on for some time about the woes of their childhood and a society that had no place for them. But as far as he could tell—what with the hood already being snugly in place—Partridge had waived that right. Perhaps, in that final moment of dread and elation all men must face, he decided to go to his maker humbly with bowed head and pursed lips.

Maybe, Pepper had thought, just maybe there is something warm and human in the man. Some shred of civility, of decency, of morality.

The noose was dropped over Partridge's head and carefully adjusted about his neck. He seemed to be having trouble standing and the guards had to assist him. The crowd held its breath as the executioner examined his handiwork: a hand-woven noose of the finest Kentucky hemp, oiled to perfection. His nimble fingers traced the traditional thirteen wraps almost lovingly, tightening the coil of rope that encircled the condemned man's throat like a jungle serpent.

There was a drum roll.

The executioner stepped back and, with no further ado, sprung the trap.

A woman screamed.

The trap door opened and Partridge plunged down several feet, the noose pulling tight and his neck snapping clear and loud as a pistol shot. Somewhere out in the crowd, there was a weeping. There was a low discussion. Children giggled. An elderly woman fainted and was attended to. But gradually, quietly, the crowd dispersed and wagons were loaded, wares packed up, and people left. Partridge's body turned with a gentle motion in the breeze and was verified dead by the attending physician.

John Pepper was one of the first to leave.

But one of the last was a tall man on horseback.

20

Kreger just stared for a time. And it was truly hard to say whether he was simply astonished, mildly shocked...or he just wanted Pepper to think so. If he were indeed concealing something, his manner was controlled and careful. "Black Jake swung ten years ago, Marshal. He's in the ground now. He's not walking the streets. I'm surprised you didn't know that."

Sitting across from him in the flickering light of an oil lamp, Pepper rolled a cigarette. He took his time. "I was there when they hung him, Sheriff. Or at least I was there when they hung *someone.*" Pepper lit his cigarette and deliberately blew smoke at the piggish face of Kreger. "Were you there? Did you see it?"

Kreger said, "No, can't say I was."

"Then what in Christ's name do you know about it?"

"I only know that when men are hung, when they are executed and duly buried, they don't make much of a habit of visiting folks by night. Only in books, I understand, does that happen."

Pepper controlled himself. Maybe ten years before he would've leaped up and laid the back of his hand across Kreger's face for smart-mouthing him. And maybe when he was done, he would've given him a taste of the boot. And maybe then he would've informed Kreger that he was nothing but the damnable offspring resulting from a union between his mother and stockyard swine. But now, he kept his cool. He filled himself with ice, kept his face as emotionless and unreadable as a marble bust.

The man who lost control in this situation would be the one who stuck his foot up his own ass.

So he was calm when he said, "That morning in Wickenburg, they led the condemned out with the hood already over his head. There was no true way to know whose neck was stretched that day."

"Well, Marshal, I'm sure it was no other than Partridge his own self."

"And what makes you so sure of that?"

Kreger licked his lips. "I mean...well, shit, something like that...you can't fake it now can you? Not like you can pay someone to take your place."

His logic was, of course, irrefutable. Pepper knew that and hated it because it was exactly what his own brain was telling him. Something which was in direct contradiction to what his heart was telling him. Hell, maybe he *was* getting too damn old. Maybe those headaches were a sign that his brain was finally going to mush. Yet, he just couldn't accept that.

"No, you surely can't hire a man to hang for you. That's true. Very true." He shrugged, deciding to downplay it a bit. Throw Kreger off-guard. "Now this sounds like something out of one of them dime novels, but what if there was some sort of conspiracy in place? You know, the sheriff and Partridge himself? Maybe they doped up some other fellow and *he's* the one that swung. How does that strike you?"

The tranquil mask Kreger wore so well began to fray around the edges, began to slide down a bit and what was beneath was most interesting. The corner of his lips jumped like a toad on a burning match. "Well, that's crazy. Sounds like one of them yellowback novels to me." He laughed nervously. "Things like that just don't happen."

"Don't they?"

Pepper let that lay a moment. Maybe the man he'd seen leaving *wasn't* Black Jake. Maybe it was someone else entirely and, God knew, he desperately wanted to believe that...but damn if his bullshit scenario hadn't unnerved Kreger somewhat. At least, it sure seemed so. Pepper knew men; he'd been hunting them all his life. And right then he knew he'd struck a chord with Kreger. But was that because the impossible had indeed happened and Black Jake was still alive or was it merely because the good sheriff was mixed up in something equally as dark and disturbing?

Pepper thought about it and thought about it some more.

You spend your life tracking men, you begin to find yourself studying behavior, patterns of personality. You learn what a man likes to eat, to drink, to smoke. You learn what kind of women he likes or if he don't like them at all. And, yes, you even learn how a man walks. Because everyone does it a little different and it's one thing that's hard as hell to disguise. And Pepper *had* studied Black Jake at one time. He'd been one of the men who'd tracked him mercilessly. And right then, he would have bet a fifty-dollar gold piece that Black Jake was not moldering in the grave but riding through Chimney Flats.

"No, sir," Kreger said, settling into his old habit of stealth and concealment, "can't believe such a thing could happen. It's too wild."

"Maybe not, maybe not." Pepper kept watching him through heavy-lidded eyes. He dragged slowly off his cigarette. "Course, it would be easy enough to prove or disprove, wouldn't it?"

Kreger just looked at him. It appeared, if just for a moment, that he might fall right out of his skin. But he recovered quick enough. You had to give him that much.

Pepper said, "Sure. All a body'd have to do is take a ride over to Wickenburg and open Black Jake's grave."

Kreger was in control again. "Well, you just can't go around doing things like that. Grave robbery and such. Besides, Black Jake's been in the ground ten years now. Won't be much left."

"There'll be bones, I suspect. Sometimes that's all you need. If you know what you're looking for."

Kreger just sat there. He didn't look at all comfortable. He grinned like a clown in a road show and said, "Course, we're just talking here. Speculating."

Pepper butted his cigarette, pulled on his coat. "Of course. But if the trail on Nathan goes dry, I might just have to take a ride on over to Wickenburg. Could prove interesting. Real interesting."

Pepper left then with no further pleasantries.

He'd planted the seed now and it was only a matter of seeing what fruit it might bear. If he knew his men (and he was pretty certain he had Kreger pegged), then the harvest was going to be most strange and most enlightening. Things might just start happening now.

Pepper liked it all. Enjoying very much his role as a catalyst, as it were. One of his headaches was coming on, but he couldn't help but smile.

21

Two days after his meeting with Josh Kreger, Nathan Partridge was crossing the Maricopa's on his way to Dead Creek and whatever waited there. He kept thinking maybe he was being foolish here, taking the word of that stupid fat idiot. Even if Kreger was telling the truth (something Partridge had a hard time believing), then he was acting on a rumor and nothing more. A bit of gossip.

And was that wise?

After he left Kreger's cabin that night he went back to the ruins of the family farm and did some thinking. He figured the logical thing to do was to hang around a spell, see what transpired.

See what Kreger was up to, if anything at all. But Chimney Flats was just too hot. Too many men were hunting him and eventually, if he had to keep killing to assure his freedom, it was all going to start adding up and folks would be asking questions. And the only obvious answer to those questions would be that Nathan Partridge was hiding out in the hills.

So, early the next morning he started out.

The country was beautiful in the mountains. Beautiful and deadly like a woman with nothing to lose, Partridge figured. It was high and wild, thick with stands of aspen and lodgepole pine, cut by stony creeks and rushing rivers all but hidden by the tangled foliage. Great knobs of volcanic rock jutted from the hilly earth like the spines of dragons. It was an eyeful, all right, but it was also treacherous and tricky terrain full of sudden crevices, sharp glens, razor-toothed slopes and rock slides. It was country to be navigated slowly and carefully.

And this is just what Partridge did.

He wanted nothing better than to ride fast and hard, but it would have been too easy for his mount to snap a leg or, and worse, for him to get thrown and busted up. No, he needed his horse and he needed his limbs intact. So slow it was.

He plugged a cheroot into his mouth and gave it some fire as the black plodded onward, ever onward. High on his mount, he started thinking how strange it all was. How he'd broken out of prison only to reclaim his money and now was being slowly and quite inexorably drawn into something that smelled just as foul as a beaver trapper's britches.

He wasn't a man who liked mysteries.

Life had enough little surprises and nasty turns of plot without a man having to seek them out. But sometimes, goddamn, if you just didn't have a choice.

Partridge rounded a series of jagged boulders and was starting up the face of a peak littered with loose, flat stones when he heard the report of a rifle and felt a bullet whip past the tip of his nose.

He heard a man shouting and another bullet thudded into the hillside, followed a moment or two later by a second and a third. Whoever was shooting was either green or pissed-off and crazy. They weren't concentrating, weren't truly aiming, just snapping off rounds in his general direction. Calmly as possible, the black nickering nervously, Partridge brought him back around those boulders where drawing a bead on either of them would have been tricky for a crack shot, let alone this crazy sonofabitch.

He swung down out of the saddle and pulled his big Winchester from the scabbard just as another shot rang out, obliterating a stone a few feet away. Cautiously, trying to make himself as small a target as possible, he peered up over the irregular ledge of the boulder. There were two of them now, he knew that much. The first shots had been from maybe a Winchester or a Henry, but that last one…there was no doubt about that huge and echoing report that seemed to shake the mountains themselves: it was an old Hawken.

They'd stopped shooting now and he couldn't pinpoint them. He figured they were in the treeline just above the peak. But that was only a guess. There was another cracking report and a bullet drilled into the boulder face a few feet away. It was followed by two more. Damn. He spotted a haze of blue smoke rising from a tangle of brush and quickly pumped three shots into it, levering without even bothering to breathe.

Then the Hawken thundered and a slug screamed not an inch from the crown of his hat. And then it all became quite clear to him. These two weren't just taking random potshots at him—there was a strategy involved. The bushwhacker was putting round after round in his direction trying to draw him out into the Hawken's field of fire. He was both surprised and disturbed he hadn't figured it out right away.

Clever. Very clever.

Partridge left his hat cradled between the rocks where his head had been and slipped from sight. Then, taking up a new position a yard or so away, he waited. The sun was huge and bright overhead in a sky just as blue and clear as crystal. It was making its way west to its deathbed, but that wouldn't be for an hour or two yet. Carefully, with as little motion as possible, he rubbed dust over the barrel of his rifle to cut down on the shine. With that nasty sun up there, he didn't want the gleam of his barrel bringing a bullet into his head.

What he wanted here was for those wily peckerwoods up there to think him dead or, at the very least, to think he was hit and incapacitated. He figured there was no way they could possibly be sure without coming in closer. And when they broke cover, he'd pop the both of them. So, he waited and waited and waited. Either they'd try and flank him or they'd get bold and swing down out of the trees. If it was the former, he had no doubt he would hear them moving through the dry brush. And if it was the latter…well, he'd pull them right in like a fly into a spider's web.

Nearly thirty minutes later, they made their move.

He saw the fellow up in the bushes pop his head up and then dart down real quickly. He kept doing it, waiting, maybe, for Partridge to start shooting, but he didn't. After a few minutes of that, the bushwhacker stood right up and made an easy target of himself. But still, Partridge did not shoot. Oh, it would have been so damn easy to core his chest and blow his heart right out with his spine, but there was no hurry.

The other bushwhacker finally showed himself.

The two of them made eye contact and communicated via hand motions.

The guy with the Hawken—a big fellow with a beard just as orange as a carrot and a crown of hair to match—edged towards the top of the rise to get a better look. He started down slowly, then slipped on one of those shiny, flat stones. He slid down the rise on his ass, but never lost his rifle. The other fellow just stood his ground up there, watching. Partridge wasn't going to shoot carrot-beard…but then the stupid shit found his footing and charged the boulders with the Hawken held out before him.

Sucking in a sharp, shallow breath, Partridge came up and already had a bead on him as he rose into view. A split-second before carrot-beard could even think of firing, Partridge already had. He put a single round right into the man's forehead. His skull flew apart like a vase filled with blood and meat. The Hawken went one way and he went the other, spilling brains over the dusty ground.

The other bushwhacker started squeezing off shot after shot, but didn't dare come down the slope just yet. Partridge again waited and waited, then bolted up suddenly, his finger already applying pressure to the trigger. There was a shot and the final bushwhacker cried out and dropped his rifle. There was a second and third and he fell over, tumbling down the slope and kicking up clouds of dust and spinning pebbles and pretty much painting that hillside a translucent red.

Thing was, Partridge never even pulled the trigger.

22

The man on the ground slowing bleeding to death had long, white hair just as stringy as bailing twine. His beard was likewise, though now matted with red. His skin was burnished brown as any Apache's and his eyes were little more than black, glistening balls peering from weathered slits.

"Bastards," he coughed, a pencil-thin line of blood flecking his lips. "Jumping…jumping my claim…twelve goddamn years…worked twelve years…you cocksuckers taking my claim…"

"Crazy old sonofabitch, ain't he?" Carl Roseman said.

He was the leader of the trio of riders that came to Partridge's apparent aid. He was a tall, somber man whose every move oozed with confidence. His face was flawlessly handsome as if it had been pressed from a mold. He wore a military-style greatcoat with shiny brass buttons. With him were Caleb Kroner and Danny Withers. The three of them wore the same handlebar mustaches and carried matching Henry rifles. The prospector's body had barely quit rolling before they appeared, waved Partridge over and introduced themselves like this was some charming afternoon tea.

"Seen men get like that, though," Kroner said as though it were an everyday occurrence and maybe it was. "They slip up into the hills dreaming of gold and silver, that great motherlode they all read about and no one ever seems to find. But they keep at it year after year after year and what have you? Crazy mountain rats like this one."

Withers said, "Nothing'll destroy a man faster than loose women and the promise of easy money."

Partridge lit a cheroot and nodded his head. "Amen to that," he said. "It's a shame what gold fever will do to a man's soul."

"It surely is," Roseman said.

Partridge didn't like any of this. All he wanted was a quick and clean ride through the mountains and then onto the trail to Dead Creek. Where maybe, just maybe, there would be a few answers waiting. But what he was getting instead were complications. Lunatic prospectors and now these three. Jesus, what next?

Withers ran a tongue over yellowed teeth. "You suppose this one and his partner were just flat-out mad or do you think there might be some real money hearsabouts?"

Partridge said, "Could be either way, I figure. Problem being it could take weeks of combing these hills before a man found their operation."

The prospector shuddered and blood bubbled from his lips. His eyes looked filmy, hazed over like those of a hound waiting for death. He kept trying to say something, but speech was beyond him now.

"He's suffering," Withers said.

"He'll be gone before long," Roseman told him. He scanned the landscape, looking as if he didn't like what he saw. He looked over at Partridge. "Well, Mister Smith, I don't know about you, but we have business elsewhere by the end of the week. If'n there's a fat vein up in those hills, we'll have to leave it to you."

Partridge blew smoke out his nostrils. "Count me out. I've got a long ride ahead of me and the sooner I get to it, the better things'll be." He hadn't honestly figured out yet what these three were up to. Part of him wanted to believe they were just innocent men out on innocent business. But he'd lived a dark and seamy life and trust did not come easy. And particularly when you were a man with a bounty on your head. "I want to thank you gentlemen for arriving when you did. You surely pulled my fat out of the fire and I think it was beginning to sizzle."

Roseman's smile was thin as ribbon. "You looked like you were doing all right. I think it was them other two that needed the help."

"All the same, I appreciate it."

Kroner scratched his privates, then prodded the prospector with the scuffed and dusty toe of one boot. "Think he's dead," he said. "Yessir, just as dead as old dogshit."

Roseman squatted next to him, took off his hat. He shooed a fly away from the old man's grimy, blood-spattered face. His lips moved silently, as if in prayer, and the others, even Partridge, bowed their heads dutifully. Roseman shut the eyes and folded the stiffening arms over the bosom.

He stood up. "I think the only Christian thing to do is to bury these men. Would you agree, Mister Smith?"

Partridge almost didn't catch that. Mr. Smith. *He was Mr. Smith.* He had to be careful. "Yes, of course."

They buried the prospectors in a common grave up in the trees. Roseman fashioned a cross out of a few sticks of wood and tied it together with twine. He sank it into the ground and mumbled a few prayers.

Partridge was ready then to ride out. He figured he'd done his civic duty and all. He also figured he'd been friendly enough, not at all evasive in questions put to him. He figured that unless these men already knew who he was, then he hadn't aroused any suspicions. The sun was sinking low in the west and the shadows were creeping up just as thick as serpents in a snakepit.

Kroner and Withers gathered up some wood and put together a nice little fire. Roseman asked Partridge to join them for supper and, despite himself, he did just that.

23

He supposed he was curious.

Yes, he needed to be on his way, but, damn, there was something about these men that just didn't wash. As it turned out, they claimed to be riding to Dead Creek as well. Claimed there was a ranch nearby that was doing some hiring. And that sounded reasonable enough. It was just that Partridge had a nasty suspicion that these fellows wouldn't have known a Texas Longhorn from a Hereford. Maybe he was wrong. Maybe. But he didn't like the idea of these men suddenly showing like they had and going out of their way to be so friendly. And he liked the idea of them riding to Dead Creek with him even less. What he had to do was make them show their hand one way or another. If they were hunting him, then it would be best to get the killing done and over with now, rather than out on the trail.

They stuffed themselves on boiled beans and biscuits. And for a time all you heard on that lonesome mountain night was the sound of spoons scraping tin plates. Partridge pretended to eat with a tranquil and easy manner. The way a man supped with friends. Truth was, he was ever-vigilant, ever-ready for the shit to come raining down hot and heavy. He balanced his plate on his knee and shoveled in the grub with his left hand (he was actually right-handed) and just waited for it to happen. If they were able to get the draw on him, then they would have to be good.

"I must say I appreciate your hospitality," he said to them. "It's rare a man meets such as yourselves on the trail. Most of the time it's just riff raff."

Roseman set aside his plate. "What sort of riff raff would that be?"

"The usual. Outlaws. Road agents. Bounty hunters. You know the sort."

Roseman's expression did not change, but Withers face seemed to tighten, the flesh nearly curdling on the skull beneath. Kroner just licked his lips, eyes darting to the fire and then back to Partridge.

Partridge himself was leaning back slightly now, the .38 Colt in its cross-draw scabbard within easy reach. He figured he'd broached it now and maybe struck a mild chord, so now was the time to play it for all it was worth.

"Yep," he said, "can't seem to recall such a lower, dirt-eating bunch of cowards in all my life as them bounty hunters. Men like that would sell their own mothers for two bits. Give me crazy, dirt-mean prospectors or drunken, pissed-off injuns any day of the week. Least they have convictions, they have pride." He shook his head as if it all disgusted him and spat into the dirt. "No sir, them bounty hunters ain't nothing but low-down garbage-eating, gutless swine. Why they'd lick the ass of anyone with a dollar in their hand. That's the sort they are. I could drop a nickel into the pit of a privy and those yellow sonsofbitches would be fighting to see who got to dive in after it. And why not? Wallowing in shit? Hell, it's their natural element."

Again, Roseman's expression did not change. He raised an eyebrow and the muscles at the corners of his lips tensed, but he held it in tight. If he'd held it in any tighter, he would have come apart from sheer internal stress. But you could see it filming his eyes: anger boiling now like a vat of wax. Kroner looked confused by it all. He looked to Roseman, looked away. Then he studied the ground blankly, just waiting for a signal from the older man as to how he should feel about it all.

And Withers? He was the best of the lot. His face was screwed-up and pinched tight as a fat lady's corset. Ready to come blowing apart in every conceivable direction. He looked like someone had shit a turd in his mouth and made him chew it.

There was a heavy, brooding silence for a moment or two, but charged with electricity like the air right before lightning struck. Up in the high country a wolf howled low and long.

Withers spit tobacco juice into the fire. "Hell of a thing to say to a man that's spent the better part of his life hunting criminal scum like you, Mister Partridge. Unless, that is, you're fixing to die."

Roseman was staring at him. "Bounty's the same, alive or dead."

Kroner licked his lips. "But the man said—"

"Shut the fuck up," Withers warned him.

So it was out in the open and what came next, of course, was inevitable. Roseman was too cautious, too controlled to make a blind play for his gun. And Kroner wasn't about to do anything until someone else did first. Which left Withers who was a born hothead and had all the common sense of a hound with its dick stuck in a fence.

He moved quick, but clumsily.

Partridge threw himself back and cleared leather simultaneously. As Withers' round went wild and high over his head, he put a slug right into his throat. It made a neat, smoking hole in his Adam's Apple and sprayed blood and meat as it exited. Withers fell over just as Partridge hit the dirt. By that time, Roseman was already shooting and his first two rounds went skyward just as Partridge put one in his chest and another in Kroner's belly. Roseman's third bullet, fired as he was going down, ripped across Partridge's forearm in a searing trail.

And that was it.

Kroner was moaning and gagging and vomiting out a froth of blood. The poor bastard hadn't even pulled the trigger. And now he was gutshot. Dying slow, but not easy.

Partridge pulled himself up, his forearm wet and bleeding. He looked over at Kroner who was still holding his Colt, though it was pressed along with his hands to his gored belly. "Drop it," Partridge told him. "Or you'll be dying a lot quicker than the good Lord intended."

Kroner made a sharp, squealing sound and did just that. He let the gun go and fell away from it, pulled up into a fetal position now, his hands and belly a red and bubbling mess.

Partridge had his eye on Roseman.

Withers was stone dead, lying there in the rocks and dirt, eyes wide and staring, mouth sprung open like a beaver trap. It looked like he was wearing a crimson and black neckerchief.

But Roseman was still alive. Sucking air like a leaky bellows, but alive.

"Well," Partridge said to him. "Maybe you should get it off your mind. Unburden yourself here and now."

Roseman was staring at the stars overhead, not moving. But he was breathing and he kept swallowing as if he were trying to keep something down. The front of his coat was wet with blood and blackened from contact burns. He wasn't long for this world. His right lung was whistling and that blood was very dark—arterial blood.

"What's it gonna be?" Partridge asked him.

Roseman looked over at him, painfully and slowly. "Go...to...hell..."

Partridge shot him in the head without a hint of drama.

Roseman had balls. He'd give him that much. A chest wound like that had to hurt like a sonofabitch, but he never cried out, never so much as batted an eye. Just took it and laid there waiting for death. Partridge knew he could've worked on a man like that with a knife for hours and never gotten so much as a grimace. Some men were born tough, though, seasoned with iron and they died the same way.

But Partridge didn't care about him anymore than he cared about Withers. Men like that lived like they were asking to die and sometimes you simply had to oblige.

Kroner was an entirely different matter.

Ignoring his gagging sounds and whimpering, Partridge tended to his arm. He went over to Roseman's horse and opened his saddlebag. There was a fine white cotton shirt inside amongst other items. He cut it into strips and bandaged his arm, after first swabbing away the blood and examining the damage by the firelight. It wasn't so bad. A nice, hurting rut carved there. But a clean wound. Just another scar to add to his catalog.

After a time, Partridge lit one of Roseman's big cigars and went over to Kroner.

24

After his days as a buffalo hunter ground to a halt, Partridge spent his days as a line rider for the Quade-Beale Cattle Company up in the high country along the Mogollon Rim. It was work best suited to a man who was unattached and favored his solitude. For up in those grassy, pine-shadowed meadows it was often months in-between visitors.

It suited him just fine.

Whatever it was that burned in him, be it hereditary or learned, he was a man who enjoyed peace and quiet. Up at the line shack, he spent his nights feeding the fire, playing solitaire, and reading books. His days were spent riding fence, doctoring screwworm, and gathering strays. And this for forty-odd dollars a month.

It was surely not a fortune, but it was a paycheck.

And after the decline of the buffalo herds, work became scarce. An entire industry was in collapse. And like most other hunters, he had spent all his money whoring, drinking, and gambling. So, he rode the range and spent his days staring up at the snowy peaks and that blue sky that went on forever, wondering how it was he could make his fortune. He decided mining was out. What he knew of it, he didn't particularly care for. There was always the army, but that wasn't much of a life. And lawman. Better pay, but an easy way to die. Too easy.

Then one day, on around sunset, as he rode his red down a rocky verge after safely tucking away his herd in a grassy meadow above, fortune or fate called his name. It called in the form of three rustlers. They were dressed in canvas mackinaws that were patched together and just as dirty as the backside of a hog. Bearded, they wore their hair long like Indians. When Partridge rode down to them, they all smiled.

"Evening," a man with a scar across the bridge of his nose said, pulling on the brim of his sodbuster hat. "These cattle hearsabout…who might they belong to?"

Partridge could smell trouble brewing, could smell it coming off these men in a thick sour stench.

"These cattle are the property of the Quade-Beale outfit."

"See?" one of the other men said. "I told you as much."

"Shit," said his partner.

They looked enough alike to be brothers, right on down from the bulbous noses to the crooked grins and missing teeth, save one was fat and the other thin. And both, Partridge noticed with some unease, had Winchesters laid across their laps.

The scar-nosed man took off his hat and hung it from the saddle horn. He opened his coat and the setting sun glinted off the blue steel barrel of an 1860 Colt Navy slung through his belt. His fingers drummed the butt of a Sharps carbine in the saddle boot. "Tell ye what, brother," he said. "We aim to rustle about a hundred head and drive 'em up to Flagstaff where we has ourselves a buyer all ready to take possession. Question being, is a shit-nothing hillbilly like ye gonna work with us or do we have to kill ye?"

Partridge could never remember being called a hillbilly in all his borne days. True, he wore his beard long in those days and up at the line shack, him and soap and water weren't exactly on the best of terms. And maybe the greasy beaver coat and threadbare buckskin pants weren't helping matters much either. "I ain't no hillbilly," he told them, not sure why the idea of that ate at him like ants on a dead woodchuck.

Old scar-nose shrugged. "Yep, ye ain't nothing but a fucking hillbilly."

One of the others said, almost apologetically, "Don't take offense none, friend. He calls everyone that."

And Partridge supposed it didn't really matter. He kept his hands on the red's cinch and thought about the scattergun in the saddle scabbard, the Starr double-action at his hip. Thought about it, mind you, and that's about all. Because he knew if he so much as scratched his privates, he'd have more holes in him than a sprinkling can.

"Ye haven't answered me question," scar-nose said. "Maybe you need some time to consider it. I'll give ye…ah…let's see…about as long as it takes one of me boys here to kill yer hillbilly ass deader than Billy the Kid's moldering dick. How's that sound, ye hillbilly sumbitch?"

Partridge just looked at him hard and mean and by that point in his life, he really knew no other way. "Don't need quite that long," he said. "I've already made up my mind. I'm going to kill you. Yes, sir. That's what I aim to do."

Scar-nose started laughing. "Well, ye crazy hillbilly sumbitch!" He laughed so hard, he started to cough. He worked up a wad of phlegm and spit it over his shoulder. "Tell ye what. Before ye kill me and these boys kill ye back and do something unforgivable with yer corpse, how's about ye tell me what yer making for risking yer scrawny ass up heres."

Partridge said, "About forty-three a month."

They all started laughing then.

"Jesus H. Christ," scar-nose said. "Ain't ye the living end? Bet when ye ain't up here doggin' strays, ye wear floppy shoes and a big red nose and ride about on one of them unicycles making folks laugh and such." He just shook his head. "Listen, hillbilly. Some rich sumbitch sits up in his big house pawing up some imported French whore and drinking champagne and chewing steaks thicker than yer pecker…while you, ye inbred hillbilly shit-eater, sits up here on the far side of the Devil's asshole, jerking off and risking yer neck and eating second-hand buff steaks tougher than my mama's backside. And all to keep that rich sumbitch in whores and champagne! What the hell's wrong with ye?"

Partridge opened his mouth to object…but this guy was right. Damn but that hurt some. He'd lived a long, hard life by that point and was spending a lot of time at the shack reading books by highbrows like Chaucer and Milton and Shakespeare (even though he couldn't be sure what they were about), trying to make up for his lack of true education and white trash upbringing...and now here was this goddamn rustler pointing at him and laughing and telling him he was stupid, making him feel like he'd been tit-weaned by a mare donkey. And this just when he thought he was gaining some smarts.

"A man pays me to do a job," he told the rustlers, "and I do it. I don't give a damn if it's ten bucks or two-hundred. He pays me, I do it."

The rustler and his compatriots were really roaring now.

"Why, ye poor dumb hillbilly. Good Christ," scar-nose said, cackling madly now. His eyes were starting to water. "Ye know how much I'm gonna make this week?"

Partridge just stared.

Scar-nose did a little quick finger-counting. He was missing two fingers on his left hand so it took a little time. "Near as I can figure four, five thousand, things go well. And that's U.S. Treasury greenbacks, son. The real item." He looked to his fellow rustlers and then back to Partridge. "What ye say ye come ride with us? Ye help us drive these head up to Flagstaff and ye'll be in for a good cut. What ye say, peckerwood?"

Maybe any other time Partridge would have done the first fool thing that popped into his head—like going for his guns—but for once, he thought about it. And thought about it real carefully. He'd held his current job for most of the year, but rumor had it down at the cookhouse (on Partridge's infrequent visits, that was) that old man Beale was going to bring back his old line rider, who also happened to be some sort of shirt tail relation. Which meant, of course, that Partridge was going to be high and certainly dry.

"All right," he told them. "I don't need this goddamned job and I could sure use the money. But if you try to steal from me or do me harm, God help you. I'll kill your ass dead."

Scar-nose looked him up and down. "Don't doubt that, hillbilly. Ye look like a low-down murderer if I ever did see one. But, hell, most of me friends are murderers, so I welcome ye." He dug out tobacco and paper and deftly rolled cigarettes for all in the gathering gloom. "Let's smoke on that. Name's Ben Kirby."

"Kid Kirby?" Partridge said.

"Been called worse. Be as it may, I'm at yer service, hillbilly. At yer service. These two are the brothers Webb." He motioned to the chubby one. "Henry." And then the lanky one. "Reese."

Pleasantries were exchanged.

"Ye'll discover in due time, hillbilly, that these two ain't much smarter than yeself. But dependable as all hell."

Partridge knew about Kid Kirby. He supposed everyone in those parts did. He was something of a near-legendary outlaw who'd made a career of robbing banks and stagecoaches. And apparently he was something of a hand at rustling cattle as well. Partridge supposed diversity was important, though. It was rumored by some that Kid Kirby rode with Sam Bass and his gang. And when Bass was gunned down by Texas Rangers, it was he who had tracked down the man who had betrayed Bass—Jim Murphy—and hand-fed him poison in his cell. That his death was not at all suicide like the law said.

This was all running through Partridge's head and he couldn't help himself. "They say you rode with Sam Bass—that true?"

Kirby blew out a cloud of smoke. "Not that I recollect, hillbilly. But, shit, them fools want to give me credit for killing that turncoat goatsucker Murphy, I guess I'll take it. Why not? But if it was me, I'd a just blew his brains straight out his asshole…or what he had of them. No, hillbilly, it wasn't me. I don't enter jail cells willingly."

Partridge knew that much was true. Three times Kirby had faced the noose and three times he'd skated away from it. And on each occasion, he'd defended himself. No lawyer needed. His courtroom antics were said to be bold and brash and oddly refreshing. Juries fell in love with him. And Kirby, using a purloined license, had even defended other men. And successfully. But, somewhere along the line, he must have returned to crime.

"What's your name?" Reese Webb asked.

Partridge told him.

That got all the rustlers looking at one another. "No shit?" Kirby said. "Ye don't, by chance, be kin of old Black Jake Partridge?"

"Yeah. Father. Less said about that the better."

Kirby nodded, pulled off his cigarette. "Amen to that. Meanest sumbitch I ever did come across. I'll only say, hillbilly, that if ye got his blood in yer veins, I'll not be crossing you no how." Saying that, Kirby put his index and middle fingers in his mouth and let go with a shrill, deafening whistle that brought riders from the treeline. "Don't be nervous, hillbilly. They's with us."

Besides Kirby and the Webb brothers, the gang consisted of a completely hairless man named Mexican Joe Avilla. He was built like a bridge support and had just about the hardest, meanest eyes Partridge had ever seen. They could've drilled holes through concrete block they were so fathomless, dark and piercing. "What's the matter with you?" he said to Partridge in a voice full of gravel and dust. "Ain't you never seen a bald Mesican before?"

Partridge just shrugged. "Can't say that I have."

"Hereditary, that's what. Even my ma was bald as a stone," he explained.

Besides Mexican Joe there was Willy Boy Horton and Prescott Jackson, both of whom had yet to see twenty. And both of which were pumped full of the sort of fool bravado and glandular machismo that got many such boys killed in that hard and violent country. They were both armed and were both ready to start killing over any and all imagined offenses. The last member of the rustlers was a fellow named Johnny Blunt. He was just as thin as a finger of straw and had a complexion like maybe he'd bobbed for apples in a vat of lye as a kid. His hair was the color of desiccated wheat, long and stringy, all tucked tightly beneath an old CSA cap.

"P-P-P-Pleased to make your acq-q-q...nice to meet you, t-t-that is," he said, pulling from a flask of shine. "W-W-What you all s-s-staring at?"

Partridge shrugged and forced himself to look away. "Not a thing, friend."

"M-M-Maybe you noticed I s-s-stutter somewhat. M-M-Maybe."

"John's a bit sensitive about it," Kirby explained. "But he's a fine man and it's been my pleasure to ride with him."

"I t-t-thank you kindly, M-M-Mister Kirby."

And that was the gang. With Partridge along for the ride (and he knew right then and there that he was, that he'd been waiting for something like this for some time) there was eight of them.

Kirby said, "Ye pretty much replacing another fellow we had with us. Apache Gerou. He got shot up awful in West Texas and we had to bury his miserable heathen ass on the trail. Poor old Apach." Kirby shook his head and it seemed the others bowed their as well. "Loved him as much as any white man can love a heathen breed devil like him. Yes, sir. Apache was quick with a gun and quicker with a knife. He could rustle up a mess of rattlers and turn 'em into the tastiest stew ye ever did have. Crazy sumbitch, though. Liked his womenfolk real natural and all. Didn't like 'em bathing and such. Those whores in Wickenburg, why they knew he was coming, they wouldn't touch soap nor water for a full week. Apach liked 'em gamey as a carcass full of flies. Heathen bastard, that's what old Apach was. Hillbilly sumbitch right from the start."

They came upon Apache Gerou, Kirby said, at a little carnival in a town called Steuberg, just outside Santa Fe. Place smelled of cowshit from five miles out. But they had a little seedy carnival of sorts going with beer tents and shooting exhibitions and pigs roasting put on by an outfit called Dr. Cagliostro's Travelling Medicine Show and Mysterious Magic Carnival. There were freaks and magic acts, shootists and juggling apes, African pythons and Egyptian mummies. Even an electric man who could call lightning down from the heavens. Doc Cagliostro himself was selling snakeoil off the back of a medicine wagon. Rancid goatpiss is what it was, flavored with corn whiskey and pine pitch. That stuff was guaranteed to do everything and anything. It cured piles and increased sex drive, made the blind see and turned barren women fertile. It also raised the dead, cured tapeworm, and took bloodstains out of britches. Kirby bought a bottle and was certain it could also strip paint from metal and make hair grow on a man's palms.

But for Kirby that was all just filler, the real attraction was Apache Gerou.

Apache was biting the heads off chickens and sticking needles through his arms and gargling with scorpions and shoving rattlesnakes into his shorts. His best bit was drinking kerosene and pissing flame.

He was a real sight.

But probably the best thing about Apach was that he threw knives with the accuracy some men shot bullets. And if that wasn't enough, he could break bricks with his head and bend metal bars with his bare hands.

Kirby bought him off Cagliostro for $500. Admittedly, he was very drunk at the time but Apache Gerou amused him to no end. Doc Cagliostro said Apache was from some horseshit town in Utah. Said his old man was some sort of part-time Baptist minister and full-time pimp name of Preacher Dan. He'd knocked up some Mescalero gal and then, when she died suddenly and in abject poverty, he decided to raise the boy himself (being the Christian saint he was), even though everyone knew said boy was crazier than tapdancing barn cats. Why even Apach's mother's people wouldn't have nothing to do with him.

Anyway, Preacher Dan kept Apach on a rope in an old hog barn that was near fallen down, feeding him scraps and letting him do his business in the hay...such were the depths of Preacher Dan's fine and charitable soul. Apache's only real vice seemed to be digging holes and sleeping in them. Now and again, of course, Apach would get loose and run about naked shaking his privates at God-fearing old ladies and devouring lower animals and fornicating with trees and such. Sometimes he'd run wild in the streets and chase wagons about on all fours, barking like a bloodhound. Maybe none of that was real acceptable, but it was livable. The final straw came though, Preacher Dan told Doc Cagliostro, when Apache chewed through his leash and slipped into a nearby pasture and made passionate love to a prize-winning cow. The cow's owner was rightly concerned, though Preacher Dan seemed to think it was not so much because he'd had relations with the animal, but because the farmer feared either the cow's milk would be tainted or it would give birth to a calf that walked upright and liked to expose itself.

That's when Cagliostro purchased Apache Gerou.

First night in his possession, Apach got loose and tried to eat a saloon cat. He was discovered later grunting like a pig and digging for grubs in a local orchard. The townspeople said Preacher Dan ran a brothel out of the back of his adobe church. It was said he put on a blasphemous sort of sex show for the local miners and cowhands. And his star attraction was Apache Gerou who was endowed such that it would've made a stallion envious. He was known as the Three-Legged Man. About the time Cagliostro took possession of Apach, Preacher Dan was run out of town.

"Tell ye something," Kirby said, "he was dirt crazy, moonstruck, but he was good at everything he tried. Once I took him in and stopped exploiting him and all, he turned into a helluva good man. I schooled him and showed him how to shoot and speak properly. Shit-crazy still, sure, but a good man all the same. Ye should've seen him, hillbilly, he was something."

"Goddamn silly bastard," Mexican Joe said, shaking his head.

Henry Webb laughed. "He's still sore on account Apach took a liking to this Stetson he had. Thing was full of fancy beadwork and what not. Apach like it so much he done humped it right to death one night."

They all started laughing at that, Partridge included, but Mexican Joe failed to see the humor in a man making love to a hat. And a fine one-of-a-kind hat, too. Damn waste, that's what.

Partridge figured he'd do his best to fill the boots of Apache Gerou…within limits. They spent the night in the line shack, the lot of them, drinking and singing and vomiting with great abandon. The next day they got down to it: rustling Quade-Beale stock and driving them down out of the mountains and then up to Flagstaff. Some two-hundred steer at fifty a head resulted in a payday of $10,000 from a rancher who'd lost most of his herd through an infestation of tick fever and wasn't too concerned as to how he replaced them.

And that was how the next six months were pretty much spent. They rustled cattle and horses and somehow, through luck or pluck, managed to keep their necks out of the noose. But things started to tighten up and cattle companies and ranchers were hiring range detectives and regulators. So Kirby and company got out while the getting was good.

But they were far from done.

Kirby decided they needed a new venture and one that he had some experience in. So, in Tombstone, they robbed a mining camp paymaster for $7000. In a lightning sweep of raids during the next month or so, they robbed six other Arizona mining concerns for a final take of upwards of $60,000. It would have been nearly twice that, but in Globe they got carried away blowing a safe with the company payroll safely ensconced within and not only blew the safe, but put most of the building into orbit.

Of course, they didn't sit still with this.

They started hitting the Union Pacific railroad on a regular basis not only in the Arizona Territory, but in Utah, New Mexico, and California. They based themselves out of a hideout at the convergence of Salt River and Tonto Creek, an old miner's shack dug into a hillside on high and defensible ground. Their favorite ruse was to stop a train on a bridge...a bridge rigged with dynamite. Then they would march out both the chief engineer and conductor so they could see for themselves what was going to happen if they didn't open the express and mail cars. It all worked very well and in six, seven months' time they had taken down no less than eleven trains and had made several hundred thousand in folding money. So much money, in fact, that they began to throw it around like rice at a wedding—the best hotels, the best whores, the best restaurants. They pissed away thousands gambling. The water was flowing and its color was green. Posses were duly organized and not a one came within spitting distance of the outlaws the newspapers called the Gila River Gang (in that Kirby's crew robbed a series of stages along that body of water).

The truly exceptional part was that they had yet to kill a single man or even wing one. But that, as it turned out, was coming next.

Sometime during this period, Partridge met and wed Anna Marie. He saw her very little and only knew for sure that she had the face of an angel and the body of a she-devil. She could do things in bed no self-respecting woman had a right doing. With that in mind, Partridge wined, dined, and proposed to her. They were married but a year and he probably spent less than five or six weeks with her the entire time.

Meanwhile, the gang's exploits did not lessen.

More trains, more stages, more mining offices. They would go in irregular sporadic bursts—a week of hell-for-leather train robbing and when the law turned up the heat, mining offices and ranch payrolls. Then when vigilantes and U.S. Marshal's posses started getting too close, they would start hitting stages. They were a fluid, flexible machine. It worked very well and seemed to keep both the law and the civilian population off balance. At least for a time.

"I'm thinking on bringing in a couple new men," Kirby told Partridge one day, who through pluck and brains had become the outlaw leader's lieutenant of sorts. "What ye think of that, hillbilly?"

"I think I'm getting goddamn sick and tired of being called hillbilly. You got the other boys saying it now, too."

Kirby thought that was pretty damned funny. "Ah, shit, Nate, don't take it personal. I ain't nothing but an Alabamy 'billy meself. First date I ever did have was with me sister. Never could be sure which critter out in the pen was me mother."

The new guys were two drifters named Pierce and Coltrane. They claimed to have quite a bit of experience fighting Injuns and robbing banks up north in the Wyoming Territory. Partridge didn't exactly trust either of them and particularly Pierce. It was a feeling that grew stronger as time passed. And one that was confirmed with what happened next. They tried to take down a Union Pacific train outside of Phoenix. Kirby was certain it was a sure thing. They hadn't so much as looked at a train in months. The express car, Kirby learned, was carrying in excess of $40,000 worth of cash and bonds bound for a Wickenburg cattle combine. They stopped the train by throwing timbers across the tracks and attacked it mounted. It was to be their usual quick and devastating raid. The sort that had always been successful.

But this time it didn't work.

As they approached, they were fired upon by dozens of well-placed rifles. Prescott Jackson took rounds in the head and chest and went down dead in the desert sand. Johnny Blunt's horse was shot out from under him and Reese Webb lost a chunk of shoulder. Considering the amount of firepower loosed upon them, it was a wonder they rode away at all. As Kirby said later, the air was buzzing with lead like flies lighting from a corpse. Partridge figured they were either expected or set-up. Maybe both.

A posse led by the Maricopa County sheriff ambushed the outlaws at the junction of the Salt and Verde Rivers. Twenty men rode down on them and a running gun battle ensued. It was only the marksmanship of the outlaws (and the posses' lack of it) that saved their hides. As it was, Willy Boy Horton was killed and Coltrane mortally wounded. But the opposing force didn't fair too well either. Six possemen were killed and five others wounded. The sheriff's right arm was shattered by bullets and later had to be amputated.

Bloody, worn, and damn near beaten, the Gila River Gang slunk back to their hideout like whipped dogs. They patched up Reese Webb and did what they could for Coltrane, but he was stone dead by sunset.

Partridge couldn't help remembering how Pierce had managed to stay out of the fray each time. He didn't do much shooting and never seemed to be shot at. Maybe it was the confusion of the gunplay...but he didn't think so. He told Kirby his suspicions. And Kirby, quite calmly and efficiently, asked Pierce if he was working with the law. Pierce violently asserted his innocence. But they saw it in his eyes and five minutes later, he was sprawled across an ancient oak table. The Webb brothers held him down while Mexican Joe and Johnny Blunt pulled his trousers off.

Partridge stood by watching and smoking.

"Well," Kirby said, pressing the blade of his bowie knife up to Pierce's balls. "We got ourselves one helluva predicament, don't we? Ye say ye didn't sell us out. But I have to ask myself how we could be so damn unlucky. Ye got any ideas?"

Pierce's face was twisted-up in terror, his flesh gone fluid. It had run now like wax, it seemed, pooling in all the wrong places. "Jesus H. Christ, Kirby! You can't...I mean, you won't..." Then he started screaming and hollering for help. Partridge silenced him by extinguishing his cigarette on the man's lips.

"Why?" Kirby asked him. *"Why?"*

But it was the same old story and who hadn't heard it a dozen times by then? Money. Pierce was a bounty hunter. Pinkerton agents had used him before to infiltrate gangs and he was pretty good at it. He headed a group of manhunters who were all fairly practiced at doing the same. The sheriff's posses had included six of his men. Pierce named them plain as day and—

And then Kirby slit his throat, saving his balls for the crows.

In retrospect, maybe they should've waited and interrogated the sonofabitch at more depth. Found out what was in store for them, but they got pretty much what they needed. After that, there was only one thing to do. Coltrane was dead and Partridge was sorry he hadn't trusted the man more, because when the fat was in the fire, that boy gave all.

But it wasn't just Coltrane, but Willy Boy Horton and Prescott Jackson. Both cold as a result of Pierce's gang of manhunters and rats.

It was an insult that couldn't go unchallenged. So what they did next was to go after Pierce's men.

25

Drawing off one of Roseman's big cigars, Partridge gathered up the bounty hunters' weapons. Then, slugging from a bottle of whiskey he found in Withers' saddlebags, he returned to the fire and fed it a few more sticks until it was blazing bright and orange like a harvest moon. He went over to Kroner who was whimpering about his mother and the Lord Jesus Christ. He searched him, being careful so as not to add to the man's agony. He found a small hunting knife, but nothing else worth mentioning save for fifteen dollars in silver.

Sitting cross-legged by the fire on the cool ground, Partridge stacked wood off to his left and arranged a few things before him taken off the dead men—Roseman's hunting knife, a bottle of whiskey, Withers' Hotchkiss .45. Off to his right was the form of Kroner, balled-up like a snake avoiding the talons of a hawk.

"Don't think there's much of a future for you, friend," Partridge told him. "Smart thing would be just to tell me what this is all about."

Kroner coughed and spat something out.

"I…need…a…doctor…goddamn you…"

"Doctor? Friend, they're rarer than honest women hereabouts. Hate to be the one to tell you, but you're a dead man. All that's lacking is a box, a plot of earth, and a preacher." He drew off the cigar, decided it tasted like burning cow dung. "Best I can do for you is make it easy. What say we start with a drink?"

In the glow of the firelight, the bounty hunter's eyes were huge and glazed, jutting from a face just as white as unbaked bread. His lips were trembling like maybe they wanted to crawl off his face and find a safe place to die. He was making groaning, choking sounds deep in his throat. His hands were clutched over his belly, but what Partridge could see was a welling, wet valley beneath them. Maybe he could've checked the wound, tended it possibly, but he knew dead when he saw it. He knew its look, its smell. And that stink was all over Kroner. Thick as rot in a coffin.

"A-a drink," Kroner managed. "God…God help me…but I'm…thirsty…"

"Of course you are." Partridge placed the bottle in the man's shaking hands, led it and them to his mouth. He started guzzling and all that led to was a violent fit of coughing and hacking in which he tore up his insides even worse than they already were.

"Easy," Partridge told him when he'd settled down somewhat. "Just a sip. Just wet your lips."

Kroner complied and just nodded when he wanted the bottle drawn away. "Yeah…yeah…better…hee, hee…I'm dying. Yes, sir." His eyes swam in and out of focus.

"Like I said," Partridge reminded him, "I can make this real easy on you or real damn hard. See, thing is, I gotta know what this is about. Why don't you tell me?"

Kroner nodded again. His chin was wet with blood and whiskey. "We just…we just happened upon you…is all. Roseman…he recognized you…from your dodger…said we could…that—"

Partridge touched his cigar to Kroner's cheek and he let out a yelp. "Now let's try the truth, son. You ain't got a damn thing to lose now. I was there, remember? Roseman said there was a bounty dead or alive and you said something about the man. 'The man said…' Something along that order."

"You gonna kill me, Mister Partridge?" he said, lucid now.

"No, but if you don't start talking straight, you might wish I had."

Kroner licked his lips. "Can...can I have another pull?"

Partridge gave him one. "Now tell me about this man."

"I...I don't know no man," he said, his breathing suddenly harsh and ragged. "Just do what Mister Roseman said. I was in the army with Mister Roseman. Mister Roseman, he—"

Partridge extinguished the cigar just beneath Kroner's left eye. He writhed and screeched in pain. "You cocksucker...you sonofabitch...*you goddamn Yankee mother—"*

Partridge struck him across the face with the back of his hand and silenced his mouth in addition to dislocating his nose. Blood funneled from his nostrils and he shuddered all over, but did not try to move. He knew better by then.

Partridge said, "Let's get one thing straight, son. I'm a citizen of these United States. That's what. War's long over. No more Yankees and Rebs. Now we're all the same. I made myself a promise years ago that I'd kill any man what called me a Yankee and, so far, I've only done it twice. But you're getting close, real close. You need to face up to the fact that you're standing at death's door knocking. You're not back in Alabamy or Tennessee getting pumped by your daddy or fingering your sister out in the barn or sitting around with the boys pissing about how the Yankees ran roughshod over the family pea patch. Death is right here and right now. And before you pass, you better do the right thing or that passing is gonna be ugly."

Kroner just lay there, bleeding and dying and hating in the light of the flickering fire. Off in the trees something chirped and something else chittered. Other than that there was only the cool breeze blowing down from above the snowline.

Partridge picked up the knife. "I told myself I'd show a little compassion this time around. That I wouldn't go about hacking up folks as is my custom, but—" and Partridge emphasized this by pressing the flat end of the knife blade to Kroner's eyelid "—God help me, you are trying my patience. So before I slice off your privates and make you gargle with 'em, tell me some truth here."

Partridge was finding himself amusing by that point. Sometimes the mere mention of physical torture turned some men to jelly. Sometimes the very idea of it was worse than the reality...*sometimes,* that is. He wasn't against using it, but neither did he take any pleasure from it. He'd seen it done and had participated once or twice himself. But unlike his old man, Black Jake, who it was said took great enjoyment in gutting a man real slow, he didn't care for it on general principles.

He dearly hoped it wouldn't come to that. If it did...well, he didn't have much to lose in the greater scheme of things.

But Kroner seemed to believe that he was some animal that went about hacking on folks, because he said, "We...we were hired to track you...to find you..."

"For the bounty?"

Kroner shook his head slightly. "No. We weren't to...to take you in. We were just to find you...follow you..." He vomited out a gout of blood and maybe some innards, too.

Partridge gave him a taste of the juice. "And?"

"Like I said...just find you...befriend you...if we could, but stay with...you..."

"Who hired you?"

Kroner shook his head slowly from side to side. "Don't know...Roseman didn't introduce him...but, ah *Christ,* white hair and tall...that face...Jesus, you'll know him when...when you see him...ugly...ugly as Satan's backside...dirt ugly..."

Partridge knew he was telling the truth now.

Someone had hired them to find him, to follow him. And whoever that was, they were after the money. There was no doubt about that. They hoped he would lead them to it. But who had hired them? White-haired? Ugly? It could have been a lot of men, but none that rang any bells in his head.

"Have another swallow," he told Kroner, guiding the bottle to his lips again.

Kroner tried to swallow, but most of it ran down his chin, dribbled from the corners of his mouth. He wasn't moving much anymore. Wasn't doing much of anything except mumbling odd little, incoherent things. Bits about Roseman and his daddy and something about a pony he'd once owned.

Then suddenly, just as it looked as if he were slipping away, his eyes snapped open clear and bright. Firelight was reflected in them like shooting stars over a dark lake. "Yeah...y-you'll know him all right...tall and ugly...mean-looking sonofabitch...ugly...*ugly*..."

Then his eyes glazed back over and he was still.

Partridge shut them and had he known any prayers, maybe he would have said one. Death was always an ugly thing to him, whether it took friend or enemy. It was black and complete. Frightening in its permanence.

He went through their saddlebags, took all the money he could find (about sixty dollars), some whiskey and tinned food. He opened the feed sacks and let the horses eat as they pleased on the oats within. He left the guns, but took some of the ammunition. There wasn't much of interest on the men or in their packs. Letters to family, most very old. A Bible, dog-eared and greasy. Tobacco. Personals. In Roseman's pack he found one item of interest.

Just a plain white business card and on it, in a flowing and elegant script:

THE EGYPTIAN HOTEL
Dead Creek, Arizona

He studied it by the fire, thinking and thinking. Wondering if there was a connection and who exactly that ugly white-haired fellow was. He tucked the card in his pocket and extinguished the fire. Maybe someone would find the dead men and have the decency to bury them.

But that wasn't Nathan Partridge.

He had other plans. And most of them seemed to be centered around Dead Creek as if it were the crux of this mystery and he figured it probably was.

Climbing onto his black, he rode on down the trail at a leisurely pace. In his mind, he knew it was coming soon. Whatever was in store for him was getting closer all the time, circling like a buzzard and just waiting for the right time to pounce, claw and peck. And Partridge went to it, whatever it was.

He went willingly.

26

"I declare, gentlemen, that the world is in a most atrocious state," Coy Farren said to the saddle tramps, hard rock miners, and soiled doves of the Bullseye Saloon on the outskirts of Chimney Flats. "Most atrocious. Why, it simply isn't safe for a god-fearing man to travel alone these days. The trails of this harsh and uncivilized land are crawling, literally *crawling*, with shootists and desperados of every ilk and color. Terrifying, that's what it is, simply *terrifying*. I do believe, as many a fine and noble preacher has descried from his pulpit, that the days of Revelation are most certainly upon us."

The patrons of the Bullseye agreed with steely silence.

They were a grimy and greasy lot, all dark-eyed and desperate. Men who spent their days high in the saddle, faces peppered by dust, wind, and weather. Men who spent their lives down in the mines, clutching and clawing for that elusive finger of gold or trace of silver. On good days, they barely made enough money to keep themselves in whiskey and beef. And on bad days—and there were more of these than the latter—they didn't even make that much.

But today they were drinking beer and the whiskey was flowing and not because of any boom, but because of the man before them: Coy Farren. He was buying the drinks and the regulars were listening, even though they weren't exactly sure what the hell he was talking about most of the time.

The Bullseye was a simple loghouse with scarred wooden tables and rough-hewn pine benches pulled up to them. The bar, as it were, consisted of several hardwood planks supported by whiskey barrels. There was an oil stove sputtering in the corner, a still in yet another. Kegs of beer and whiskey behind the bar. The air was heavy and hazed with smoke, stunk of unwashed bodies and urine.

A naked Injun whore was seated on the bar top whilst two men took turns pinching her nipples and sliding their fingers into her, both arguing amongst themselves as to whether she was worth the price.

Mamie McGill, the proprietor, fixed them with an evil stare, her face yellow in the lamplight. "Ye'll pay, all right, ye right bastards," she promised them. "Ye've already been handling the goods, haven't ye? So pay up and put yer willies in her and be done with it. I'll hear no more of this."

They paid up and mounted her in turn.

Coy Farren turned away. "Drink up, gentlemen," he told the others. "Drink up, I beg of you. You'll excuse me, I'm sure, if I don't join in your celebrations, but, alas, I am plagued by something of a weak constitution. An inherited malady, I do say." He pulled out a big, tooled leather wallet from inside his broadcloth coat once again and every eye in the place was on those greenbacks he flipped through. Hungry, wanting eyes. "I'm afraid I'll have to take leave of you, but, please, do have another drink on me."

The men and their whores grunted in assent and raised empty glasses. All save a Cavalry sergeant and his soiled dove. They were fucking near the door in plain sight atop heaped filthy beaver hides that were rank with the secretions of dozens of such unions. Coy Farren purposely did not look upon them as if such a sight would wither his refined gentility. They groaned and grunted and sweated and strained.

He pretended not to notice and everyone else had stopped noticing such things years before. He set a note down on the bar top. "Good lady, if you would be so kind."

Mamie McGill began filling steins with beer from the vats behind the bar. She drew whiskeys and set them before greedy, soiled fingers. She was excessively fleshy like a woman from a renaissance painting, large and robust, breasts like feedbags that were illy-contained by the strained bodice of her calico dress. Her thighs were meaty and powerful, arms like slabs of trembling pork. Her face was a round, distended ball, multi-chinned, eyes tiny and close-set in that sea of oily flab.

"Aye, rounds for everyone," she said in her shanty Irish brogue. "And a fine man you are, Mister Farren, providing for these poor and desperate souls."

When she had refreshed all their drinks, she stuck her corncob pipe back in her mouth and puffed contently, watching, ever watching. She didn't especially care for Coy Farren. Although he waxed poetic and at great length, affecting the speech and mannerisms of some high-born southern gentleman, he was dressed in dusty, trail-worn clothes like some peddler or tramp. He pretended to be some dandy fallen on hard times, though his poke was full to bursting. An enigma, yes. Her heart told her that he was not as he seemed. That if you were to strip away the bullshit he had troweled on in layers like stucco, there was something malignant and vicious beneath, something coldly intelligent and predatory. Like a rattlesnake, it waited in darkness to strike.

Not that any of this bothered Mamie McGill. It took one to know one. She didn't fear the man (truth was, she feared no man, had broken and devoured many like a female spider casting aside the leeched bodies of its lovers), but she knew something repulsive when she saw it and that something was Coy Farren. His kind slithered under logs and in dark, wet places.

He was up to something. She had no doubt of this. But what he didn't know, was that so was she.

One of the miners pulled out a harmonica and another started to sing a Scottish dirge about failed life and missed opportunity. Nobody but he seemed to know the words, but a few others joined in, grumbling out choruses they made up as they went. Some beaten, drunken ranch hand stood up to join in and fell straight over like a domino, proceeding to vomit on himself. Again, no one noticed.

Coy Farren mingled amongst the others at the tables. "Please, please do enjoy yourselves, my good and multitudinous friends. I say it is a rare day when friends can gather and imbibe and wish one another well. You do me great honor, each and every one of you, by your presence and good cheer. God bless you, one and all."

Mamie McGill filled her pipe and lit it with a match scratched off the bar top. She looked towards two men seated at one of the tables and motioned them over. They came without hesitation, one in a buckskin cloak and the other in a woolen poncho and denim shirt. They were thin, desperate-looking men, both corded with muscle and hungry as starving cats.

Mamie made sure Farren was discoursing freely once again, then she said, "Our Mister Farren has a good deal of currency he wishes to part with. Mayhap we'll help him out, eh? He's a tenderfoot, maybe, but take no chances. Follow him back to that wagon and take what needs to be taken in the way it needs taking."

The men went outside without a word. They waited in the darkness with their horses for Farren to come out.

Inside, Coy Farren said, "Well, I suppose it would be in my best interests to get back to my wagon. It being unprotected up in the hills with only my womenfolk to tend to it, frail and lovely creatures that they are. With that, gentlemen and ladies—" he bowed and tipped his bowler hat to one and all "—I shall take leave of you. May goodness and mercy follow you all. Perhaps, one day, we'll meet on the trail and on that day, my friends, I can guarantee you my hospitality. In fact, I can guarantee you an experience you won't soon forget. Most certainly, I'd love to have you one and all for supper one day."

With that, he left amidst good-byes and farewells and good lucks. Not a one of which was meant nor intended.

As he unhitched his horse, the moon was big and bright in the sky like a single winking eye. The landscape glowed eerily under its glare. He rode off, taking his time...making doubly sure his pursuers would not lose him.

Certain they were following, he smiled a toothsome and moony grin.

27

In September of 1864, Coy Farren and his brother were recent arrivals to Elmira Prison Camp. Neither knew if the other were alive and would not discover this for some time. They spent most of their days in their respective wards, crowded in with hundreds of other prisoners in the rat- and lice-infested barracks. The roofs were unsealed and leaked incessantly. The floorings were of rough green lumber that was warped and splintered. Bunks were three-high and extended the length of the wards to either side, leaving a narrow aisle in-between that housed the stoves. The bunks were designed for two men, but were packed with four and had blankets only for three. The beds were rough-hewn planks covered with foul-smelling straw tainted and discolored by human waste. Others too weak to make it into a bunk were sprawled on the drafty floor. Each morning, it seemed, a few more were dead.

And that was what life was like there, day in and day out. A tight, cramped, ugly world that stunk of rotting flesh, body odor, shit, and vomit.

Rats entered freely through rents in the floors and nibbled at appendages left unguarded and chewed on those either too weak to fight or dead and festering.

His first night there, Coy Farren saw a slat-thin man dressed in rags capture a rat as it scurried along the floor. He seized it and quickly, expertly, snapped its neck, tucking its limp body into the filthy folds of his tattered shirt. His eyes were huge, black holes punched into the sallow, flaking skin of his face. That night, after lights out, he heard the crazy man chewing on something, slurping and snapping and crunching.

"He's right out of his head," one of the prisoners told Farren. "He eats the most god-awful things…"

A month later, the crazy man became more secretive than ever. And one night they saw him remove a board from the wall and retrieve the bloated, stiffened body of a dead puppy. It was crawling with maggots. Grinning, he fed on it as the others watched in horror.

But it was the last straw and they beat him nearly to death out of pure outrage and maybe terror. Terror that they, too, could possibly become like him—a skull-faced ghoulish thing feeding off the dead.

But hunger and deprivation could do strange things to a body. Hideous things. Men went hungry so they could trade their rations for tobacco. In the prison, it sold for a dollar a pound. It would be cut into small squares and re-sold as "chews". Tobacco and food were the primary mediums of exchange. The camp was overrun by rats and particularly fat ones were considered a delicacy. A plump rodent would buy you five chews or even a loaf of bread.

Both Coy and John Lyle Farren were captured with the survivors of their company just outside Purcellville, Loudon County, Virginia following a bitter battle with Union forces. They were herded into cattle cars for the long push north which ended in

Elmira, New York, site of the infamous prison camp. By the time they arrived, dozens of men had died from their injuries, from disease and dehydration. It was rumored that more than a few had taken their own lives with secreted weapons.

Black soldiers marched them from the train depot and through the streets to the camp. Rain was falling and the day had gone gray as lint. Many men dropped from fatigue and were either dragged or carried or kicked into motion by their captors. It was not a proud nor dignified moment for the rebel forces, but they had heard of the horrors of Andersonville, and figured the Yankees were just returning the favor.

Coy Farren was uninjured as he passed through the huge and heavy swinging gates. Tired, disillusioned, and hungry (not having been fed in nearly four days), he was marched into the muddy stockade and got his first real look at Elmira Prison Camp. It was enclosed by a sixteen-foot tall planked fence supported by deep-set posts. Three feet from the top was a parapet walkway upon which guards were stationed, an unpleasant-looking bunch if ever he saw one. There were rows of two-story wooden barracks and beyond them other nondescript buildings.

It was a dire and forbidding place and even the falling rain couldn't dispel the thick, fetid odor that hung in the air. Farren knew that smell. He was a soldier; he knew what death smelled like.

They were formed up into ranks and before long a senior Union sergeant dressed in a mottled slicker came out to inspect them. His name was Penning and he had a head like a concrete block riding atop shoulders that were squared and sharp. He walked with a pronounced limp and had eyes that belonged in the skull of a bird of prey. He carried a stick with him that was nothing more than a length of unfinished maple. There were holes drilled near the end so it would whistle when he swung it.

"Well, you're here, I take it, each and every goddamn one of you," he said with a voice that was rough and raw and had no more humanity to it than the growl of a jungle cat. "Now I have to drag my ass out into the rain and look upon you." He spat at their feet. "Miserable, sickening, pathetic lot. That's what you are. But we'll take care of you, God, yes, you're in good hands now." And then he started laughing, cackling really. It was an awful, mocking sound on that sodden day.

One man made the mistake of asking for water and Penning turned on him and jabbed the end of his stick into his belly. Then he clubbed him over the head until his face turned red with the exertion of it all. "Water? *Water?* What in Christ's name do you think is falling from the sky, you goddamned southern trash?"

After that no one asked for a thing. They stood tall and erect and silent like statues in a park despite numerous injuries, exhaustion, and despair. A few however dropped to their knees and others couldn't stand in the first place.

Penning stood over them. "Fine lot you are. Don't they teach you Rebs to stand at attention?"

A young corporal with an eye patch momentarily forgot himself. "Sir," he called out. "These men are sick. They are—"

But Penning's stick came around in a lethal, whistling arc and caught him in the mouth, scattering teeth like dice. The corporal was knocked unconscious and Penning spat in his face. "To the hospital with these boys," he said to a group of black soldiers standing nearby. "And after that, to the grave." As the soldiers made to move a man with a bandaged, swollen leg he stopped them with his stick. "Leave this one."

The injured were hauled away by the blacks with as much care as possible which, under the circumstances and evil glare of Penning, wasn't much.

Penning's face was not handsome, but brutish and coarse, the face of a swine rooting in the mud. Beneath the cheekbones on either side were matching ancient scars, the flesh there sucked in giving his cheeks a cadaverous hollow look. Farren was later to learn that he had been left for dead days after Gettysburg by Confederate guerrilla forces. His leg was blown to so much meat and he'd been stabbed and shot numerous times. A guerrilla, as a final parting indignity, had bayoneted Penning through the face, piercing both cheeks. When he was found by Union soldiers, there was still a dirty boot print on his jaw where the guerrilla had stepped down to ease the withdrawal of his bayonet.

But Penning had survived.

Six months later, he was fitted with a wooden leg and transferred to the so-called "Invalid Corps" which was comprised of men not fit for active duty. He then entered the military prison system.

The man on the ground, a graying sergeant, just stared up at Penning. There was hatred in his eyes which boiled and seethed like acid. Penning gazed down at his wound; he could tell by the smell that it was gangrenous. He pressed the tip of his stick into a bulging mass just beneath the kneecap. The sergeant squirmed and screeched, his face wet with sweat and rain, spattered by mud, but he would not cry out for mercy.

This obviously displeased Penning. "You need attention, Reb. If you beg, I might see that you get it."

The sergeant had bitten through his lower lip. He looked up at Penning and smiled with red-stained teeth. Then he hawked up a wad of phlegm and spat it onto Penning's boot.

Penning laughed and brought his stick down with everything he had, puncturing the wound. A vile stench of decay oozed from the blackened pus that ran from the morbid laceration.

The sergeant screamed and went unconscious.

No one ever saw him again.

Penning walked back and forth before the ranks of POWs, sneering and snapping and kicking men in the groin and pummeling them with his stick. He told them how Jefferson Davis was screwing their wives and sodomizing their sons down south, but regardless of what he said, no one would rise to the bait. So indiscriminately, he hobbled through the ranks, swinging his great and bloodied stick, and felling men like a lumberjack dropping trees.

In time, pleased by the moans and whimpering of beaten and abused men, he said to them all, "Good day to you, gentleman, and welcome, welcome one and all."

And that was Farren's introduction to the world of "Hellmira", as it came to be known.

He and the others were stripped of everything they carried but the clothes on their backs. Unless wounds were severely infected or freely bleeding, they were not tended to. The prisoners were forced into the barracks and a new life, a living death began for them. Men not packed into barracks were herded into the innumerable ragged tents of ripped and moldering canvas which flapped forlornly in the breeze.

The commandant of the camp was Colonel William Hoffman who bragged that he had killed more men than any other regular soldier and no one doubted it. But his tools were not rifle and bayonet, but starvation and disease.

Adjoining the cookhouse was the mess hall, more of a shed than anything. Those that were healthy enough to stand and walk were marched in here. Those that weren't, starved. There were no seats—prisoners stood and ate. On a good day a meal could consist of beans, bean soup, maybe a shrunken specimen of salt pork and a scant slice of light bread which was made from unbolted cornmeal, thick with indigestible bran which the men either couldn't keep down or (and worse) could—leading to a variety of gastrointestinal disorders. But those were the good days. More often than not, the diet consisted of bread and water.

Disease, of course, was widespread. The lack of fresh vegetables caused scurvy. Chronic diarrhea was acerbated by drinking stagnant water and water infected with insect larvae and human excrement. Small pox reached plague proportions. An epidemic of pneumonia killed men by the dozens. Unburied bodies were stacked outside the hospital while inside the wards were crowded with the sick and dying and many were lying in the corridors, awash in their own waste.

To make matters worse, there were never enough blankets, clothing, or shoes. That winter the lucky ones had the remnants of boots, others wrapped rags around their feet, and still others (more than not) stood in the deep snow on swollen, frost-bitten feet. Countless limbs were amputated. Without proper supplies, there was simply no combating the disease, the cold, the filth, and starvation.

As further humiliation, townspeople had erected high platforms outside the wall from which spectators could (for fifteen cents) look down on the droves of prisoners suffering every known deprivation.

In the center of the camp there was a one-acre lagoon of polluted water called Foster's Pond, a backwash of the Chemung

River. It served as a communal latrine and garbage dump. It was clogged with rotting matter, feces, urine, and hospital waste—it was, in essence, a huge festering mass of putrefaction. A breeding ground for millions of insects and countless contagious disease germs, a pestilential organic soup of miasmic rot. The stink of it was overpowering and particularly nauseating during the warm months. It enclosed the camp like a shroud. Finally, with so many ill and dying, drainage ditches were dug to drain away the filthy waters.

In November of that year, Coy Farren, an ambulating stickman who weighed barely over a hundred pounds, was removed from the barracks and billeted in one of the over-crowded tents due to a smallpox outbreak. By this time, he was well used to the raving and the dementia, the heaped cadavers swarming with worms and beetles. He, like the majority, had become something less than human. A walking skeleton with sunken red pits for eyes. He was beyond compassion and mercy, stumbling about gibbering to himself and hallucinating.

In that tent packed with dirty bodies and dying bodies and the hopelessly insane, he witnessed a secret. He watched a soiled and hollow-eyed group of men covet a particular section of the dirt floor. All day long, they hovered over it, very often pissing and shitting themselves rather than abandoning it. One evening, just before sunset, they revealed their secret. That section of dirt was actually a false floor and beneath it, a pit of bones—dog, rat, and human. Many of the bones were old and yellowed, others were fresh and still stained with their owner's blood. All were gnawed, most had been snapped open for the bounty of salty marrow within. The men retrieved their bones and fondled them, chewed on them, played with them. One of them withdrew a human skull and slavered it with passionate kisses.

Such were the depths of pure and bleak insanity.

A week or so later, he bumped into his brother, John Lyle. He was still big and burly and looked as if he could snap logs with his bare hands. But his eyes were blank, they were dead and sunless pools.

Not that Farren was surprised.

All the men in Elmira had that look about them. Emaciated, spiritless, just walking corpses searching for an empty grave.

"Come with me, Coy," he said, leading him away by the arm and, by Christ, he *was* solid and well-fed. "I want to show you something."

In a nearby tent, just off from the others, a group of men huddled about a stove. There were strips of meat laid across the surface, sizzling. The smell was intoxicating. Before Farren could inquire as to whether it was dog or rat, a hot and juicy filet was shoved into his hand. He gobbled it down and it was very rich, very sweet, unlike anything he had ever before tasted. At first he was repulsed...sickened by the fleshy aroma and honeyed flavor, it was almost too much to digest. Then his stomach settled down and demanded more. He stuffed himself as the others stood around grinning and laughing low in their throats.

That's when Farren saw that they had all filed their teeth to points.

John Lyle grinned with a mouth of spikes. "Yessum," he said. "Good ets."

And then Coy knew, God help him, but he knew.

But his mind was a black and predatory thing by then and meat was meat and blood was blood and he only knew his belly was full. And he wanted more, always more. The flavor was addicting. There was nothing else like it.

Before long, he was leading the nightly hunting parties looking for the fat ones, the new arrivals. They were the best.

At Elmira, human evil was given full reign.

28

The two riders clung to Coy Farren like buzzards to bad meat.

They had his scent thick in their nostrils and, to them, that smell was money. They'd both seen his wallet, the cash that bulged in it. If nothing else, that was worth killing him for. But the fool had also bragged about the money he had back at his wagon. Silver, he said. And Mamie wanted it all and she'd get it.

They were patient.

They hung back, their mounts plodding along as silently as possible. Nothing but the gentle thudding of hoofs. Farren was well ahead, moving at an even, unhurried pace up the trail into the foothills that twisted and turned like a snake crossing water. There were few clouds that night and the moon was bright, shining up there like a silver piece. The trail, the jutting rocky bluffs, and the encroaching pines were washed by its ethereal glow.

The one in the buckskin cloak was named Taveres and his partner in the woolen poncho was Garrison. They were both ex-convicts. Both practiced road agents. And both would kill a man for two bits or a good cigar. Recently, they were in the employ of Mamie McGill: she fingered the targets and they took them down. She didn't trust them with anything that required any real thinking—stages, banks, trains—but they were most useful when it came to emptying the pockets of rich miners or ranchers sitting on a fat payday. The hills were littered with the shallow graves of their victims.

"Suppose he knows we're back here?" Garrison asked in a low voice.

Taveres shook his head. "Don't suppose so. If'n he did, he wouldn't be taking his time, now would he?"

"Don't suspect so."

"Just some dandy, green as a sapling," Taveres said. "Trust me, this un's gonna be easier than picking up the clap at the Bullseye."

They both laughed low in their throats at that one. Mamie's whores back there...Jesus, a man had to have serious lack of respect for his dick to be sticking it into any of that stuff. All those broads were road-weary. They'd been passed around more than a cold in a schoolhouse. Bagged-out, ragged-out, nothing but bargain basement slunk meat by that point. Most had worked mining camps and army posts single-handedly. They knew their business, but had more crabs on them than a Pacific beach at low-tide.

They lost sight of Farren suddenly.

The trail twisted into a stand of willows and for a moment there they could see his silhouette riding tall and proud and then he was swallowed by shadows as a mist of clouds fell over the face of the moon. When they made the bend, he was gone completely.

"Dammit," Garrison spat, "now where the hell is he?"

Taveres halted his gelding. He studied the dark woods, the rolling hills, the fingers of skeletal rock. A thousand hiding places and in the darkness, one as good as the next. He licked his weathered lips, wiped a trickle of sweat from his brow. Squinting his eyes, he thought about it.

Luckily, the moon peeked back out, the countryside once again dappled by patchy illumination. It saved him from doing any real thinking, which was never a good thing. It came hard to him, that thinking business. That reasoning nonsense. Thinking for him was like a blind and armless man trying to rope a calf: it just didn't work when you lacked the basic equipment. He would never admit that he was stupid (even though his old man had told him repeatedly when he was a kid that a ripe bean fart had more smarts). He just figured a man should be impulsive, should decide on the spur of the moment. So, pretty much, as you might figure, he routinely blundered into situations blindly. And this is what led him to a life of petty crime, led him to prison, led him teaming up with Garrison, and led him to Mamie McGill who did his brainwork for him.

He decided they'd move on, play it as it came.

Garrison agreed and on they went. They rounded the bend and went up another hill and then off to the left where there was a clearing. Near the tree line they could see a wagon parked, a team of horses picketed nearby. A fire was blazing away in a pit. The air smelled of wood smoke and pine breeze.

"Don't see nobody," Garrison said.

"Maybe they's in that wagon there," Taveres suggested. Which made a certain amount of sense…except Farren's horse was not around.

But he must've rode in there, though. Where else could he go? He said he and his womenfolk had themselves an old medicine wagon and that wagon in the clearing certainly fit the bill. It even looked like there was some old writing on the side, but faded and weathered gray. No, dammit, this had to be the one.

"Let's ride in," he told Garrison. "Keep your gun leathered. We're jes two boys out on the trail what needs to warm up at that fire a bit. Got it?"

"Yeah, I get it."

Taveres figured he probably didn't, but in they went.

The campsite was deserted. Wood was chopped and piled. Oats were set out for the horses. There were a few wooden barrels and crates stacked about, but nothing more. Strange. By that point, Taveres was not only thinking about the money but about the women, too. He had a hunger for a woman. A real woman, not one of those creatures back at the Bullseye, all of which had seen more dick than a privy pit. He wanted something clean and fresh that wasn't crawling with disease like a hospital chamber pot. Something that maybe smelled of soap and perfume rather than sweat and leather.

Crickets were chirping off in the woods and somewhere a cicada buzzed. There was a funny smell clinging to that wagon. Taveres couldn't be sure, but he thought he'd smelled something like it once in Kansas City. And that had been when he'd hid out in the dark and dripping cellar of an abandoned slaughterhouse.

"Awful quiet out here," Garrison said. "Cain't say I care for it much."

Taveres gave him an evil, withering look. Dumb bastard was always imagining things. Smelling Indian war parties where there were none. Refusing to cross burial grounds because of spirits. Claiming certain buildings were haunted.

Taveres hated that sort of talk with a passion. But out here, Jesus, it did sort of get under a man's skin, now didn't it? The wagon sitting there with that stink clinging to it like vines, horses silent and waiting, those huge and dark Arizona hill pines pressing in like witnesses to something about to come. A stick snapped out in the woods and Taveres started. He was looking at the wagon, the rolling script on the side that you could no longer read. There were pictures there, too. Women, men, what he thought were snakes. He thought for a moment one of them moved.

"Stop it," he said.

"What?" Garrison asked.

"Nothing."

He stood with him by the fire, warming his hands.

"How long we gonna stand around?" Garrison wanted to know, an edge to his voice. "Let's get to it. They's probably in the wagon."

Taveres wanted to play it cool for a time. Just stand about harmlessly and wait. He figured if Farren was hiding out in the woods, he'd come back in when he saw they were real peaceable and the like.

A horse snorted in the woods and they looked at each other.

"I'm going after it," Taveres said. "You wait a minute or two and then check out that wagon. Do what has to be done."

Taveres took off, unleathering his 1860 Army revolver and pressing himself into the shadows. First thing he noticed right off was that the crickets had stopped chirping. He started wondering if maybe he'd misread that sound. It had sounded like a horse, but what if it wasn't? Could have been a big grizzly rooting and if a man came on one of them at night, he was going to be food. Taveres swallowed that down and moved as silently as he could.

"Mister Farren?" he called out, trying to sound concerned and friendly. "You out here?"

Nothing.

The woods pressed in from all sides, the shadows thick and crawling. He wasn't a smart man, but even he knew he wasn't alone out there.

There was someone, someone...

Brush crackled behind him and he whirled violently around, but a hanging tree limb snagged the long barrel of his Army and he couldn't bring it up quick enough. At least not quick enough to stop something from colliding with the crown of his skull and putting out his lights like a shade was drawn in his brain.

29

After Taveres had left, Garrison made his way to the back of the wagon.

First he circled it several times, even looked under it. Taveres thought he was crazy with his feelings and premonitions and what not, but he trusted implicitly in them. Most of the time they turned out to be nothing at all, but more than once they'd saved his bacon. And those feelings were rioting in his head. *You want to stay alive, you best ride out while you still can.* And it bothered him somewhat, as you can well imagine. But if he rode out, Taveres would catch up with him and things wouldn't be pleasant.

His feelings were also telling him that he wasn't alone.

Someone was close.

He could feel their eyes crawling on him like spiders. He pulled his gun, an 1860 Army just like Taveres' except lacking the fancy engraving, and held it tight in his grip which had gone decidedly greasy with sweat. He took hold of the latch on the door and pulled it open. The door swung outward soundlessly. A stink came wafting out. A hot and high stink that reminded him of the straw in a monkey cage. But worse, just as black and flyblown as a wormy body locked in an August closet.

Garrison stepped back.

He licked his lips and he could almost taste that noisome smell on them. Nothing had a right to stink like that. Nothing good. Nothing that walked by daylight. This was the smell of subcellars and drainage ditches.

Gun held out before him, he started in. Things like boxes and sacks were heaped on the floor and he had to crawl straight over the top of them. Other things were hanging from the ceiling and they brushed his hat as he moved forward. He was about six feet into that black heat when he realized how handy a lantern would have been. It was just too murky in there. No way he could see anything. If there was money or women (which he doubted) how was he supposed to see them?

His heart filling in his throat, his mouth full of sand, he crawled forward. It was hotter now and that stench was so bad his stomach was filled with cold, shifting jelly. It was putrid. It was mean. It was savage.

He reached into his pocket and brought out a match. Part of him begged him not to light it, not to look, just to get out. But he scratched it with a dirty thumbnail and the bowels of the wagon suddenly leapt out at him in the flickering light. He saw a moth-eaten red velvet curtain drawn just before him. Patches of mildew threaded its surface. He heard breathing on the other side, hoarse and ragged. Then he saw what was hanging from the timbers overhead and what decorated the walls.

He let out an involuntary scream and the curtain suddenly parted.

The match went out but not before he saw what was behind that curtain, the numerous sins in concealed. And not before one of them, a dark and slithering shape, jumped out at him.

He tried to bring the Army up, but something flashing and silver which caught the moonlight sliced into his wrist and nearly cut his hand free. Then it sank into his chest, his shoulder, and his throat with a meaty thud.

As he died all he could hear was that whistling/throaty sound and the meat cleaver coming down again and again and again.

Death was welcome.

30

When Taveres opened his eyes again, his head was throbbing.

Whatever had hit him had hit him hard enough to give him an entirely new hat size. That was the first thing he noticed. The second was that he was sitting in front of the fire. And the third was that he was completely naked and bound with ropes in a sitting position, back up against a barrel. Coy Farren was sitting on the other side of the fire.

"Well, I see you've joined us," he said and his voice was not the voice he'd heard earlier at the Bullseye. This voice was cunning, evil-timbered, almost a growl. "And how welcome you are, my dear friend. How very welcome."

The fire was blazing away and there was a big black pot suspended by a folding iron tripod. Something was bubbling away in there and damned if it didn't smell good.

Taveres struggled against his tethers, but it was hopeless. He was completely at Farren's mercy. "What the hell is this about?" he asked, trying to keep the terror out of his voice. He was naked and defenseless. He'd been in prison. He knew some men had a taste for exotic things, vile things. He knew—

"How much is your life worth to you, friend?" Farren asked of him.

Taveres just stared, trying to find words that would easily diffuse this situation, but none came. Either his brain was too big and he couldn't locate them or his mouth was too small to speak them. So he just started rambling: "I...I...I have money. I got plenty of money and if'n you set me free...you can have it, yes sir, it's all yours."

Farren just laughed. He pulled a few onions from a sack and expertly peeled them with a hunting knife, dropping them in the pot. "I must say that is most kind and considerate of you, my friend. As my father was wont to say: You are rarest of men, one of breeding and compassion. But, unfortunately, I already have your money. I have your friend's as well. I'm afraid you'll have to do better. For as you can plainly see, you are at my mercy. Yes, sir. Most assuredly you are at my mercy."

Taveres was shivering, but he knew he couldn't lose his head. He had to think his way out of this. No easy thing for him. "At the Bullseye...there's money there...I can help you get it...please, Mr. Farren, please just let me go..."

"I must confess your pleas are moving me. Are they moving you, Lyle?"

"Yessum," a gravelly voice said. "Moving me, yes."

Taveres smelled something like old meat and a huge man moved into view. He was bearded and filthy. He wore a sleeveless beaver coat and for a moment, one crazy and shuddering moment, Taveres thought that it wasn't a coat at all, but greasy fur sprouting from his gigantic hide.

"Did you meet my brother John Lyle?" Farren asked. "Perhaps not. Well, now you have the honor. John Lyle is a man of few words whilst I am one of many. But you'll enjoy John Lyle—" Farren was smiling now, a dark and lethal smile "—and he'll enjoy you. Yes, sir."

Taveres felt like a jar of ants had been dumped on him. Everything was crawling and trembling and prickly. And although he was not an intelligent man, he knew he was in serious trouble here. He knew that there was something very wrong about these two, something degenerate, something corrupt.

John Lyle just stood there grinning like a wooden Indian and the firelight flickered and turned his image to a shifting orange, his face a mask of creeping shadow. Light glimmered off his teeth and Taveres saw they were sharpened like stakes, tools designed for rending and tearing. He recalled stories he had heard at his grandmammy's knee, tales of flesh-eating ogres that lived in the black forest waiting, always waiting for lost children to fill their stewpots with. He knew then that John Lyle Farren was one of them.

"Did you bring the taters, brother of mine?"

"Yessum." He dropped a cloth sack at Coy Farren's feet. "Taters."

"Excellent, excellent." Coy examined them and sliced them carefully, dropping them into the stew. Then he took a long fire-blackened spoon and stirred the mixture. The odor was spicy, rich.

"You see, I have no real interest in killing you," Coy Farren admitted. "But that doesn't mean I won't. Course, if you can offer me something valuable, I might be inclined to set you free."

"Anything," Taveres said in a high, whining voice. "Anything, anything! You jes ask me, Mister Farren, you jes see what I can do for you! Ask! Ask!"

Coy Farren laughed and it was a bad sound like a scream in a mineshaft. "Yes, yes, yes. I can see you are a man who wishes to be of service. And why not? When a man's life is at stake, he'll do just about anything to preserve that precious commodity. And you...heh, heh, you are in a most tricky position, sir. Would you agree with that, Lyle?"

John Lyle made a grunting/snorting sound that might have been a laugh. "I would agree with that, yes. I would," he said.

"W-What can I do for you? There must be something you want."

Coy Farren thought about it. He drummed his spidery fingers on his tattered broadcloth coat, then wiped them on his pants as if there was something unpleasant on them. "Thing is, we're here on business. Looking for a man name of Nathan Partridge. Do you know of him?"

Taveres brightened. "Yes! Of course! He jes escaped from Yuma Prison. Everyone's looking for him...the law, bounty hunters. He's got a good price on his head or so I hear. I...I know something about his wife..."

Coy Farren leaned forward, elbows on knees. "I am listening, sir. Most attentively. Pray continue."

So Taveres spilled what he knew. It wasn't much, but it was more than the Farren brothers knew and it interested them. Interested them greatly. The story was the same one that Sheriff Kreger told Partridge himself, except backed-up by the facts—Partridge's wife supposedly perished in a fire but no body was actually found and some folks speculated that she just up and moved and maybe, just maybe, the money had upped and moved with her. Dead Creek was a place that was mentioned.

"If'n any of that's true," Taveres said, "and it jes might be, then I bet he went after her...her and all that money."

Coy Farren looked pleased. "See! See, Lyle, if you connect up with the right sort of people, *quality* people that is, things begin to happen. Did I tell you as much?"

"You did," John Lyle said. "Yes."

From inside the wagon there was a sudden bumping, thumping sound. Then all went quiet again.

Pale as plaster, Taveres said, "What the hell was that?"

Coy Farren just smiled. "Just ma, that's all. Tending to her needs you might say." He stirred the stew and motioned to John Lyle. The big man pulled out a skinning knife and cut Taveres' hands free. "There. Consider this an act of good faith on our part. You help us and we help you."

Taveres thanked him. Grateful for any little thing. He massaged his hands, working the numbness out. He was starting to believe that he might just get out of this. Things were definitely heading in that direction.

Coy Farren took up a tin plate and spooned a helping of the stew onto it. "You will, of course, join us for supper. You are our guest and we would be terribly remiss if we did not see to your needs, if we did not satisfy your hunger. Good friends breaking bread together. It's a fine thing. Would you be inclined to say that is correct, Lyle?"

"Yes, I surely would, my brother. Yes."

Taveres took the plate that was offered him. Resting within a steaming clot of grease was a slab of pale meat that was falling from the bone beneath. Meat that he soon enough noticed had fingers attached to it.

"Pray enjoy," Coy Farren said.

"Special meat," John Lyle said. "Ever et it before?"

Taveres was waiting for some punchline, something that would tell him this was a grand joke. But none was forthcoming. The grinning, malefic faces and deranged eyes of the Farren brothers shined in the firelight.

"I you want to live," Coy Farren said, "I suggest you eat."

And then, something twisting up inside him and breaking down into a wet insane laughing/sobbing, Taveres did just that.

31

When John Pepper came to, he was laying facedown, spread-eagle on the floor of his room at the Gila Hotel in Chimney Flats.

He came to with a blind and surging panic, scrambling madly to his hands and knees while the room spun around him like a carousel. His eyes watered and tears ran down his cheeks, his limbs shaking as if he were a colt fresh from the womb. And that's pretty much how he felt: weak, clumsy, unsure, and, yes, frightened. He lowered himself back down to the floor. His heart was pounding and he was breathing very fast, very close to hyperventilation.

Easy now, he told himself.

He had to think here. He had to sort this out and make sense of it. There was a logical, reasonable explanation here. All he had to do was think of it. But the more he thought about it, the more concerned he became for he had no clear memory of what had happened. There were vague shadows in his mind...but try as he might, he could give them no solidity. It was like trying to recall dreams halfway through the day. The memories were there, just out of reach. He could catch glimpses of them, blurred images, but clarity would not come.

After a time he pulled himself up onto the bed and stretched out.

He remembered waking that morning. Remembered cleaning up and going to the café across the street. He had a good appetite for the first time in weeks. Ham, eggs, cakes and syrup. He ate everything. He chatted with ranchers and townsfolk. He enjoyed their company, maybe glad that there were decent people in this town, that not everyone stank rotten like their sheriff. Then he came back up to his room to take a brief catnap, do some thinking about recent events. He had a slight, tugging headache.

He remembered coming up the stairs, but nothing more.

Not walking the corridor or opening the door.

But what he *did* remember was that the headache had worsened by the time he made the lobby of the Gila. That his hands and feet were tingling oddly. That his left arm began to feel numb and then, and then—

Nothing.

Propping himself up with pillows, he sighed and lit a cigarette. Okay. Okay, then. Whatever was going on in his head was getting worse. He needed to see a doctor. Granted. But it was a hell of a time for something like this. Though the trail of Nathan Partridge had cooled somewhat, the trail of his father had reappeared. The more Pepper thought about it, the more he was certain that it *was* Black Jake he'd seen leaving Kreger's office. If that was so and he'd somehow survived the noose, what could his connection be with the dirty lawman? Something to do with Nathan and the money?

Pepper was inclined to lean in that direction.

He didn't know much about Sheriff Josh Kreger, nothing beyond what his senses, what his heart told him, and that was that Kreger was a low-down, slimy weasel who had about as much to do with real peacekeeping as nuns had to do with brothels. So maybe he was something of an unknown quantity, but Black Jake was hardly that. Pepper had studied him thoroughly. He could've written a book about the man. But what it all came down to was this: everything that murdering sonofabitch ever did (or would do) was motivated by one single inescapable factor—greed. He lived for money. For the feel, the taste, the smell of it. He liked it like some men liked fast women or gambling or a taste of hootch.

That was Black Jake Partridge. A greedy man who would use and abuse, maim and kill men and women and probably even children if it would fill his pockets. That was one thing that could never change.

Whatever was going on here, Pepper began to wonder (and not for the first time) if he was up to it. Maybe he should wire Tom Franks, the U.S. Marshal for the western district of Arizona,

Franks was his boss. The one who handed out assignments. Maybe Franks could send another man to handle this. But that was only wishful thinking and he knew it. There was no one else with his reputation, his experience, his record of success. And that is exactly what Franks would tell him.

No, only death or out-and-out infirmity would get him out of this.

He kept telling himself just to see it through.

This whole assignment was getting more interesting day by day and, if nothing else, curiosity would keep him going. There were mysteries here and it was going to take a good man to bring them to light.

He didn't doubt that.

And ten years ago…hell, *three* years ago he was that man. But he'd been slowing down lately, he just didn't seem to have his edge anymore. And that would have been bad enough, but he was sick, too. Brain sick, he figured. Something was going on up there. Something bad and maybe even something terminal. Thinking that way, he decided if he was already dying, then he was going to give this last chase everything he had. Better to die game in the saddle than wasting away in some hospital ward with nothing but old, sick men and memories for company.

Enough, he thought.

He stood up, adjusted himself before the mirror and splashed water on his face and neck. He strapped on his ivory-handled Colts and pulled on his sheepskin coat and leather chaps.

Time for business.

32

He supposed that maybe it bothered him more than he was ever willing to admit. He hadn't seen much of his niece Anna Marie as she grew to womanhood. Her mother, Katherine, was Pepper's favorite sister (he had six others, all deceased but one). Maybe in retrospect, he should've spent less time on the trail and more time with her, the only real family he had. And especially after her husband George died of tuberculosis. Katherine was a capable woman and she'd continued to run their dry goods store in Phoenix, but she was soft as butter at heart. Anna Marie walked all over her. Had Katherine been a rug she could not have absorbed more boot prints. Anna Marie needed a strong male figure in her life, but she had none. Katherine had not remarried. Pepper remembered, even as a little girl, Anna Marie had been very confident, very headstrong, very sure of herself in every way. She was smart, but she was also wily. And when she became a young woman with a plentitude of natural beauty and charm, boys and men fawned over her. She had something they desired greatly and she put it to use.

She was wild. She was hungry for something more than a storekeeper's life.

And maybe that's what had fascinated her about Nathan Partridge. For, if Katherine was to be believed, Partridge could not necessarily be blamed. Anna Marie pursued him shamelessly. Katherine was even of the mind that they had had relations before marriage.

Pepper never doubted that a bit. No more than he doubted that Partridge was not the first. His niece was not a whore, she was no slut in his way of thinking, but she was independent and freethinking.

No, he hadn't liked her marrying Nathan Partridge—him being the son of old Black Jake and something of an outlaw himself—but, even had Pepper been present at their courtship, he couldn't have stopped it. Once that girl set her mind to something, mountains trembled and seas divided.

This is what he was thinking about as he rode up into the hills to the ruins of the Partridge farmhouse. He'd been up there when he first arrived, but only for the most cursory examination. Hoping, maybe, that he'd find the escaped convict. Now he returned.

He rode down the snaking overgrown road through stands of spruce. Birds were singing and squirrels chittering in the trees. Butterflies roamed the meadows and a buck broke cover suddenly and made for the deep thickets.

He found the farm much as Partridge had, neglected, going back to earth.

The barn was weathered and collapsing. The fields thick with wild grasses. The windmill tower rusting. The loghouse itself nothing but a jackstraw tumble of blackened timbers and boards. Only the chimney stood straight and tall.

Pepper tethered his horse to the hitching post and struck out on foot.

Smoking a cigarette, he casually patrolled the grounds and took it all in—the smells, the sounds, the sights, the very *feel* of utter desolation. He could almost sense all the memories raining in the air, the ghosts of children playing in the meadows and beneath the gnarled elms, the phantoms of adults building and cleaning and hoping for a good crop. Yes, it was rich here.

He imagined it would have been almost unbearable for Partridge.

He stood before the derelict house, just looking. What he saw told him that the ruins had been pushed about, dug through, and recently. Old dark ash was disturbed, fresher gray ash from below exposed. Timbers were pushed aside, darkened planks heaped. The fire had not done this; it was the work of an orderly mind.

But whose?

Tramps? Bored children? Treasure hunters? Maybe even bounty hunters or any of dozens of others hungry for that hidden money. Maybe. But maybe Partridge himself. Possibly.

Squatting down on his hands and knees, he followed the path through the wreckage.

Yes, things had been cleared here, too. The trapdoor of the root cellar had been forced open and the floor of the cellar itself had been dug into and dug deep. Pepper had no intention of hopping down there for a look, but it was obvious that someone had done some heavy work here. They'd been looking frantically for something.

Partridge?

He guessed as much. But that was just a guess, nothing more. There was no evidence to prove some treasure hunter hadn't done it and maybe it had been done by several men over a period of days all seeking the same thing.

But, for some reason, he didn't think so.

He was crawling back out, keeping his head low so he didn't bang it on the precariously nested timbers overhead when he heard his horse whinny nervously. He stopped. Waited. Listened. Yes, there and there. The sounds of hoofs coming through the brush, but slowly, carefully. He listened again. Yes, those riders were circling the farm, staying off in the trees.

Pepper crept to the opening and peered over a central fire-blasted beam.

He could see riders out there, but in the shadows of the foliage. They had stopped now, three of them that he could see, staring in his direction. Pepper looked around. It was a good jog to his horse and that through the open where there wasn't so much as a bush to hide behind. There was no other cover within a stone's throw. If they had come to do some shooting, they'd cut him down if he tried to make a break for his horse. He could see the shapes of rifles they held.

He would wait.

If they were here to chat, they would have ridden right in. Innocent men did not hide in the trees.

Pepper pulled his twin Colts and made ready. Lately, his mind had been obsessing with the idea of his imminent demise. Maybe it was the problems with his head and maybe it was just age, but the idea of death was always close at hand. As he crouched there, he wondered if it would be today. Would these gunmen be the ones? Would it be their bullets?

He couldn't allow that.

He was too close to something big here and he wanted to know what. He didn't want to die with questions on his mind.

He steeled himself and waited for it. Because it was coming. He could hear their horses spluttering. He wished he could get to his Winchester in the saddle boot. It would have made this all a lot easier; he could've picked them off the moment they broke from the treeline. But with the Colts...well, he'd have to wait until they were real close to get any true accuracy.

He clenched his teeth and narrowed his eyes to slits.

Come on, you bastards. Come and get it.

And then they did.

With wild whooping war cries, they rode out of the trees at full gallop and he saw there were four of them. Four Apache raiders. They carried Army carbines and their dark manes of hair were tied back with headbands of red flannel. They wore the traditional leggings and breechcloths, but gray Army shirts and leather cavalry boots. Just another small band that had tired of the deprivation of the reservation and had bolted, returning to the raiding they knew so well.

Pepper had no time to sort it out.

They charged his position, firing their carbines from the hips. What they lacked in accuracy they more than made up in aggression and battle fury. Bullets went over his head, chewed into timbers, kicked up clods of earth. But he stood his ground and held his fire until they were in range and when he started pulling the triggers, it was with definite targets in mind. When they were close enough for him to see the blood boiling in their eyes and the fanatical rage on their faces, he showed his pistols and let lead fly. The nearest raider lost his face in a spray of bone and blood, flipping right out of the saddle with a scream on his lips. The man to his left caught three bullets in the chest and slumped over in his saddle.

And then it was over.

The other two broke off the attack and retreated, still hollering and screeching. Unscathed, they made for the trees and vanished. The other raider who'd had most of his chest blown to confetti went with them as his horse followed in swift pursuit. But its rider was dead or near death and Pepper knew it.

Clouds of gun smoke and dust hung in the air as he crawled out of his hidey-hole and walked over to the dead Apache. His horse had stampeded off somewhere. With his boot, Pepper flipped him over. His face was nothing but a smoking pit of bleeding muscle and ligament, tightly sculpted over the skull beneath. His rifle lay nearby. Pepper picked it up and examined it. An Army carbine, all right. No doubt stolen from some shipment either by this man or one of dozens and dozens of other gunrunners plaguing the Territory.

Sighing, Pepper dragged the corpse by the feet over to his horse. He draped the body over the hips of his mount and then climbed onto leather, riding back down to Chimney Flats at a slow, unhurried pace.

33

"He's dead," Kreger said.

Pepper dismounted and tied his mount's lead to the hitching post. He stared at Kreger. "You trying to tell me the town doc can't patch this fellow up?" he said, taking hold of the glossy black hair of the corpse and lifting up the head so Kreger could see there was no face left to speak of. "Thought maybe some ointment and bandages would fix this buck right up."

Kreger's face darkened and not just because of what Pepper said, but because a few townspeople had gathered and heard. One of them giggled.

"No call for that," he said. "No call whatsoever."

One of Kreger's deputies, a lanky man named Tilbury with a perpetually frowning, unhappy face stood there with his thumbs hooked in his gunbelt.

"Get undertaker Clew. Tell him to get this body in his wagon and off the streets," Kreger told him.

Tilbury nodded his head. "Yup. I figured as much." He strolled away.

Kreger looked at Pepper tiredly. "I guess we better go inside."

In the office, Pepper went to grab himself a cup of coffee, then remembered his last experience with it and just sat down. He had the Apache's rifle with him and he set it on the desk before him. He started rolling a cigarette.

Kreger hung his Stetson on the hook and then his gunbelt. He poured himself a cup of coffee, sipped it and made a face. He spit some grounds out. "Damn," he said. He sat opposite the marshal and leaned back, interlocking his fingers behind his head. "No need, Marshal, to run your mouth like that."

Pepper stuck his cigarette between his lips. He struck a match off the desk. "You don't think so?" He exhaled a cloud of smoke, feeling an odd throbbing behind his eyes. "Well, I would think you'd know a dead man when you saw one. Funny, though, how I come a-tooling down that road out there and, goddamn, if you ain't standing out there, checking your pocket watch and all, almost like you're *expecting* me to come riding in with a dead man."

Kreger looked uneasy. "What the hell you mean by that? How could I know what sort of trouble you'd get yourself into?"

"Sometimes I wonder."

Kreger looked at him and it was truly hard to say whether it was mere hatred or apprehension on his face. Whichever, he was not amused by any of it. Not whatsoever. He opened his mouth to say something and Pepper launched into his version of the events at the Partridge farmhouse.

"...I suppose they could've just been passing by, but I have to wonder." He leaned forward so Kreger could see the complete distrust on his face. "You don't suppose someone might have sent them, do you?"

"Sent them?" The sheriff wetted his lips and shook his head. "That's crazy."

Pepper leaned back. "Sure it is. Sure it is. I keep having all these damnably crazy thoughts in my head. First I think I see Black Jake Partridge riding from your office when we both know he's cold and dead in the ground. And now I think maybe someone sent some Apache renegades after me when that just can't be." He was staring at Kreger hard and mean in the eye now. "I mean, hell, no one knew I was up there, right? Well, I *did* stop by and talk with you before I went up there, but it's not like you would have passed the word."

"You can go right straight to hell, Pepper!" Kreger cried, looking pissed-off and confused and beside himself. "I'm sick of your goddamned accusations! I have half a mind to wire the Marshal's Office—"

"Go right ahead. And while you're at it, wire the Army."

Kreger looked like he'd been slapped. "The Army? What in Christ for?"

Pepper shrugged. "Well, Sheriff, I mean lookit the facts here. You got renegade Apaches up in those hills. Blood-hungering heathen devils out praying on God-fearing white folks like myself. The Army will have to get involved in this. It is their job, you know."

Kreger looked like maybe he wanted to say a lot of things, but instead he merely pressed his lips shut. It suddenly dawned on him that Pepper was playing him again and he grasped for control. "Being that I'm the Sheriff here, Mr. Pepper, I believe that will be my call. As for *your* version of events, they'll be looked into. For all I know you might have just killed an innocent man. Yes, it calls for an investigation." He folded his arms, cool and confident now. "One man armed with pistols turned back four wild injuns with carbines, no less. My goodness. What a tale that is!"

Pepper knew what he was doing. It was very transparent. Not to say it didn't bother him, because it did. He was long since tired of playing these games with the sheriff. But he had no other choice, not until something broke open in one direction or the other.

He stood up. "Kreger, you're into something rotten here. We both know that. The smart thing to do would be to come clean. I can help you out of it, I'm sure. Maybe you should consider taking me up on that before it's too late. I'll be at my hotel if you come to your senses."

Kreger watched him leave and when the door swung shut, he buried his face in his hands. Pepper didn't know a damn thing. Because if he even guessed at any of this, he would have known it was far too late to do anything.

34

Back at the Gila Hotel, Pepper was down on his hands and knees.

It felt like someone was driving spikes into his skull. Dizziness raged in his head, buzzed and droned as if his noggin was full of hornets. He squinted his eyes shut, dared not open them because every time he did, the room not only spun but blurred, misted, seem to lose solidity. His fingers were tickling and he needed to vomit.

Lowering himself down until his face pressed against the cool hardwood floor, he lost consciousness.

35

It was near sunset and Kreger sat at his desk. His supper— steak and potatoes—was untouched before him. He was rocking back and forth in his chair and staring around his little office. The wanted fliers tacked to the walls. The gun case. The barred door leading back to the cells. The pot-bellied stove in the corner. His life, his world. And how long before it all came crashing down around him?

Tilbury, the deputy, was sweeping around him. It was his nightly duty: cleaning up, making sure the prisoners were tended to, locking the gun case. Just the odds and ends Kreger himself often seemed to forget about.

Kreger sipped whiskey from a flask.

"You keep drinking that stuff, Josh," Tilbury said, "you won't be of much use to anyone."

"Sometimes I wonder if that wouldn't be for the best," Kreger said under his breath, but it was loud enough for the deputy to hear.

"Maybe what you ought to do is just call it a day and go home. Get some rest, relax. I think that's what you need. Maybe a day off. When's the last time you had a day off? I can't seem to recall."

"This job. You don't get a day off."

"Hell, that ain't right," Tilbury said, leaning on his broom now. "You got me. You got Danny. You even got old Frank anytime you need him. We can handle things. Take a day off. Get some rest."

"I'd like that."

"So do it."

"I can't."

"And why not?"

Kreger shook his head. "Right now...it's just a bad time to be away. Too much going on."

Tilbury didn't seem to believe that. "There's always something going on. Take a day off anyway. I bet it'd do you wonders."

"Maybe I will. Just not right now."

Tilbury shrugged. "Well, it's up to you. Not worth killing yourself for. No job is." He continued sweeping, humming some melancholy dirge low in his throat. Ten minutes later, he was finished. "What time's Danny coming in?"

"I told him to take the night off."

Tilbury just looked at him.

"I got a rancher coming in to see me. Just some business we got to discuss."

Tilbury didn't look like he believed that either. He pulled on his coat and left without another word. Kreger kept drinking, waiting for his visitor to show. He knew he would.

He took another drink.

36

On around midnight, Kreger heard a rider coming with the sound of shoes clomping in the road. The sound of spurs on the boardwalk. The door eased open and the wind it brought was chill and damp. The figure standing there was gaunt, silvered by moonlight, his duster flapping around him. He had a smelled of graveyards and gallows.

"Come in, Mr. Jones," Kreger said.

Jones stepped in, quietly closing the door behind him. He walked about the room stiffly as if he were looking for something. But he wasn't; Kreger knew that. It was just his way.

He sat down across from the sheriff and Kreger could only see the right half of his face for which he was grateful. It was not an unhandsome face, he supposed. Lean, sharp-edged. The sort of face a woman might have called *intriguing*. And it was that, all right. Full of lines and hollows and ridges. A face of experience and hard-living. But menacing, threatening under the shadow thrown from the brim of his hat.

"I guess it didn't work out so well," Kreger said, finally breaking that oppressive silence.

"No, it did not."

Kreger licked his lips. "Did all I could do. He came in here, said he was going up to the farmhouse, and I passed it along to you."

Jones nodded grimly. "Two of my boys are dead."

"Pepper said he got two of 'em."

"He did at that."

Kreger sighed. "The other one's over at the undertakers. If you want him."

Jones turned now, giving Kreger a full view of his face, the left side which was a mass of scar tissue. Hideous. As if that half had started on fire and someone had put it out with an axe. "What in the hell would I want with a corpse?" he said, his voice cold as ice in a cistern.

"Well...I...I mean...it's there is all."

Jones glared at him and his dark eyes were unforgiving repositories of every black secret and atrocity known to man. He looked away, plugged a cigarette between lips thin and dry as strips of jerky. "Question now is what comes next. It's something I've been thinking on." He lit his cigarette with slow, deliberate motions of his spidery fingers.

Kreger took a pull from his flask. "Belt?"

Jones shook his head slightly. "Lost the taste for it some years back. Muddles the brain." He dragged off his cigarette.

Kreger set the flask down. He decided he wouldn't drink either. Anything to make "Mr. Jones" happy, anything at all, so he'd get out, go back to whatever grisly and ghoulish pursuits a man like him whiled away his time with.

But Jones wasn't going anywhere.

He blew smoke into the air. "Pepper's going to be more trouble, apparently, than I thought. I don't relish the idea of killing a lawman, but I've done it before and I'll probably do it again. Today, I'd hoped my boys would have removed him. Made things much easier."

Kreger shrugged. "Well, they say he's plenty good."

"So were my boys...or so I thought." Smoke curled from Mr. Jones' nostrils. "But they were Kiowas. They don't understand tactics, those people. All they know is attacking, raiding, charging in for the kill." He made a low chuckling sound. He did not smile. "Pepper must've known how they would come after him when he saw them. He drew them right in. Clever, that."

Kreger decided he *would* have another drink. "What are you going to do about him?"

"Maybe you should do something about him."

Kreger steeled himself. "No. I won't get involved with that. You know our agreement, Mr. Jones. I'll tip you off, steer things your way, anything I can do to make finding that money easier. But I won't have any hand in killing."

"Selective morals," Jones said as if he had no use for such things.

"Maybe. But a man has to have some rules. Otherwise, well, otherwise—"

"Otherwise we'd all be common criminals, eh? Animals? Outlaws just like me?"

"I didn't mean—"

"Shut the fuck up. Nothing I hate worse than sniveling, whining little cowards like yourself who feel the need to continually apologize."

Kreger felt redness touch his cheeks. He was not the child that had been bullied in the schoolyard anymore. That person was long gone. He was a fair man, he thought. Reasonable. But he could only be pushed so far. "That'll be enough."

Jones finished his cigarette, crushed it under his boot. He stood up. "You're becoming a liability, Sheriff. You don't have the stomach for this sort of work. God knows whatever possessed you to think you'd make a good lawman."

Kreger glared at him now, knowing it wasn't a good thing, but not caring. "I *am* a good lawman."

Jones spat on the floor, that evil face filled with triumph. "What you are, you spineless little sonofabitch, is a disgrace. Letting a man like me sour you, corrupt you. You have no self-respect and I have no respect *for* you."

Kreger felt his anger begin to subside. He had to go slow here. He had to remember who and exactly *what* he was dealing with here. If Jones had been a desert snake, his tail would have been in full rattle now. If pushed, he would surely strike. And he was easily as venomous as any creature God had put on the face of this dismal planet.

He began walking away towards the door, his spurs jangling.

Kreger saw his gunbelt hanging on the wall.

Jones wheeled around quickly, a big .44 Colt Dragoon in one leathery fist. "You're a liability, Kreger. It's only a matter of time before you start talking to Pepper."

He was right. Kreger knew this; he'd been thinking that very thing. He sat up erectly in his seat, knowing he was a dead man and also knowing he could only die once. "God damn you, Partridge," he snarled. "God damn you straight to hell."

Black Jake attempted a grin and it was horrible.

Kreger stared, did not blink, did not flinch.

He thought of his wife who'd left him many months before and he wished he'd been a better man, a better husband, and, God yes, a better lawman. He heard thunder and saw lightning. And these were his final sensory impressions before his skull flew apart like a Ming vase.

37

In Dead Creek, Nathan Partridge laid in bed and smoked a cheroot, blowing smoke rings in the air. A girl named Lily Keen lay next to him. He was certain she had yet to see twenty and wouldn't have been surprised if she was much younger. But like a man taking a swan dive off a chair with a noose around his throat, he did not care. Wasn't much he did care about...outside his money, that was.

"How old are you?" he found himself asking, even though he knew he really didn't care.

She brushed a strand of red hair away from one taut, smallish breast. "Seventeen. As of last winter, I'm seventeen."

Partridge nodded, pulled off his smoke. "Now how's about the truth?"

"What are you? A preacher? A minister?" She scowled at the thought and rolled away. "Don't matter if'n you are, honey, because I've serviced them, too."

Partridge laughed at that. He was truly surprised how easy it was to smile again, to laugh, to be a human being. His situation was surely not the best...yet, he lived it, trials and tribulations and all, as a free man. And that, in the final analysis, is all that really mattered. "I'm a preacher like you're a nun, honey."

She smiled and her face was lovely in the mid-afternoon sunlight. Golden, glowing. Marked by experience and hardship, but lovely somehow. He squeezed his eyes shut and decided this is how he would remember her: golden-faced, bright-eyed, that red hair falling over her bare shoulders like tongues of flame. Yes, he would file that image away. Save it. Savor it. No one could take it away from him.

"What if I was to tell you I was fifteen?" she said. "And what if I was then to tell you I've only been doing this for a month?"

He traced a rough, callused finger over her bare forearm. "I'd say you learn fast."

"And what about my age?"

He had to answer that carefully, he supposed. "I'd say a person has to get by the best they can. And that's all I'd say about it."

She seemed to like his answer. She rolled back in his arms and kissed him hard on the mouth. Then she went on to tell him how she'd come west with her mother from Indiana, searching for her father who'd come out to Arizona Territory to make his pile in the mines. He never did and they never heard from him again. Nobody was even sure if he made it this far. Her mother had died the summer before of consumption (though the actual cause was never ascertained) in Globe and Lily was pretty much left high and dry without any means of support. Except one.

"I hope to, someday, get out of this. I don't want to spend my life whoring."

Partridge believed her. The brothels in Dead Creek (of which there were many) ran from your bargain establishments where a man could get a slap and tickle for two bits to your high-dollar whorehouses where you could drop hundreds or even thousands. But it was a mining town and prices had a way of inflating when money was being pulled out of the earth. Lily worked for the pretentiously named Silver Dollar Emporium for the equally pretentious Lord Johnny Max Silver, a high roller, dandy, and inveterate gambler who tooled about town in a private carriage, decked out in a black Prince Albert suit, silk vest, black tie, boiled white shirt, and Italian leather boots. He sported a silken top hat and walking stick and more upper crust attitude than a privileged Bostonian men's club. But you could rub shit all day long and it still wouldn't shine. And a pimp would always be a pimp.

The Silver Dollar Emporium's prices were mid-range.

It was not and would never be the equal of the Moonlight Tea House or sport the imported French delights of the ultra-elite Royal Parisian Theater. The Silver Dollar boasted vaudeville acts ranging from belly dancers to magicians to comedy troupes. When the prostitutes weren't employed servicing men in the bedrooms upstairs or the velvet-curtained booths in the theater, they spent their time shilling drinks, picking the pockets of drunken cowboys and miners, dancing for a price, and encouraging rich ranchers to throw down more money at the notoriously rigged gambling tables.

"Suppose you know this town better than anyone," Partridge said.

She shrugged. "As good as anyone can. But, hell, this town grows by leaps and bounds everyday. And will, until the gold runs out."

"Ever heard of a place called the Egyptian Hotel?" he asked.

"Sure. Everyone has. It's a high-dollar joint like the Royal Parisian. Don't bother going unless you got a few thousand in your poke. Even the drinks there'll cost you twenty dollars."

A whorehouse then. Interesting. He had figured as much. Roseman had had a card from there…was it purely accidental or was it connected? Partridge took another drag off his cheroot. "You know who owns it?"

"The Egyptian Hotel? Not sure, some lady, I think. Whoever she is, she must be damn rich. You ought to see that place…it's something, all right." Lily shook her head. "Just once I'd like to see some real money."

"You know what that woman's name might be?"

"No idea."

"Ever seen her?"

"Nope."

But it was enough to start with. He climbed back on top of Lily and before long he forgot about the Egyptian Hotel and who might own it.

38

Later, walking the muddy streets of Dead Creek, he was surprised by all the bustle and activity. Chimney Flats, despite its wild streak, was positively quiet and tame by comparison. Dead Creek was like an ant hive, constantly in busy, industrious motion.

The town was built right up the side of the mountain, centered right around the mineral lode, no doubt. Buildings and stores and ramshackle structures of every possible description clung to the hills and slopes. There were houses packed so tight on those grades that if you fell off your front porch you would've landed on your neighbor's roof. It looked, if anything, like a city a child might have thrown together. Without plan, without organization. Like a handful of dice tossed to the wind. Roofs and chimneys, headframes and fingers of machinery jutting in every which direction and possible angle like weeds sprouting from a rock pile. And surrounding all this sprawling squalor were immense tent cities and shacks and the ever-present heaps of slag, mountains in their own right.

Streets were cut up hillsides and down hollows, strung between homes and buildings and shanties in a knotted, snaking profusion. Low-lying areas were seas of mud and hilltops were so dry a good wind could have blown them away.

And everywhere, packed in amongst the confusion were gin mills and parlor houses and saloons of every description ranging from adobe edifices to huts with blankets for doors. There were gambling houses and brothels and shops and mining offices and stables and cafes and everywhere, people. Children running through the filthy streets, chasing makeshift balls with sticks. Whores and prospectors and dandies and shopkeepers and dirt-caked miners. Partridge heard English spoken, Spanish, half dozen European tongues. Gold brought professional hardrock miners from all over the world. And the lure of it turned hardworking men into amateur diggers. And it also brought out those who would mine the miners—soiled doves, card sharks, tinhorn gamblers, and petty criminals. A raging, stormy sea of human dreams and human waste. And in the midst of it all, preachers spouting psalms from the tops of wooden crates, herders in search of a flock. They might as well have looked on the dark side of the moon.

Partridge had been to plenty of mining towns.

But it was usually to rob and run. He'd never actually stayed long enough to watch the machinery of gold fever in action. It was really something to see.

He knew how places like this worked. Some prospector struck a rich vein and every panhandler and saddle tramp in the Territory converged on the place. Soon enough placer gold was being gathered in pans and rockers and sluiceboxes. But that played out fairly quickly and the digging, the tunneling began. If there was enough there, the big mining concerns descended like buzzards on fresh meat. They bought the rights and pretty soon owned all the countryside and built homes and erected stores and miners came in droves. All of them working themselves to death six days a week, ten hours a day for $3. The mining companies got rich and the miners dropped like flies in a fan and were instantly replaced by a half-dozen other hungry men. There was always plenty of work for those who didn't put much value on their lives. Single-jackers, double-jackers, muckers, drillers, powermen. They channeled out drifts and slopes and gutted the hills and mountains and blasted shafts through solid rock and soon enough the landscape was so scarred and broken from dynamite and shovel and corrosive chemicals that not even a weed would grow there.

And, in time, the gold would play out and the town would be nothing but a dusty wound on the countryside.

As Partridge walked he could hear not only the voices of the townspeople and miners, but the sound of gunfire and dynamite detonating up in the hills and down in the shafts. The ground seemed to rumble underfoot. The air stunk of sulfur and caustic fumes and rotting garbage.

He found a saloon and ducked inside.

There were maybe a hundred men inside drinking and fighting and laughing and boasting. A bearded man banged away on a piano in the corner that hadn't been tuned since before the War Between the States. The air was thick with a haze of smoke, the reek of unwashed bodies, spilled beer and cheap whiskey.

"Pull up a stool," an old man said to Partridge. He had salt-and-pepper hair and a matching beard. His face had more lines in it than a survey map. "Go ahead, pilgrim. Sit down and I'll buy you a drink. You're a stranger and I know it and I better set you straight before your pockets are empty and you're fighting for crumbs."

Partridge took the stool and sat down.

"Maddie! Beers over here! Two of 'em and make it quick!" The old man tugged at his beard, staring at Partridge as if he just didn't know what to make of him. "What's your tag, pilgrim? Gibbons is mine. That's what folks call me. Around these parts, you ask for Gibbons, goddamned if they won't steer you straight to me quicker than a young man fucks. Yes, sir. Gibbons, all right. Got me a Christian name, too, but I'd sooner stuff hot coals up my ass than reveal to you what it is. One of them biblical names and all. Not my fault, you see, my old lady, shee-yit, she was crazier than a hound humping a gopher hole. Ate, slept, and drank the Good Book. Probably wiped her ass with it, too, when I wasn't looking for all I know. Anyway, what'd you say your name was?"

"Smith'll do," Partridge said.

The old man put his hands on his hips. "Ha! You don't look much like a Smith. But that's your business, partner. Yes, sir. I'll just call you *pilgrim* because we're all pilgrims here seeking that which we shall never find."

Partridge just grunted.

The beers appeared in glasses not much cleaner than the rest of the town. But it was good, warm, but good. Partridge took half his glass in one swallow. "Appreciate it," he said.

"You here to make your fortune?" Gibbons inquired.

"No. Just passing through."

He looked disappointed. "Oh, well, no matter. See, I told myself that the next greenhorn I saw pass through that door that looked honest and dependable, I was going to help him out. And that's the truth." The old man crossed himself. "Shit, I know what you're thinking—that I'm running some scam here. Not so. See, I'm a rich man. That's the truth. I might be dirtier than a boring rig, but money I do have. And it's all tucked safely away in a bank in Phoenix. Yes, sir. See, I already made my pile. Took me fifteen years of hardrock scrabbling, put I finally hit it. And hit it big. Look around, pilgrim. Tell me what you see."

Partridge did. Dirty men crowded shoulder to shoulder. That was all there was in this place. Unless you wanted to count the stools and the jury-rigged bartop.

"Don't even answer that, pilgrim. I'll answer it for you. What you're seeing is the underbelly of mankind, all drawn here for a few nuggets of gold. Only one man in a hundred will make anything to write home about. Me? I'm richer than a bank vault. Got more money than a Republican. I'm lucky, that's what. Lucky."

Partridge sipped his beer. "If you already made your fortune, what are you doing here?"

"Ha!" Gibbons laughed and slapped Partridge on the back none too gently. "Fair question, that one. Well, pilgrim, I'll tell you. I made it. I dug my fortune out of the ground. I was an independent. It's the only way you can make any real money. You work for the big mining concerns and your pockets will always be emptier than a promise and you'll always be in debt to them. Yes, sir. But now as to your question—" he scratched at his shaggy beard "—it's one I've pondered myself. All I wanted to do my whole life was make my pile and leave. And when I had it safe in the bank, all I could think about was starting again. Crazy? Touched in the head? Yes, sir, pilgrim. That's me. But I guess, deep down, I love the lifestyle. Either that or I'm just plum too damn old or stupid to know a good thing when I got it."

Partridge was originally inclined to think Gibbons was a liar. But now…well, he wasn't so sure. Maybe he *was* rich. Then again, maybe he'd just spent too much time in the darkness, rooting like a mole.

Gibbons said, "No, a man has to be independent or his goose is surely roasted and served up. I'm glad you're not here to mine, pilgrim. Nothing ruins a man's life and soul quicker than gold. Yes, what you see around you is men who break their backs day in and day out so they don't have to work at an honest trade. It's no easy life." He swallowed his beer in one gulp, threw some coins on the bar and his glass was instantly refilled. "Yes, sir, you work for the company, you gotta make your quota. You don't, you're fired that day. No ifs or buts about it. Ten hours a day down in them shafts that are hotter than the Devil's own asshole. Swinging a pick until your muscles go to putty. Pick handle so goddamned hot you could light a cigarette off it. Yes, sir. Heat and pressure and breathing that foul air until your lungs are full of dust and you got the cramps so bad you can't stand straight for three days running. *Damn.* Then you got your cave-ins. You got inexperienced men blowing explosives and sometimes you with 'em. You fall five-hundred feet into a water-filled sump. Or maybe you drop into a pocket of scalding water and boil up prettier than a lobster. You ever seen a man get broiled like that? No? Good and God bless you. You'll never get that stink out of your nose."

Partridge just stared at him. He was an amusing fellow. He talked nonstop, hammering out words rapid fire. But he supposed any man that worked by himself down in the earth day after day had that right. "Don't sound like much of a life," was all he could say.

The old man smiled. "It ain't. But it's the only one I got. And I cling to it like a turd to a dog's hairy ass."

Partridge finished his beer. "You know of a place called the Egyptian Hotel?"

Gibbon's eyes widened. "Hell, yes! Best steaks in town! Entertainment, the finest! And the women—" he kissed the grubby tips of his fingers "—beautiful! Just beautiful! But you better be a rich man, pilgrim. Because they don't give it away for free."

"Been there?"

"Once, pilgrim. Only once. Dropped three-hundred on a woman and three-hundred more gambling. Ah, but what a night it was!" The old man positively glowed with the memory. "What a night! Ha! These days my business is about as stiff as a ribbon in the wind, but, now and again, it takes a notion and stands taller and prouder than a flagpole on a winter night. Where you hail from, pilgrim?"

Partridge thought about lying to him, but didn't see the point. In this heaving sea of bodies that was Dead Creek, he rather doubted he'd be recognized or even sought. "Yuma. Yourself?"

"Sedona. Ran a livery there. Did pretty good. Dry goods, too. Can you imagine me as a shopkeeper, pilgrim?" He burst with hearty laughter. "But it's true! Then I got a taste of the gold fever. Told the old woman I was going for a walk and I never came back! Ha! Course, she don't mind now at all, being rich and what not. Still lives in Sedona. You ever been to Sedona, pilgrim?"

Partridge's face went grim, his eyes narrowed. "Yeah, I was there. Once. Just the once."

39

They rode into Sedona on a blistering hot July afternoon: Nathan Partridge, Kid Kirby, Mexican Joe Avilla, the Webb brothers, and Stuttering Johnny Blunt. The sun was smoldering in the hazy yellow sky like a burning coal. The air was stillborn and stagnant. You could smell nothing but dust and despair. Hear grass crisping and adobe melting. See horses languishing at troughs and dogs sprawled under porches, the lot of them baking in their own skins.

The Gila River Gang were dressed identically in black coats and flat-crowned hats of the same color. Dressing alike had been Kirby's idea; he figured any witnesses would get their stories confused by men wearing identical clothing. The others weren't sure, but they let it ride.

Nobody paid much attention as they rode in past saloons and hotels and liveries. Those that were on the dusty streets were anxious to get off them and into the shade. A few watched them from benches on the boardwalks, but not with any special interest.

For the past three months they had been tracking Pierce's gang of bounty hunters, the very ones that had ambushed them as part of a sheriff's posse at the Salt River. Word reached Kirby that three of them had been killed during the gun battle and a fourth died shortly later. But word had also reached him that no less than eight of their member were still alive and together. And still operating as something of an enforcement wing of the Pinkertons, running down horse thieves and bank robbers, infiltrating their gangs wherever possible.

"But all that's done and gone," Kirby said when he found out. "Done and gone. Them sonsabitches are walking dead men and all they need is somebody to remind 'em with some iron in the belly."

And so it was.

They tracked them to a saloon in Sedona called the White Spur. It was owned by one of the manhunters, a fellow named Skinner. It was here that the bounty hunters ran their operation. It was their hideout and re-grouping area. Where they licked their wounds and poured over wanted dodgers.

And it was here, Kirby decided, they would die.

So, on that fateful day that was hotter than Mexican peppers in a frying pan, the Gila River Gang entered town and rode through carefully until they came first to a seedy hotel called the Donover House and a cash store right next to it. A rutted dirt road cut past them, a corral, and a smithy shop, a Chinese laundry and a weathered livery barn. Just around the corner was the White Spur.

It was in a two-story cracker box building with an assayers office around the side. Out back was a stable. It was weathered gray as ash, the clapboarding warped and splintering. Three or four horses broiled outside, their coats thick with flies buzzing and nipping.

"That's her, hillbilly," Kirby said as they passed. "Just one big graveyard waiting to happen."

They were all thinking about their fallen comrades, those poor bastards killed as a result of Pierce's underhanded double-dealings with the law. Prescott Jackson, Willy Boy Horton, and Coltrane. All dead as bones in a ditch now. Dead but surely not forgotten. It was in the eyes of the Gila River Gang as they dismounted and tethered their mounts to the hitching post: stern, unforgiving, relentless hatred

They walked up to the peeling door of the White Spur.

Kirby was in the lead. He tried to open it, but it was locked.

There was a sign tacked up to the side of the door. It read:

OUT A LICKER
GIT SOM MEBBE TOMORAH
MEBBE NOT

"Out of whiskey," a voice behind them said.

They all turned and there was a boy of eleven or twelve standing there in a sweat-stained cotton shirt and boots three sizes too large. He had a cherubic, pleasant face. He grinned broadly. "White Spur's out of whiskey," he said. "Won't be none in for a few days. But you can try—"

"We're looking for some friends of ours, son," Partridge said. "Fellow name of Skinner and his bunch. You know of 'em?"

"Surely! They's bounty hunters! They chase down shootists and outlaws!" He seemed proud of the fact and, Partridge supposed, to a boy, men like that probably seemed bigger than life. "Are you lawmen?"

"Yes, we are. Could ye point us to 'em, young master?" Kirby said, tossing the kid a silver piece. "Be mighty obliged if ye could."

The kid looked at the piece and grinned. "It's real!" he said. But he still didn't know what to make of this bunch. Maybe he wondered why Mexican Joe carried a sawed-off shotgun and the Webb brothers carried carbines. But money was money.

"Real as rain, son."

The gang all gave him friendly smiles, save Mexican Joe who was screwed-up tighter than bedsprings. He was all attitude and rage barely concealed. He'd traded his blood for acid and his flat, dark eyes were so intense, so predatory they would've scared worms out of pork.

The kid just looked at him and his Adam's apple bobbed as he swallowed. "Right this way," he said. "They's out back, I reckon."

The kid led them to the barn out back and knocked until a hoarse voice called out. He pushed open the door and the gang filed in after him. Partridge was the second one in and he made a quick mental count. Yup, eight of them. Eight men. Three were playing cards at a table. Four others lounging on bales of hay. A fifth hitting off a bottle of shine.

"Need to see a man named Skinner," Kirby said, stuffing a plug of tobacco into his cheek.

The man with the bottle stepped forward. You could already see it in his eyes that he knew this was trouble. He watched Kirby's boys fan out behind him. "I'm Skinner, stranger. What can I do for you?" Then he looked at the boy standing there. "Mike, you go on home now. We have business with these gents."

And Partridge figured you had to give him that. Regardless of what sort of weasel he might be, least he didn't want the kid catching lead.

When the door had shut and the air smelled of the dry, hot stink of hay and feed and motes of dust and chaff were drifting in the beams of sunlight from the windows and numerous holes in the roof, Skinner's men became pensive. Nothing good could come of men armed as these strangers were. Nothing good at all.

Kirby let one hand drift down to the double-action Colt riding at his hip. "Well, Mr. Skinner," he said, spitting tobacco juice onto the table and fouling the cards. "You know a man named Pierce?"

There was silence for a moment. Everyone of Skinner's men knew what this was about. Their eyes were all beady and darting like those of rats in a sewer. They were armed, but how fast could they reach iron?

"Jesus Christ," one of them said in a whisper, "that's Kid Kirby..."

"Yer right, friend. That's who I be. And I've come to do you a hurt."

Skinner licked his lips. "The hell you say."

And then it happened. The bounty hunters went for their guns or maybe just one of them did and the Gila River gang cleared leather and started pulling triggers. Mexican Joe's shotgun boomed twice and split a man in half as he reached for his pistol. Partridge and Johnny Blunt dropped three more before their fingers found their belts. And Kirby pulled his Colt just as Skinner went for his and it was Kirby who won that race as three bullets drilled into Skinner's belly and burst him like balloon full of red. A third and fourth slug turned his face to a bleeding jigsaw puzzle and he stumbled over a bale of hay, pissing blood in wild, spraying loops.

The other three didn't even bother: they just reached for sky.

Kirby said, "Fuck the lot of 'em," and turned away.

The five other gang members, Partridge included, kept shooting until they ran out of bullets and the surviving bounty hunters were broken and bleeding things laying in heaps. It looked like their shirts were stuffed with raw meat. Mexican Joe, still not sated, reloaded his scattergun and gave each of the dead men a final round that blew them into tangles of red confetti.

"G-G-Guess that's it then," Johnny Blunt said, leathering his Shofield. "They's d-done exp-p-p-...they's done dead. Yessum."

It all came down within the space of about thirty seconds and well over fifty rounds had been spent. The gang stepped back out into the unforgiving sunshine and rode out of Sedona. They were never stopped. Never questioned. Never pursued. It was a duck shoot from beginning to end and a very satisfying one.

It gave the Gila River Gang a certain sense of triumph, of accomplishment.

Which was good, because what came next gave them anything but.

40

Partridge bought Gibbons another beer and he sat listening as the old man reeled off one story after another. But he wasn't really listening; he was thinking about the Egyptian Hotel. He had it in his craw now and like a bad memory it just wouldn't leave him alone.

"You sure you wouldn't be here to claw some gold out of those hills? No? How about silver? Maybe copper's your bit, pilgrim. Could be. Money in that, too."

"No, I'm not here to mine anything."

Gibbons shook his head. "Damn. Damn it anyway!"

Partridge just looked at him.

Gibbons laughed. "Crazy, that's what I am. I know you're probably thinking I got more shit between my ears than a filled slop bucket, but it ain't so, pilgrim. See, what I said to you earlier was true. I'm looking for a greenhorn I can help out. Why? You might rightly ask." He took a pull of his beer. "See, I've been lucky. I set out to do something and, goddamned if I didn't do it. I'm set. Lately I've been thinking the good Lord has been mighty kind to a man like me. And I thought to myself, well, how can you repay that? And it occurred to me I can only repay it by doing some good deeds to some souls in dire need. But that wouldn't be you, pilgrim?"

"Not just yet. Maybe tomorrow, though."

The old man slapped his knee. "Fair enough! Now, you need help or you need anything, you ask for Gibbons. Okay? I'm your man! Hot damn, it just occurred to me!"

"What?"

"That I'm like your guardian angel!"

Partridge opened his mouth, then closed it, not really sure what to say to that.

"I'm serious, pilgrim, truly I am!" Gibbons stood up and danced a quick jig. "Goddamn, if I haven't just gotten the calling!"

Partridge didn't know whether to laugh or thank him or high tail his ass for the hills.

"Gotta be pushing off?" the old man said. "You're looking a might ancy, if you don't mind me saying so."

Partridge told him he had to make a trip to the privy.

Which was the truth and a lie. He needed to, but he also needed a reason to get away from the old man. He was a good sort, but Partridge had business in this town and he needed his anonymity. He slipped out back to the alley where there was a row of privies lined up like doll houses, all nailed together out of odds and ends and stinking like open sewers. It was filthy inside and Partridge relieved himself quickly, stepping over a man vomiting in the dirt. He passed the first privy and the door swung open.

He was staring at the twin barrels of a shotgun. "You be Nathan Partridge?" a voice asked him, its owner stepping into the light. He was dressed in greasy buckskins, sported a matted beard that could've been used to sweep floors, had more eyes in his head than teeth in his mouth.

Partridge went cold inside, but tried not to show it. "No, sir," he said, very calmly, "there must be a mistake. Bedford's the name, Forrest Bedford."

The man kept the shotgun on him, his eyes darting about like something peering from a cave mouth. "Like hell you are," he said. He passed a tobacco-stained tongue over the nub of a single tooth. "You Nathan Partridge and you a wanted man."

Partridge felt it coming, felt death closing in. He could already smell its black, tomblike odor settling over the alley. Death was coming. "You've got the wrong man," he said. "I don't know what your beef with this Partridge is, but it sure as hell don't concern me."

And he almost had him with that—the old mountain rat looked confused for a moment or two. "You look like who I think you are and that's good enough. Now, be so kind as to unbuckle that there gun belt and do it real slow. Left hand, mind you."

Partridge brought his hand down to the buckle, but never made it.

Gibbons stepped up behind old broom-beard and brought the blade of a folding shovel down on the crown of his skull. Broom-beard collapsed like a preacher's tent in a high wind.

"Never did care for bounty hunters," the prospector said. "Why, I remember one time down in Mexico...well, pilgrim, maybe another time. I think you'd better be off. And good luck to you. You'll see me again. I got that feeling. Lessen it's just my piles acting up again..."

With that, he turned and was gone.

Partridge just stood there. More good luck. Seemed like he could hardly do anything wrong these days. But how long could that possibly last? Good luck and a crazy desert rat for a guardian angel. He went back out into the street and nearly got run down by a Concord coach. The driver called him a few select names and led his team away.

Partridge just stood there.

It said, EGYPTIAN HOTEL on the rear of the baggage boot. He figured it was a sign from above. Maybe Gibbons was some sort of angel after all.

41

That damp gray morning in Wickenburg when they duly hung Black Jake Partridge was the beginning of a new life for the condemned. There were probably precious few that could boast of such a thing. It took money and it took a certain amount of political maneuvering, but it worked out just fine. So fine in fact that Black Jake was able to watch his own hanging. And afterwards, to continue on with his career. And all of it seemed to be about to reach culmination. For he was so close to Nathan and the money now, he could literally taste its dirty tang on his tongue.

Up in the hills above Dead Creek, he sipped coffee from a dented tin cup and continued doing so as riders came in. He did not make a move towards his .44 Colt Dragoon. He merely waited, his ears attuned like those of a mountain cat. He listened to the horses, the way they galloped.

No danger, they were his men coming.

There were three of them. All that was left of his little gang of raiders, all that was needed now: Santos, Noguerro, and Torra

Dead Tree. They were once Kiowa warriors under the firm and sly hand of Santana, the Kiowa chief. But then came the reservation and complete bitterness. They escaped and went about raiding with twenty of their brothers. But it wasn't until they fell in with "Devil-Face" Black Jake Partridge that they truly learned the time-honored white man's arts of robbery and murder.

They tethered their horses and came over to him.

"He is in town," Torra Dead Tree said. Raised in white mission schools, Dead Tree spoke Spanish, English, and a bit of French. He could also quote openly from the Bible and Shakespeare. He was no savage, but, at heart, that's exactly what he was.

Black Jake took off his Stetson, picked a bit of lint from it. He ran long fingers with knobbed knuckles through his thinning white hair. "Then, gentlemen, I'd say things are looking up. The wind is blowing in our direction."

And that was good. Black Jake had been beginning to worry. Sure, Kreger had steered Nathan towards Dead Creek, but that was only part of the plan. Once on the trail, Roseman and his boys were to either find and follow him or befriend him and ride in with him. But that hadn't worked out real sweet, being that word had reached Black Jake that Roseman and the others were dead.

So this was good news. Things could still work out. Maybe.

"Yes, I think this may turn out profitable for all concerned," he said.

Santos and Noguerro who could speak very little English, understood nonetheless and grinned happily to one another.

Torra Dead Tree did not smile. Like Black Jake he was incapable of it. His face was weathered and burnished, a flap of leather left to dry and season in the desert wind. "I worry, though," he said. "Your son...yes, we can best him, I think. Maybe. But he is a good man with a gun and, apparently, not afraid to use it. But this other...the marshal Pepper...he could be trouble. If we can finish before he arrives—"

"What makes you think he's coming?" Black Jake inquired.

And although he was incapable of smiling, Dead Tree's eyes twinkled now with amusement. "He's coming. Have no fear of that."

Black Jake sighed, knowing it was true.

He was well-acquainted with the ragged determination of that man. Pepper had been one of the deputy U.S. Marshals that had hunted him originally. Some men were capable of forgetting, of giving up, but not John Pepper. He was compulsive. He was obsessed. Black Jake was pretty sure the lawman would have to die. He saw no other way.

And, honestly, that surprised him.

That he actually considered another way, a way he might be able to let the man live. Killing and Black Jake were old friends. There was usually no thought about sparing lives. If someone presented a problem, he killed them. It was just another indication that he was getting on in years and had no business living the life any longer. Which was one reason he wanted Nathan's loot—it would be more than enough to retire on and spend his remaining days in luxury.

But Pepper could be a problem.

Black Jake knew from Kreger that the marshal already suspected his identity. Somehow, that wily bastard had put it together. And that definitely was trouble.

He lit a cigarette and stared into the weak, dying fire before him. It all came rushing through his head—his son, the marshal, the money. Damn, but it was getting complicated.

He thought: Pepper, you sonofabitch, you're too damn old for this. Maybe you're not as old as me, but you're too old for the game. We both are. We're both getting slow and there's no point pretending otherwise. I see it coming, yes, I do. One of us will be moldering in the grave before this is through. Maybe both. Yes, sir.

Santos and Noguerro sat down, backs against a few ungainly boulders that thrust from the earth. With their knives they cut thin strips of jerky and sucked on them, savoring the juice.

Torra Dead Tree did not join them. He squatted down by Black Jake. "What should we do now?' he asked.

"We wait. We wait and we see. Tonight, perhaps, I'll go into town and see what transpires. Beyond that, we can do nothing."

Black Jake sat there staring into the fire and drinking his coffee which, like his blood, had gone from hot to tepid. But it was age. It was surely age. The Kiowa renegades were devoted to him, thinking he was some great warrior. But once he had the money, he would have no further use for them and he sure as hell wasn't going to share it with them. No, he'd kill them. There were only three left and he could take them easy. And take them without remorse.

It had always been his strong suit.

And they would understand nothing less.

He respected them as they respected him. Their sadism was second only to his own. They enjoyed killing in all its forms. And they were particularly good at torturing men in the most heinous methods imaginable.

Black Jake thought about Wickenburg.

Thought about Sheriff Bill Teller. Teller was corrupt and greedy and, like Kreger, a lawman in name only. He was the one who had arranged everything for Black Jake. The selection of the prisoner that would hang for him and his escape. That morning, only Teller was allowed to see the condemned man. The condemned man being an alcoholic drifter name of Niles. Physically, he was a near match for Black Jake. And shot with morphine and hooded, no one knew the difference. Teller brought him in the night before, kept him in a cell until morning. And only after the hood was slid in place were the deputies allowed to see him.

For five-thousand gold, Black Jake was a free man. Of course, six months later he came back and killed Teller in order to keep the secret. It was just something that had to be done. And, truth be told, Wickenburg was much better without that sonofabitch.

Shortly afterwards, Black Jake joined up with Torra Dead Tree and his braves.

42

Maybe "joined" wasn't the proper word here, for they'd ambushed him in the Black Mountains of western New Mexico. Two months after he was "executed", they came upon him one afternoon as he whiled away his time trying to sort out his future. He had guns and they needed them and four of them came out of the rocks silent as shadows.

They were on him before he could draw his weapon.

They had knives and had every intention of using them. Black Jake pulled his own and it began. One renegade got in close, too close, fueled by desperation and blinded, perhaps, by arrogance. Black Jake avoided his thrust, took hold of his mane of black hair and yanked back his head and slit his throat. He blinded another with a slash across the eyes and gutted a third. Then something hit him over the head and he tumbled into blackness.

It was night when he woke and he was in their camp.

They had let him live because it wasn't their way to kill sleeping men. There was no thrill in it. They wanted him awake so they could hear him scream. That was their game. He was bound and gagged, tied to a tree stump.

Although Black Jake didn't understand their language, he knew that the lean and desperate raiders gathered around the fire were discussing only one thing: his death. The Kiowa, he learned, could be very patient when it came to deciding on how to best kill a man. Would they burn him alive? Skin him? Cut him into pieces? Drag him behind their horses? Shove burning embers down his throat and up his ass? There was very little limit to their creativity.

From time to time, one of them would circle him and study his face. They seemed to be in awe of him. Maybe because he'd taken out three of them before they got to him. The Kiowa did not take bravery and savagery in battle lightly; they were impressed by it. They respected it.

Eventually, one of them came to him, sat cross-legged before him. Later, he would know this man as Torra Dead Tree, but for now he was merely another heathen savage. He was dressed in worn buffalo skins, carried a jug made from the bladder of a bison. He pressed it to Black Jake's lips. Blood. They were offering him blood. To decline it would be a sign of weakness, an insult. Animal blood was a common drink among the Kiowas.

Black Jake tasted it on his lips. It was still warm. Rich and red and coppery, he swallowed down what was offered. He had drank blood before; it was not a new thing.

"Tell us who you are," the renegade said. "Where you come from."

So Black Jake did. He gave Torra Dead Tree the truncated version of his life. The guerrillas he'd fought with during the war. The gangs he'd rode with. His escape from the noose. He told him the truth, knowing it was not acceptable to lie to a Kiowa warrior.

After some discussion, they let him live. He joined up and became one of them. He learned they were from Texas and had been pushed westward by the Army who was busy rooting out and crushing renegade Indian bands.

They both had reason to hate the white man.

Their raids were lucrative, but no one was getting rich. They were living, they were surviving and while that was enough for the Kiowas, it was not enough for Black Jake. Two weeks after he gunned down Teller, he and ten of the Kiowas raided a mining office in the Maricopas. Seven of the braves were killed in the ensuing gun battle. A barrel of kerosene ignited and engulfed Black Jake. Torra Dead Tree had taken his burned body away and nursed him back to health. But the left side of his body…it would never be the same. He was disfigured, hideous, but as a consolation, no one would ever look in his face and recognize him as Black Jake Partridge.

The price of freedom was often high.

After a time, he was more Kiowa than white. The Kiowa were buffalo hunters and although the buffalo had all but vanished, they were still hunters. Black Jake wore skins as they did. He spoke their language. He saw compassion and mercy as a weakness (an easy thing for him in that this was already ingrained in him). He lived in a house made of hides and bones. He burned dung for his fire. And, like them, sometimes he roasted his meat and sometimes he ate it raw, cutting off mouthfuls and swallowing it birdlike, half-chewed. He sucked on fat and he drank blood, learning to truly like the taste.

Together, they lived in the mountains and raided down into Mexico for women and into the Territories for money and goods. They regularly attacked the wagons and trading posts of the comancheros, taking their money, their whiskey, their horses, any plunder they could lay their hands on. They robbed stages. Their favorite prey became miners up in the hills. They robbed and murdered dozens.

It was a very satisfying life.

Black Jake showed them how to strip and maintain their rifles. The quickest way to decapitate a man and hang his head like a trophy from your saddle just as Bloody Bill had shown him during the war. He easily became the most sadistic of them, devising new tortures and revising old ones. Together, they raped and plundered and robbed. They stuffed hot coals down the throats of captives. They plucked their eyes out. They glorified in what Black Jake referred to as "the shearing": slowly peeling a man of his flesh. An ongoing process that could be prolonged for hours and hours while the victim begged for his death. The Kiowas were particularly impressed by the more imaginative methods he came up with.

In a tiny adobe village on the San Juan River in northern Mexico, he introduced them to the Medieval method of execution known as quartering. The village priest who knew the whereabouts (supposedly) of a cache of Army carbines that Black Jake wanted, but refused to admit to this, was the victim. His ankles and wrists were bound tightly with ropes. The other ends tied to the saddle horns of four powerful bays. The bays were mounted by four of Black Jake's renegades, who led the horses off until the priest was lifted from the ground. Step by step, he was drawn taut like an X, suspended above the ground, legs and arms straining. Still, he would not tell though his face had gone red and sweating and his joints and ligaments could clearly be heard popping. Finally, Black Jake gave the signal and each of the mounted Kiowas let loose with a wild and whooping war cry, slamming their heels into the sides of their mounts. The bays charged off and for one split second, the priest was pulled tight as wire…and then there was a hideous, wet rending and ripping sound and the horses charged away, each dragging its respective rope and respective limb. The priest, an armless and legless trunk, squirmed and raved and bled into the dry, parched earth. He lost consciousness and died soon after.

But he was not the last man to be drawn and quartered for the Kiowas loved it.

Black Jake showed them other methods of torture and execution. Victims were "pressed": staked out and piled with heavy stones until they were crushed. They were impaled on sharpened stakes. They were buried alive head first, their legs from knees to feet still above earth. And, in one of Black Jake's darker moods, a Mexican bandit was tied to a cottonwood tree and his head sewn-up in a burlap sack. Unfortunately for him, there were also two extremely pissed-off diamondback rattlesnakes in there with him. The snakes struck him repeatedly and by the time they cut the sack off, his face was a swollen-purple black contusion. So bloated from venom you couldn't find his eyes or nose, they were completely swallowed in that fleshy bag that had once been a face.

And that was how Black Jake lived with the Kiowas.

He enjoyed it, but as time passed age began to set in and he began to think of a quiet and easy life for the very first time. Sixty had come and gone several years before and he was not as spry anymore. He wanted out.

But how?

Then Nathan escaped from prison and he got a few ideas.

43

Black Jake came back to reality, finding it amusing how easily his mind drifted between the past and the present. It was becoming a fluid thing and maybe one day, it would not come back at all.

Old, he thought, that's what.

His memories, though dark and violent, were treasured. He could close his eyes and relive his accomplishments at any time. It was a good thing to be able to remember everything so clearly. Sometimes he thought of the war. He'd rode with Bloody Bill Anderson and his Confederate guerrillas. They supposedly fought for the Confederate cause, but in reality they robbed and raped and murdered and the war was just an excuse. He had been involved in the atrocities at Lawrence, Kansas and the Centralia Massacre. But all the murdering and robbing and pillaging came to a screeching halt in October of 1864 in Missouri when Union troops crushed the guerrillas and Bloody Bill was killed in the ensuing battle. Black Jake was among the raiders who tried desperately to recover the body, but it was hopeless. There were folks who said Bloody Bill hadn't been killed at all, but rode off into story and myth.

But that was bullshit so rank it smelled just plain bad.

Just a charming folktale that helped to ease Confederate sympathizers still smarting from their loss at the hands of the Union. There was no more reality in it than the story of Sleepy Beauty or the fucking tooth fairy.

Black Jake had seen Bloody Bill catch bullets in the head. He was killed, all right. No less dead than a carcass full of maggots. What happened after that, he got from eyewitnesses. Bloody Bill's body was decapitated and the head impaled on a spiked telegraph pole. The ravaged body was dragged through the streets of Richmond where, Black Jake had heard, it was spit upon and chamber pots were dumped upon it. A rather undignified end, but one befitting a very undignified man.

Black Jake himself was typical of the men that rode with Bloody Bill. Although he held Confederate loyalties of a varying degree, his true interest was not in paying back Union troops and sympathizers, but in the robbing and murdering of civilians. In any war, there was money to be made. And swearing your allegiance to one side or another gave you the perfect vehicle in which to fill your pockets.

When he thought about the war, he was unconcerned as to its outcome. He was only saddened that it had ended.

But maybe for him, it never had.

His thoughts returned to his son. They were not warm nor fatherly.

"Right now," he said, "I'll bet Nathan is slipping about in town, thinking about his beloved. Yes, I do believe so."

That money was getting closer all the time.

44

It was two days after Josh Kreger's murder that John Pepper rode out of Chimney Flats. He passed by the ruins of the Partridge farm on his way out. Maybe he sought inspiration, maybe answers to all the questions buzzing in his head. But there were no answers. There were only mysteries.

He kept wondering if he was in any shape to be sorting any of this out. In fact, he didn't really wonder, because he now *knew* he was in no shape for it. His head problems had not lessened, they had worsened. But was he taking it easy? Was he resting like he should've been? Hell no, he was off on another hunt. This time to Dead River and just maybe Nathan Partridge and maybe even his father, Black Jake.

I'll not give up, he thought then as he followed the trail through lodge pines and rocky knolls that thrust from the ground like skeletal knuckles. I will not give up and I will not give in. I will die like a man with a gun in my hand. Nothing less is acceptable.

He'd been thinking about Black Jake, certain now that sonofabitch was still alive. He couldn't pretend to know how it had been fixed, but it had. And with the way his mind had been turning of late—when it was turning and not filled with slashing knife blades of agony—he was more interested in Black Jake than his son. He'd get Nathan if it were possible, but it was the father he burned for.

If I can do nothing else, Pepper thought, then let it be planting that murdering monster in the ground where he belongs. If I can do this, I can die at peace.

He kept to the trail and a meadow opened up off to his right. It was wide and flat and grassy. Pines pushed in from all sides. He could see the remains of a campsite. But what drew him in was the smell of death. It hung in the air like a shroud, a sweet and appalling odor of rotting flesh. It could've been an animal, it could've been a lot of things.

But, somehow, he knew. He *knew*.

He tethered his blue roan to a fallen tree and stepped down, his head beginning to throb slightly. But there wasn't time for that. Not now. He moved through the tangled witch grasses, hoppers vaulting before him. Butterflies drifted over the meadow like pale, fluttering leaves.

He examined the campsite.

And did not like what he found.

Dread that was as thick and cold as tar oozed in his belly. He could hear blood rushing in his ears. Feel the dull thud of his heart. He found the remains of a woodpile scattered about. The grasses were pressed down from the hooves of horses and the wheels of a wagon. He felt a certain sickness settle into him. He went to the fire pit. Ashes. Charred logs. But a strange odor still present as he squatted by it—burnt meat. Taking a stick, he rooted through there and—

Oh, dear sweet Christ.

He just stared at what he uncovered. Stared and kept staring as an echoing darkness filled him. There were human remains in the pit—the slat of a rib, a pelvic wing, what might have been a shattered femur. All blackened by flame. He dug further and, yes, God, yes, here it was—the final damning proof. A jawless skull, the crown of which was bashed in. He slid the tip of the stick through one charred eye socket and fished it out. He set it on a log and it leered at him with a fathomless neutrality. It had secrets, it had seen horrors, but it would not speak of them.

Pepper thought: Somebody tried to burn up the evidence. But why? What was the reason for that?

He pulled himself to his feet, his back protesting with more snapping cricks and creaks than an old roof in a windstorm. He kept studying the campsite, thinking, thinking. That stink of decay led him into the woods. He knew he was alone and had known it from the first moment he entered the meadow...yet, his scalp tingling with fear and apprehension, he unleathered one of his ivory-handled Colts. He licked his lips and pushed through the pine boughs. What he was feeling, what he was sensing here turned his blood to ice, made something go bad inside him. He didn't like the thoughts that shivered in his brain. They were dark, they were unspeakable. Yet, they persisted.

Dangling from the stout limb of a ponderosa pine there was a body.

It was covered with hundreds of flies. It was bound by the wrists with a length of hemp rope and suspended off the ground. It had been there, broiling in the heat, for several days. Bloated and putrescent, it had gone soft as grayed toadstools. The legs had fallen off, the femurs pulling out from the sockets of the pelvis. They were sprawled beneath the body, ripe and worried by animals, carpeted in ants. Pepper swallowed down hard and shooed the flies away from the body itself. It turned in the gentle breeze with a slow, lazy roll. It was full of maggots, but he saw it had been stripped of flesh, divorced of meat right down to the bones beneath. Just a blood-stained skeleton, the face hacked and plucked, peeled to the skull. The jaws were sprung open as if in a scream.

Nauseated, Pepper forced himself to examine it closer.

The reddened bones were scathed with marks. He knew no animal had done this: these were the cuts of a knife. He'd seen such signs before…but never like this. Never so methodical.

This man and the remains of the other in the fire pit, they had been butchered. But was it for sadistic pleasure or something far worse?

Pepper cut the body down and left it where it lie. Climbing back on his roan he was thinking about Coy and John Lyle Farren. And what he was thinking was horrible indeed.

45

"It's very hard to say with any surety," Dr. Packard told Pepper that morning. "I'm not a neurologist. I am not a specialist in such matters, you see. But I have been in practice for thirty-odd years. There's precious little I haven't seen."

Pepper felt uneasy, but he did not show it. He simply listened to Packard as he talked around the subject. Pepper had gone to see him that morning, figuring he could only put off the inevitable so long. Packard gave him a complete examination, but seemed most intrigued with Pepper's eyes, his symptoms.

"Just lay it out, Doc," he said finally. "I'm not a young man. I've lived a full life. I don't expect it to go on forever."

Packard ran thin fingers through his sparse white hair. "I see trouble, Marshal. That's what I see. Your left eye is dilated, but your right is not. This is a sign of brain injury. But you tell me you have received no trauma to the head and that, in combination with your symptoms—"

"C'mon, Doc." Pepper felt like a worm on a hook dangled before the snapping jaws of a big pike. "Tell me now."

"Yes. Yes, of course." He cleared his throat and looked about his examination room—the books, the medical charts, the shelves of chemicals and instruments. He looked everywhere, it seemed, but at his patient. "You have, I believe, one of two things. Either an embolism to the brain or a carcinoma."

Pepper felt his blood drain into his boots. He was thinking these things and had thought them for some time, but to hear someone else speak them…it was terrible. No other word described it. "Yes?" he said.

Packard nodded. "A carcinoma, or cancer, will mean a slow and painful, debilitating death. But I'm not certain this is what you're suffering from. The other symptoms are not clearly in place. So, I tend to opt for the embolism theory. An embolism is caused by a blocked blood vessel, Marshal. Perhaps by a blood clot or foreign matter. This embolism puts pressure on your brain causing the headaches, the dizziness, the vision problems. Unfortunately, it will continue to expand like a pocket of blood and, sooner or later—"

"Burst?"

"Yes. Yes, I'm afraid so," Packard said. "Death will come quickly when that happens."

Pepper felt his face go tight. His flesh went gray. There was a mounting pressure behind his eyes. He swallowed. "There is no operation? No cure?"

"Not at this time, no. Maybe one day. Back east at one of the teaching hospitals there may be an experimental procedure, but its chances of success would be slim, I'm afraid."

Pepper thanked and paid him. In some way he felt sorry for Packard, for having to tell people the things he did. It was surely not a pleasant task. But he supposed for every man a doctor had to condemn to death, he saved five more and delivered five more babies, bringing life into the world. It balanced things out. Packard gave him a bottle of laudanum for the pain, but there was little else he could do.

Pepper went to the nearest saloon and swallowed three whiskeys in rapid succession. It calmed him somewhat, but it did not brighten him. Like the black depths of the ocean, sunlight would never touch him again.

46

It was, of course, the dire culmination of the past several days which began when Josh Kreger's body was discovered. Deputy Tilbury found it and immediately fetched Pepper. The man was distraught and confused. It took some time for Pepper to put it together, but eventually things began to make sense. All Tilbury knew was that Kreger had an appointment with a rancher that night. It didn't take Pepper long to arrive at the conclusion that his assailant was no rancher but Black Jake Partridge himself. Whatever sordid business had passed between them, Black Jake had concluded it in the same way he concluded all his business affairs. With the undertaker, Pepper had briefly examined the body. He'd seen enough dead men, enough gunned-down dead men, to know that Kreger had taken a blast from a large caliber weapon. His head was nearly destroyed by it.

Black Jake's trademark weapon was a big Colt .44.

Pepper needed no more convincing: that sonofabitch was alive.

Later that afternoon he visited Kreger's cabin. It was cluttered, messy, desperately needed a woman's touch, but there was nothing out of the ordinary. He examined Kreger's effects—his books, his guns, magazines, mementos from places he'd visited. Stuffed beneath a loose board he discovered a ledger. Most of it was concerned with the sheriff's financial doings—how much he paid his deputies, how much it cost to keep prisoners, expenditures such as rifles and new horses—but in the back there were a series of scrawled notations. Most were figures and the reoccurring name of Mr. Jones, usually referred to in quotations. It didn't take much deduction to figure out that "Mr. Jones" was merely a pseudonym. And it didn't take much more to guess who "Mr. Jones" really was.

Kreger had written down two other figures that were interesting: $80,000 and $100,000. Both were circled in red and followed by question marks. Pepper knew those figures well. The second was how much money the newspapers claimed that Nathan Partridge had squirreled away. The first was nearer to the actual figure the Gila River Gang had taken from their final bank robbery.

Yes, it all began to fall into place.

Pepper could, from the scant evidence at hand, assume that Kreger and Black Jake had been scheming together to get Nathan's stash. It made perfect sense. Partridge escaped from prison probably because his wife had been guarding that money and she had supposedly died in a fire. He would be coming for his loot. So Black Jake approached Kreger and offered to split with him, if they were able to recover it. That much seemed to make a certain sense…but what of the scribbled notations of a place called Dead Creek and an establishment referred to as the Egyptian Hotel?

Pepper knew there was only one way to sort that out.

So, the next day he made plans to visit Dead Creek. But first, despite himself, he decided it was time to see a doctor.

47

Like Nathan Partridge a few days before, Pepper rode up through the Gilas and marveled at the beautiful scenery. But he didn't marvel long as he steered his roan through the maze of canyons and gorges and rocky bluffs. The thickly wooded expanses of pinions and junipers and chaparral were and always had been excellent hiding places for bandits and renegade Indians. So like a man shaving with a straight razor, he kept his eye on his business.

Even if his mind was elsewhere.

He was thinking about the campsite, the human remains he'd found. He couldn't get it out of his mind. The body hanging from the tree had been almost ritually sliced and peeled with a knife. He was sure of that. But that had not been the cause of death. There were numerous hacking injuries to the bones of the neck, chest, and head. Like somebody had killed the poor bastard with a machete and then strung them up. But if they were dead before being hanged, then peeling them was not for torture surely.

It had to be for something else.

And there was only one thing that Pepper could think of and it filled him with horror.

He thought: Good Christ in Heaven, such a thing and here of all places.

But it had happened before—the Donner expedition being but one example. But that was out of necessity. And this, this was surely out of choice. The hills were thick with game and Chimney Flats had no shortage of eateries or victuals. If it was the

Farrens...then what in God's name had happened to them? What had turned them into monsters?

Pepper shook his head, steadied his mount, and carefully rolled a cigarette. The tobacco helped to clear his head. To chase away the leering and reaching shadows, the bogeymen and their chattering teeth.

His mind sought more pleasant topics and found not a one. All it could mull over was his own impending death.

Dr. Packard had told him that if it indeed was an embolism, it could rupture at any time. As he put it, five minutes from now or not for five months or five years. But, he added, with continuing severity and worsening of symptoms, it seemed clear that whatever was going to happen, would happen soon. And that could mean either a quick death (if he was lucky) or a stroke which would leave him severely impaired if not a complete vegetable. And if the latter was the case, Packard told him, he may well pray for death. It was all very hard to take. Like a fist full of gravel, it was hard to swallow. Pepper had known there was trouble brewing in his head for some time, but part of him had hoped it would be a passing condition. That death, when it did come, would be a bullet or a sudden heart attack in his sleep. Something quick and complete. But surely something that would give him little or no time to contemplate his own ebbing life, his own mortality.

It was not good for a man to dwell on such things.

But not thinking about it was near impossible. It was a natural rhythm now like breathing or pissing. Pepper figured this was his last run and he had to make good on it. Had to use what time he had left to its fullest measure. That got him to thinking about Nathan Partridge. He was becoming of less and less interest to the marshal. Yes, he was a criminal and a thief and, yes, he had killed men. But his actions were fueled purely by greed. And Pepper could understand that. Like love or hate it was a distinct part of the human condition. He didn't respect the man, but he could understand him.

But Black Jake on the other hand...well, he was an entirely different matter.

The man was treacherous, he was a sadist who enjoyed murder. It gave him pleasure. He was, in Pepper's opinion, a thoroughly vile and evil creature. Like a large and venomous spider, he had to be crushed under boot. Such a creature was blasphemous and unfit to live. And with that in mind, Pepper decided that his mission in life (what remained of it) was to hound that bastard right back to the grave he was absent from. He would bring him to ground and crush him. And the way to do that was to find his son. And maybe, if his luck held, he'd get to Nathan before Black Jake did.

Because Pepper had no doubt about one thing.

Black Jake wanted Nathan's money and he would kill him to get it.

It was a hard ride for Pepper. It seemed every few hours he had to stop because the headaches got the best of him. The days to Dead Creek passed slowly and painfully. And more than once there were particularly bad spells where his hands went numb as frostbite and his vision blurred like a runny watercolor. When this happened, he had to rest. Near sunset on his second day on the trail, a headache hit him and hit him hard like a railroad tie to the skull. It was so bad his eyes rolled back into his head and he shook with convulsions, pissing himself somewhere in the process. It was then he took his first spoonful of the laudanum. It was a purplish liquid with a bitter, unpleasant taste. Packard told him it was merely a solution of opium in alcohol. It was habit-forming. It would work wonders at first but gradually lose its potency.

Pepper sat there by a small fire, waiting for darkness, his head throbbing and…and then, ecstasy. It was like falling into the folds of the softest, warmest velvet. It fell over him, wrapped him up, held him. He grinned and even giggled once or twice.

He'd never known such peace in his life.

Exquisite.

Dying wouldn't be so bad if you could die like this. He laid out his bed roll and settled into it under the cold eyes of the stars. When sleep came, so did the dreams. And they were doozies. Not just dreams, but sagas, surreal adventures. It was a shame he had to wake, but wake he did.

48

Coy Farren said: "I think, perhaps, we've made a slight mistake, dear brother of mine, an unforeseen error, a minor *faux pas,* and possibly an inexcusable transgression that could lead to certain troubles of varying degree."

John Lyle—big, mean, and about as intelligent as horseshit in a shine box—just stared at his brother in complete confusion through red-rimmed eyes. He did not comprehend what his brother was saying and rarely did. But he was certain it was important. Had no doubt of it. He did not question, he accepted.

Coy Farren pulled a dipper from a wooden barrel of water next to the wagon and drank carefully. He replaced the dipper and secured the lid with his long and delicate fingers. "What I mean, Lyle, is that we could have possibly brought trouble down upon ourselves." He sighed heavily. "I blame only myself. It was a matter of hurry and haste, was it not, Lyle?"

John Lyle scratched at his tangled black beard which hung to his chest like the pelt of a black bear. "Yes, I do believe it was such."

"You see, it was I and only I who hurried us along unforgivably when I should have been concerned about covering our tracks. Do you see what I'm saying, Lyle?"

"Yessum." The big head nodded up and down like a dummy at a dime carnival.

Coy ruffled his brother's wild locks, knowing that John Lyle did not understand in the least. He rarely did. When thinking was involved you generally left John Lyle out of the picture. Coy accepted that. Plotting and strategy were purely his domain. Mother was of no possible use and father, the good Major Farren…well, he was of even less. So it fell on Coy to see the family through the tangles, turns, and chock holes of life on the frontier. And at their campsite in the hills above Chimney Flats, he had made a major and possibly costly mistake. When they broke camp, Coy generally took it upon himself to see that things were put in order upon their departure. That no *scraps* of evidence were left lying about.

But in Chimney Flats he hadn't done so.

All he could smell was the cool green of Nathan Partridge's money and it had blinded him to all else. Greed had hurried him along, forced them onto the trail sooner than was acceptable or necessary.

Coy slipped a thin cigar from his broadcloth coat and lit it with a burning stick from the fire. He watched the sun sink lower in the western sky like a great bleeding eyeball and wondered, just wondered. If someone was to happen upon their campsite, if they were to nose about…well, it would not be good.

Coy Farren, he thought, you have come too far and too long to throw it all into the dustbin now.

They were camped off the main trail a few miles outside of Dead Creek. From their position, they had an excellent view of the town that clung to the rocks below. To either side was thick forest and wildly rolling hills. They were tucked away in a small clearing. They were safe. They were hidden from prying eyes and no one could approach them without being seen or heard.

Still, Coy was concerned.

He blew out a bluish cloud of smoke that danced on the wind, dissipated. He heard a moaning from the woods and smiled thinly like a rodent lording over a dump. "Lyle," he said, "stoke that blaze up a notch or two. It is near time, I think."

John Lyle did as instructed. He carried an armful of wood to the fire that he had earlier split into kindling. He dumped it on the ground and began feeding the blaze, slat by slat. He stared at the flames with almost ritual awe, a savage contemplating the hunger of his god. The fire was reflected in his vacant, dead eyes. A ribbon of drool hung from his lips and he wiped it away with one filthy hand.

Coy entered the woods, ducked beneath the boughs of pines and found himself in a small clearing. Two women were bound and gagged, tied to either side of the trunk of a squat oak. Both were gagged with strips of flannel. They were both Papagos, mother and daughter. Their tribe had long ago been removed by the army to reservation land, but they had stayed, eeking out a meager existence in the hills. The mother was thin and rawboned, her flesh seamed and furrowed like brown leather dried by desert winds. Her eyes were rheumy. She did not seem to understand what was happening and probably by that point in her wretched existence, she expected only the worst from whites.

And this time in particular she would not be disappointed.

Coy towered over her, cigar planted firmly in the corner of his mouth. He stared at her with flat indifference. He prodded her with his boot. She tried to shrink away, but the ropes held her taut. She refused to look at him. He squatted near her. She would not do. She would not do at all.

Pulling a skinning knife with a long, curved blade from the rawhide sheath at his belt, Coy drew it gently over his thumb. It drew blood instantly. Cigar still smoldering in his lips, he sucked the blood from the cut.

"You will excuse my manner, madam," he said and quickly, like a cat striking its prey with drawn claws, he slashed the knife against her throat. Her eyes went wide and the wound parted like pouting lips, a tide of redness splashing down over the gray dress she wore. She trembled and shook and died quickly enough. "Accept my apologies, please," Coy said.

He moved to the other side of the tree.

Her daughter was quite the opposite. She was full and plump as a ripe cherry. Well-fed, she spent her nights being passed around silver camps in the mountains. It was humiliating and dehumanizing, but she was paid in food. As much as she wished. Coy feasted his eyes on her and liked what he saw. Like a starving man eyeing up a platter of meat, he grinned with a cold, glaring appetite. He jabbed her repeatedly with his fingers. She was fat and soft like a newborn. Her eyes were huge and terrified. They glistened like black pearls in a streambed.

Coy cut her loose from the tree.

Her ankles and wrists were still bound. She stumbled along the ground, inching herself forward like some colossal worm. He kept kicking her, steering her in the proper direction like a mule. She gasped with each blow. She tried to speak but all that escaped her gag was a muffled groaning.

When she was near the wagon, Coy let her be.

The fire was blazing like a pyre, hot and ready for an offering. Coy watched it and listened to the squaw's garbled moans. Inside the wagon something thumped, something shifted, something slid.

"Tend to your dear mother, Lyle," Coy said and his voice was hollow-sounding like water dripping in a cave. "And do be so kind as to look in on the Major if you would. See how he's getting along."

The squaw squirmed and writhed in the grass.

Coy thought of finding her. Of the two of them coming into camp earlier that day begging for food. But food is not what they got.

Coy took out a burlap sack and set it before the fire. Carefully, as if he were handling precious antiquities, he unrolled it and marveled at what was revealed. The gleam of silver, of razored edges, the tools of a craftsman. The squaw saw them and contorted afresh at the horrible import of it all—the saws, the knives, the bone snips, the cleavers. Yes, the tools of a butcher.

John Lyle returned and, without being told so, tied a length of rope to the flannel that knotted the woman's wrists together. He threw the other end over the stout limb of a poplar. With a great exhibition of strength, he pulled the rope and gradually hoisted the woman off the ground. She fought and twisted like a cat in a bag, but it did her no good. When her feet were four or five inches off the ground, Lyle wound the rope around the trunk of the tree and tied it off.

He stood by his brother, breathing slowly and shallowly as if he had barely exerted himself. He stared at the woman, taking no joy or sorrow from her predicament. It merely was. Like a rabbit in a trap or hog ripe for butchering, it was nature's way. And this is how John Lyle saw it. Whatever he had once been, he was now only what the woman saw: a bearded giant divorced from morality or the ingrained taboos of his race. All of that he had left at Elmira. Along with his sanity.

"Never et an Injun before," he said as if it was the most natural thing. "Never once."

Coy laughed and patted his brother's back. "And you are feeling somewhat uncertain of it? Is that what you are alluding to, Lyle?"

"Yessum, that would be."

Coy laughed again. "We are but the products of our environments, are we not? We are taught certain things are right and certain things are wrong. We are taught that a white is in all way superior to the darker, less enlightened races. But, trust me, dear brother, flesh is flesh and blood is surely blood. Remember your biblical teachings, Lyle: 'For the blood is the life.' Do you see now, my brother?"

John Lyle grunted. "I begin to, yes."

Coy went to the woman, traced one finger along her cheek. "Fat and tasty, I do say. My dear, you make my mouth to water, my taste buds to blossom richer and sweeter than Virginny azaleas in the springtime. Oh yes, my dear, oh yes. I am grateful for this sacrifice you make onto us." He pressed his lips to her cheek, then his tongue. "Do accept our hospitality. It is yours for the taking. All that we have is yours. And all that you have—" he grinned with narrow, yellowed teeth "—is surely ours."

John Lyle began gnashing his sharpened teeth as if he meant to devour her right then and there.

Coy stopped him with an outstretched hand. "Now do remember your manners, Lyle. A table must properly be set for gentlemen to even consider breaking bread together. Wouldn't you agree? After all, we are not animals. We are not barbarians. We are men. And Southern men at that."

"Yessum, men. Southern men."

Coy pulled out his skinning knife and got to work as his brother stared and drooled like something from a Neolithic cave.

He thought: Oh yes, my fine rich Mr. Partridge, the Farrens will surely being paying you a call. You can count on that. And you will so enjoy our company as we will enjoy yours.

Beneath the gag, the woman began to scream.

49

Nathan Partridge thought: This has got to end, one way or another. None of it has been easy and that goddamn money has been nothing but trouble. I escaped prison to get my loot and it's been one merry chase ever since. Lots of killing and lots of frustration and it don't look to be over just yet.

He sat on a bench on the wooden boardwalk outside a cigar store just across from the Egyptian Hotel. It was his second day in Dead Creek. Afternoon. He pulled his hat down low and tried to merely blend in like paint on a wall, hoping no one would recognize him. He honestly didn't want to kill anyone else. His hands were so red with blood by then he knew they'd never come completely clean, but there was always hope. Hope of deliverance and, hell, maybe even redemption. You could never tell.

What he was thinking about right then was this spell of good luck he'd been having these past weeks since slipping out of Yuma Prison. It seemed that fate had shined on him every step of the way. Every encounter, every problem, every snit of trouble seemed to come around to his liking in the end. A good thing, yes, but how long could it possibly last? When would the darkness come down around him? Because he figured he had to be near out of good luck. And when the tables were finally turned on him, it was going to be bad. Real bad. When the hurting came it would come in spades.

Dead Creek was bustling and it never seemed to be any other way. Wagons and gigs and buckboards tooled through the hardpacked streets of sand and gravel. Riders passed on their mounts—rich men on proud stallions, working men on tired nags, prospectors leading trains of heavily-laden mules. People came and people went of every description and economic bracket. Not a one of them paid a nickel of attention to the lean, mustached, hard-looking man sitting before the cigar store. In that vicinity, desperate men with eyes dark as burned wood were no rarity.

Partridge was watching them, studying them, all the while thinking: Lookit em come and go and bustle and hurry. Miners and cowhands and whores and storekeepers and drivers of every sort. By Christ, even the children in this damn place are in a fucking hurry and then there's me, all the time in the world and not a blessed place to go.

No matter.

He looked through them and beyond them and pretty soon they were not there, just noise in his ears that might have been insects that needed swatting. He'd gotten good at shutting out the world when he was doing his bit in prison. You wanted to keep your sanity, you got good at such things. It was just one of those hard lessons he had learned like an errant boy getting his daily dose of the switch. Didn't matter if he was swinging the sledge and breaking rocks or hauling gravel for a new road or pressing mud into adobe bricks, he was there only physically. His mind was occupied elsewhere. And it was that ability that kept him from screaming at night or making a mad dash for the wall and getting a few slugs in his spine as payment.

There were some things in life a man had to do that he could not think about and some places you didn't want to dwell on.

Right now, he looked through the mulling crowds at the façade of the parlor house across the way. Built from red brick, it had dormer windows and balconies on the upper floors. It had its own carriage house and outbuildings and a drive that wound around it like a lazy snake. Judging by the carriages waiting outside, it was, as Gibbons had said, purely the province of men who pissed green by the buckets. A set of carved, white-washed steps led up to an ornate oaken door that might've been pulled from some European castle. To one side it said EGYPTIAN in gold leaf and to the other, HOTEL. Yeah, it was some kind of place.

After about two hours of watching and waiting, his eyes felt like they were full of ground glass. He needed some sleep, but he couldn't abandon his vigil. Not just yet. He had a room across town, but he wasn't about to go there. Not until he saw something. So he waited and watched, sinking down farther on the bench and pretty soon he had dozed off.

He dreamed of Anna Marie.

Dreamed he was back in Chimney Flats. He had just escaped from prison. He rode through the desert and arrived at the farmhouse and to his surprise, it was still standing. He walked through the door and she greeted him. She was naked and she told him it was good he'd returned at last. Then she pulled out a pistol and shot him.

He came awake sweating and he was not alone.

"Had yourself a good one, pilgrim? Yes, sir, been known to have a few bad ones myself from time to time. Can't say what yours are about, but mine are always about cave-ins and collapsing tunnels. But to each his own, I suspect." Gibbons had a picnic basket with him. He pulled out two bottles of beer and slid one into Partridge's fist. "Have a swallow, pilgrim, you'll feel better. No, you don't look good at all, if you don't mind me saying so. I knew a fellow once, was laying track he was, there was an explosion and he got a railroad spike straight through his head. Right through his goddamn skull, mind you. Survived it, too. Left the spike in there. Made it hard to find a hat that fit…point being, pilgrim, you look worse than he did."

Partridge thought: Old man, you have no idea the shit I've been wading through.

He sucked off his beer and it felt good on his throat. Felt cool and wet like spring water. He took another pull. "What brings you here? Just passing by or are you keeping any eye on me?"

Gibbons laughed. "Can't get nothing past you! Yup, like trying to geld a grizzly, that's what. Little of both, pilgrim. See, I've been looking for you. I told you I was your guardian angel and so I am. What bothers me is that if I can find you, I figure others can as well."

"What others?" Partridge said, testing him.

"Any that might wish to find you."

"And why would they want to find me?"

Gibbons shrugged. "Don't know and don't wanna know. I just have this feeling, see, that you might be a wanted man."

Of course he did. And why wouldn't he? He'd been there when that bounty hunter popped out of the shitter with that mean gleam in his eye. The old man wasn't dumb. He knew. He knew, all right.

Gibbons opened his picnic basket and gave Partridge a sandwich. "Roasted pork. Good for you. Put a little meat on those bones and, by God, case you haven't noticed you're getting a tad thin. Starting to look like something they hang on a wall in a spookshow to frighten the kiddies."

Partridge ate his sandwich. Like the beer, it was good. He hadn't realized how hungry he'd been. Lately, he'd been so obsessed, so driven, so single-minded, he often forgot to wrap his stomach around something. He finished the sandwich and then the beer.

"Don't mind me mothering you, do you, pilgrim?"

"Someone's got to."

A carriage came tooling up the road and people fell out of the way to let it pass. It was a black four-wheeled, folding top phaeton drawn by two thoroughbreds. It was just as shiny as polished mahogany. The spokes were gilt and glimmered like gold in the sunlight. It pulled up before the door of the Egyptian and paused there, horses snorting.

"Quite an outfit, that," Partridge said.

"Think so?" Gibbons said. "That rig ain't nothing. Wait'll you see what gets out."

The driver was a squat, powerful looking black man who looked like he'd been drop-forged from black steel. Sort of man that could've chewed iron and spit ten-penny nails. He was dressed in a pair of knee-high English riding boots, just as black and shiny as oil on water. He wore a red velvet tuxedo with starched, knife-edged tails that nearly touched ground, a stovepipe top hat of the same material. He opened the door and those white teeth in his bootblack African face glistened like diamonds in moonlight. His eyes were like silver dollars.

"Christ in a brothel," Partridge said. "I guess I've seen everything now."

But Gibbons shook his head. "No, pilgrim, you have not. Just wait a time and you will."

The crimson velvet driver opened the door and out stepped something that truly made Partridge sit up and notice. A man stepped out and what a man. Tall, slender, he was dressed in a midnight blue tailored Prince Albert suit with bejeweled cuffs and flaps. His vest was silken and so was his top hat. There was a rose set in his lapel and he brandished a walking stick with a gold lion's head on top. His face was carved marble, his mustache waxed and sharp enough to stick a toad with. Everything about him drooled money and position and a raw, unflinching arrogance.

"That would be Lord Johnny Max Silver," Gibbons said, whistling under his breath, "and I don't believe that 'dandy' is appropriate here. Something out of a fairy tale, methinks. A king stepped down from his throne. That high-rolling sonofabitch owns the Silver Dollar, three or four other parlor houses, a half-dozen saloons, an ore refinery, and a silver camp up in the hills. Word has it every time he squats and shits, he squirts out fifty-dollar bills."

Yeah, he was something, all right.

But Partridge soon forgot about how outlandish it all was. Because he saw the woman that stepped out next. She wore a long dress of purple silk, lace teasing at the ample cleavage on display. She carried a parasol and sported a frilled satin hat that did nothing but accentuate the auburn tresses that flowed to her shoulders and beyond. Her lips were full and dewy, her eyes huge and dark like expensive chocolate. Yes, she'd changed somewhat, but only for the best.

Partridge had everything he could do not to get up then and there. But he held himself down, knowing it was surely not the time.

"She does something for you, doesn't she, pilgrim?" Gibbons said. "Yes, sir, she owns the Egyptian. Quite a dainty dish to set before the king, eh?"

"You ain't just whistling Dixie," Partridge said, filled with emotions as wild as a raging sea and completely unclassifiable. "She's exactly as I remembered, only better."

"Know her?"

"Yes," he managed. "She's my wife."

50

Like a stake through the heart or a bullet to the head, it all ended for the Gila River Gang the day they robbed the Cochise County Savings Bank in Charleston. Kid Kirby had gotten a tip on it—near to a $100,000 in greenbacks and silver coin. Payroll and operating money for a mining concern and a cattle combine. More loot then they'd ever seen before at one time.

This was the big one.

The Gang had laid low for a time after the killing of Pierce's gang of bounty hunters. There was a lot of nonsense printed about it in the papers, none of which was true. They made it out to be some dime novel gunfight when in fact it was more along the lines of a prize turkey shoot. No matter, Pierce's people had wronged the Gila River Gang and now they were toes up, the lot of them. While Kirby and his crew hid out, they robbed nothing or no one.

It was all part of the plan.

Kirby's plan.

By that point in their careers, they had gained a certain notoriety and every stage, train, bank, and payroll office in the Arizona Territory were expecting them. So they did nothing for nearly two months, giving ample time for the dust to settle and guards to go down. Money was running short, but Kirby told them it would serve them well playing possum when the time came. The newspapers had lost interest in them and the general consensus was that the Gila River Gang had ridden into history.

Again, on Kirby's order, they wore matching black coats and flat-crowned hats. They carried Colt Peacemakers and sawed-off Greener shotguns. They came to get rich or die trying and, if need be, to take as many with them as needed.

Charleston was a milling site for the silver ore of nearby Tombstone. It had grown by leaps and bounds in the year or so since Kirby had last been there—general stores, hotels, meat markets, restaurants, boarding houses, and more saloons than bristles on a hog's backside. But the mills were its lifeblood and they sucked in workers from just about everywhere.

It was late September and although it could not be considered cool by any stretch of the imagination, it was much more pleasant than that blistering day they'd ridden into Sedona. The sky was bluer than the eyes of a Swedish immigrant and only lightly brushed by feathery clouds. It was warm, but a breeze was blowing and dust was whipping around in gritty clouds that had been stirred up by the mills themselves. People were in the streets, but they were busy—pulling wagons, loading feed, brooming down the boardwalks. Very few lounged about.

Kirby and Partridge rode out front, followed by Johnny Blunt and Mexican Joe. The Webb brothers took care of the back door. Nobody paid particular attention to them given that the streets were bustling with horses and gigs and ore wagons making for the mills.

The bank was sandwiched between a saloon and a Chinese laundry. It was a two-story affair with a brick front and false cornices. The windows were clean and shining, the gold-leaf lettering in them looking quite new.

Kirby, Partridge, and Mexican Joe went in, while the others stayed outside keeping an eye on things and on picket duty with the horses. They were not hitched to the post out front; when Kirby and the others came out, they would need to ride out fast.

Kirby and Partridge had planned the entire thing out and they saw it all coming down in a very businesslike manner. There were three cashiers inside and a man with a shotgun in a cage opposite. But that was no surprise being that Kirby had been there previously.

As he and Partridge went to the windows and produced their pistols, Mexican Joe pulled out his Colt and told the gunner to drop his weapon. The gunner just sat there with his shotgun over his lap. Apparently he never thought he'd actually have to use it. He stared at Mexican Joe and his Adam's apple bobbed up and down and right then and there you could see he was considering something dangerous.

"Don't do it," Mexican Joe told him. "You'll never make it."

Kirby and Partridge pulled feed sacks out from under their coats and shoved them to the cashiers.

"Open that safe," Kirby told them, "and fill those bags. And if ye don't, I kill all ye right here and now. Ye got ten seconds."

The head cashier, a small and birdlike man with an eyeshade and sleeve garters, opened his mouth and then wisely shut it. He nodded and went to the safe, working the combination. It all went very well up to that point.

Mexican Joe was still waiting on the gunner. "Drop it," he said.

And maybe that poor dumb bastard had read too many goddamn dime novels for he thought he was a real tricky character. He made to lower the shotgun and then tried to bring the big weapon up real quick and easy and failed miserably. Mexican Joe shot him twice in the chest, the second bullet spearing him through the heart. He made a wheezing, whimpering sound and fell straight over, dead as a plank.

But that little episode was like a signal for the shit to start spraying.

While the head cashier and his assistant stuffed the bags and Partridge kept his gun on the other one, Mexican Joe drilled the gunner and in that moment of fervor, the other cashier made a wild dash for a Remington .44 under the counter. He got it up and out all right, but not before Partridge shot him point blank just beneath the left eye. His face seem to shatter like a window, going to shards and splashing off the bone beneath. Such is the kiss of .45 caliber slug at close range. He lurched backward, fountaining blood and bone chips, but reflexive action made him jerk the trigger. The Remington went off like a canon and Partridge felt the bullet pass so close to his right arm it singed the hairs on his wrist. It went past him and found Mexican Joe. It went in through his rib cage, tumbled through his internals, glanced off his spinal column, and exited his lower back in a fist-sized hole.

Mexican Joe went down screeching.

Partridge cried out and put two more slugs into the cashier. He was already dead by then, sprawled across the hardwood plank floor, having shit himself and vomited out most of his blood.

The cashiers had stopped filling their bags and Kirby screamed at them. "FILL THEM COCKSUCKERS AND FILL THEM NOW!" he said. "MOVE YER GODDAMNED DEAD FUCKING ASSES WHILE THERE'S STILL BREATH IN YER FUCKING LUNGS!"

Bathed in sweat and trembling with fear, they did just that and kept doing it with amazing speed and agility as the specter of death hovered over them. The bank stunk of burnt powder and voided bowels and running blood.

Partridge went to Mexican Joe, but he knew it was hopeless. He was bleeding like a water bag with a hole in it. Blood was everywhere and Partridge almost went down on his ass in it. He cradled Mexican Joe in his arms and that tough, leathery face was white as flour. That great bald head had gone just as yellow as a skull in a crypt. He tried to speak, but blood and bile ran from his lips and all that came out was a horrible gurgling sound.

"Sorry," Partridge said. "I'm sorry."

They got the bags—six of them—and it was no easy business trying to carry them out and hang onto their guns at the same time. There was a seventh and eighth bag, but they were full of coin and Kirby decided to leave them.

They got outside and Johnny Blunt was shaking like a leaf. He already had his shotgun out and was ready to shoot, even if he didn't know at what.

"M-M-Mexican Joe…w-w-where is J-J-Joe—"

"He's dead," Partridge told him. "Or goddamn near to it. Mount, dammit, mount!"

They got the money bags tied down to Partridge's and Kirby's horses and it was then that whatever had not yet gone wrong, suddenly did just that.

It started when storekeepers emerged from shops opposite, armed and crazy. Bullets starting lighting in the air like pissed-off hornets. Kirby and the others started blasting and it became little better than a massacre. Armed men and unarmed ones were cut down in the ensuing confusion. Johnny Blunt emptied his shotgun, tossed it, and pulled his pistols. He tried to cut a swath through the mayhem and killed no less than three gunmen before a cowhand stepped from a saloon with a twelve-gauge shotgun in his meaty fists and gave Blunt both barrels at close range. The impact knocked Blunt right out of the saddle like a bottle struck by a brick. He flew off leather, nearly torn in half, crashing into the dirt in a mutilated heap.

The cowhand made to reload and Henry Webb passed by him and put the barrel of his Greener scant inches from his nose and pulled the trigger. The cowhand's face vaporized in a fleshy blur of blood and mucilage. The discharge threw his headless corpse back and through the batwings of the saloon where it collapsed in a ruined mess.

They started to ride out and made it maybe half a block when a sheriff's posse came riding straight at them. Henry Webb was blown out of the saddle, six or seven rounds passing clean through him. His brother Reese took two or three and beyond that it was pretty hard to tell exactly what happened. By the time the posse rode at them hell for leather and Henry started catching led, Partridge and Kirby started shooting. They knocked four possemen from leather and winged two others. Reese Webb, screaming a wild and wailing rebel yell, filled with a blood-maddened rage for his brother's death, rode out ahead of the others and emptied his pistols into the posse. Which, by that time, consisted of three or four men who were trying to shoot and trying, without much success, to get control of their mounts who were running in circles, petrified by the gunfire. Partridge saw Reese catch another slug or two, but it didn't even slow him down. He galloped in with his Greener in his fist until he got up close and pretty and could see the sheriff himself who was still trying to reign his steed. The sheriff tried to get a decent shot, but his horse wouldn't allow it. He shouted. He hollered. He swore. Finally, he tried to throw himself from saddle, but it was just too goddamn late. Reese gave him both barrels at close range and his chest imploded like a rotten melon. He dropped sideways off his horse, but his foot was caught in the stirrup and he was dragged in a crazy circle while the other posse horses stomped on him and all you could hear were the sounds of gunfire and people crying out and those hoofs snapping the sheriff's bones like dry slats of kindling. Finally, his horse broke free and made a run for it, pulling his corpse with it through the dusty streets. By that time he was crushed and bloody and mangled, looking like about two hundred pounds of raw meat stuffed into a lawman's outfit and boots.

And that's about how it all came down.

This is how outlaw gangs died. With screams and whimpers and pain and blood, buckets of it. A blaze of glory? Maybe. But more like an awful convergence of fate and crazy circumstance. A mess. A great, horrible fucking mess.

Partridge was riding out of town with Reese Webb by his side and then he happened to look where Kirby had been and he was gone. His horse galloped at their side, but he was nowhere to be seen. Partridge looked behind him and it was impossible to tell whether he'd been hit or had just fallen out of leather like a rodeo clown. All he could see were clouds of dust and people mulling and that was the last he saw of Kid Kirby.

He got hold of Kirby's horse and they rode out of town like the devil himself was nibbling at their backsides. By providence or the grace of God, they were not followed. They rode past the mills and into the rocky countryside beyond. Reese was barely staying in the saddle. He was painted up red and had taken a round in the face that had blown off most of his lower jaw. Under that sodbuster hat, his pale, blood-spattered face looked like a fright mask with huge and staring eyes, jutting upper teeth and nothing but bloody sinew and flesh below. With each lurch and sway of his nag, he nearly went ass over teakettle and kissed the stony desert floor. He reeled and rolled like a drunken man.

Partridge was unscathed save for a stray bullet that had creased the crown of his skull and knocked his hat off. It was a superficial scalp wound that bled profusely nonetheless, two snaking fingers of red wetness trailed down his face through the sweat and dirt. Kirby had already mapped-out their getaway and Partridge followed his route. They rode north through a dry riverbed for the better part of two hours until it intersected with a shallow stream. They followed the stream for what seemed hours and somewhere in that time, Reese died and dropped from his saddle. And the sad thing was, Partridge never even noticed.

He had been leading and Reese was behind him.

Now and then he looked back and Reese was always slumped in the saddle...and then he was just gone. There was no point going back for him. Partridge rode for three days and finally made Chimney flats. Anna Marie took care of him and it was her idea to bury the money—well over $80,000 in U.S. Treasury greenbacks—beneath the root cellar. The newspapers had a field day with what they called the "Charleston Massacre" and speculations ran wild. The strange thing was, Kid Kirby's body was never found. The others—Mexican Joe, Johnny Blunt, and the Reese brothers were identified as members of the Gila River Gang. Partridge shaved off his beard and cut his hair, looked like a very different man.

A week later, a posse led by the district U.S. Marshal came and arrested him.

But not for the Charleston thing, but for a train robbery six months before. Apparently, he'd been identified. He was questioned in depth about Charleston, but even the bank cashiers could not positively say that this clean-shaven man was one of the robbers. So Partridge skated a life sentence and got ten years for the train robbery. He was quickly convicted and sentenced.

And then life for him was the desperation and suffering of the Arizona Territorial Prison at Yuma.

51

Partridge had no trouble getting through the door.

Gibbons came with him and although they both looked a little worse for wear and a little trail-weary, they had money. Partridge had near a hundred dollars, all things considered. Gibbons had much more than that. They went into the salon and had drinks. There were fresh-cut flowers and crystal glass and velvet-upholstered furniture. Satin and silk draperies. Garish oil paintings that would've made a preacher blush. It was warm and dim in there, tapers set out in gold candelabra and it smelled of perfume and body oil and pleasures of the flesh. And there were woman, of course—blonde, brunette, red-heads. There were even Asian and high-yellow girls. They were thin and regal, fat and busty, girl-next-door pretty and exotically beautiful. If there wasn't something on display to put iron in your pants, then your iron had long ago rusted.

"Well, pilgrim," Gibbons said, arm around a colored girl with seductive, slanting oriental eyes, "you go do what you feel you have to, but stay out of trouble. Look around you for the love of sweet Jesus and Mary...you sure she's worth it? You sure you need to bang your nail into her when you're stuck dab in the middle of the garden of earthly delights?"

Partridge told him he had to see her. It was why he'd come to Dead Creek.

"Well, suit yourself. I'll be here when you're done." He laughed and nuzzled a buxom blonde. "Hell, maybe I won't be. In fact, I'm damn near sure I'll be in a tub with my friends here spanking the nasty and singing church songs. Yes, sir, praise the Lord and his creations. I have a feeling the old mast'll be rising this day!"

Partridge excused himself and went to take care of business.

52

He waited until she was alone.

She had rooms on the upper floor.

A man the size of a small mountain range tried to keep him out, but Partridge cold-cocked him with a pistol butt and locked him in a closet. Then he entered her rooms. He found her in a small, lavishly-furnished parlor.

At first, she did not recognize him.

Maybe what she didn't recognize is what prison had done to him. He was hard and wiry now, put together like he'd been carved from oak. His face was lean and sharp, the cheekbones wanting to thrust from the flesh under those dark and merciless eyes. He sported a black mustache that trailed to his jaw line.

"What the hell do you think you're doing in here?" she said and that voice held an edge he had never heard before. Oh, it was her voice, all right, but now it was used to giving orders and having them followed. It was so acid and sharp, that the words nearly stuck in the wall. "You turn around and march your goddamn ass right out that door while you still can!"

But Partridge did not move.

He stood there, staring, staring, drinking her in, sucking her down like a parched man at a creek. Thing was, her taste, it boiled in his stomach like lye. "Hello, Anna," he finally said. "You look well."

She was sitting on a loveseat upholstered in lush purple velvet, a ledger book on her lap. Ever the conscientious businesswoman. She looked and looked again and then it seemed her jaw would hit the carpet. She tongued her lips nervously and gathered herself. "Nathan," she managed. *"Oh dear Christ."*

"You're looking pretty healthy for a woman who perished in a fire."

She sighed. "You don't understand."

"No, can't say that I do. Thing for you to do is enlighten me and enlighten me right now. I killed more men than I remember getting this far. So it had better be good."

She set her ledger book aside. She started to get up, then sat back down. "Would it do any good if I said I missed you?"

"It might help."

"I did," she said, but the words were flat as fallen cake. "You probably think I just ran off with the money and forgot about you. It isn't so. Believe me, it isn't. Let me explain."

"You had better."

He took his hat off and sat opposite her on a sofa that nearly swallowed him in softness. He had never felt such comfort before. He positioned himself so he could easily see the door (which he had locked) and the entryways to the adjoining rooms. He was wearing his Schofield .45 low on his right hip. He'd left the .38 in its cross-draw scabbard in his rented room, thinking such a set-up marked him as a shootist. And he didn't need additional reasons for people to notice him or throw down on him.

There was a cut glass compote tray filled with freshly-rolled cigarettes. He helped himself to one and was surprised at how smooth they were. Money and position surely had their advantages. "Let's get one thing straight, Anna," he said, letting that rich and pleasant smoke drift from his nostrils. "If anyone decides to come to your aid, I will kill them. Any of your boys come busting through that door I'll shoot them fucking dead. And maybe you, too. Is that clear?"

She swallowed. "Very."

So he listened and she talked.

"It wasn't easy being Nathan Partridge's wife. It was damn hard is what it was. Anywhere I went in that town, I could feel 'em all looking at me and pointing at me behind my back. Wife of an outlaw. Wife of a criminal. Despite it all, I loved you and I kept faithful, but it all got to be too much…"

During their year of marriage when he was a free man, she said, she saw very little of him. She was stuck on that farm in a town where she knew no one. And Nathan himself had no friends and neither did she. After he was sent away to prison, she languished up in the hills all by herself. But she remained faithful and loved him and wrote him letters and even visited him twice. No, it wasn't much, but as much as she could endure. But time dragged out and she was alone, so very alone. Ten years in prison seemed like an incalculable amount of time. But after the first three years, she convinced herself it really wasn't that awfully long. If she had had friends it would've been easier. But she was an outlaw's wife and few, if any, would have much to do with her. Her mother was dead and there was an aunt back east she did not know and beyond that, there was only Uncle John. But John Pepper was a hard and empty man in her way of thinking. Emotionless and cold as a wooden Indian. He preached his high morals and precious ethics, only he didn't seem to apply them to his own life which was one spent hunting and killing men. She did not like him and never had. It was common knowledge within the family that he had a son somewhere that he had abandoned during the war and who was he to espouse virtue? Besides, he never had cared for her lifestyle or her choice of husbands.

"So I was alone and you were gone and I was going out of my mind. That's the truth, simply put. So one day I woke up and I was depressed and angry and I began to make plans. Money wasn't a problem, besides the buried loot we had over five-thousand in the bank. It was then I visited Dead Creek. I told people it was because I had family there, but the truth was I liked what I saw. It was a boom town and the proper investments in the proper places could bring in a lot of money. So—"

"So you bought this place, built it up, and then burned down the farmhouse," he said.

"Yes, more or less. I used ten thousand of the robbery money, but no more."

He dragged off his cigarette. "And now you're a successful madam and me? I'm just a wanted man who's very desperate. Where's my money?"

"I have it. I still have all of it. I even repaid the ten grand I borrowed. I kept it safe."

He nodded. That was something. At least he had that. "And you built this place up for us, am I right? So that when I got out we could share all this?"

She blushed slightly at the idea and he knew instantly it wasn't true. Yet, she went on, the shit running from her mouth: "Yes. Only I had hoped you'd finish your term so you could be a free man. But now...I don't know..."

"But you've been faithful to me?"

"Yes! Of course I have."

"Bullshit," he said. "Who was that slick squeeze of pig shit I saw you with?"

"Lord Johnny Max Silver. He is a business acquaintance. No more."

Partridge butted his cigarette and stood up, going over to her. She bristled with unease and maybe even fear. He could see twin reflections of himself advancing on her. He could also see that she no longer loved him. Maybe she never had. But all that was mute.

"As your husband, I have certain inalienable rights, do I not?" He came in close and grabbed her lace bodice and before she could more than gasp, he tore it right down to her flat belly. Those magnificent breasts he'd dreamed of in prison were on full display. Milky white and full and jutting with promise. They trembled as she breathed. He pressed his face between them and pulled one into his mouth, sucking and licking at it until the nipple grew hard as a thimble. He worked both of them and she did not stop him. He tore the rest of her dress free, then the lacy things beneath. His tongue swimming in the hot ocean of her mouth, he unzipped himself and slid his length into her. He rode her hard, slamming into her with powerful thrusts. All you could hear was the sound of flesh slapping flesh and Anna Marie's sharp breathing. And then it was over and he had come and so had she…to the surprise of both of them.

Slumped together on the loveseat in various states of undress, they smoked and drank wine and talked about old times and it was all as empty as a drum. But they went on like that, on either end of the loveseat, not touching and careful not to. But they were shadows to each other and nothing more.

Eventually, there was silence.

Partridge broke it by saying, "I locked a fellow in the closet down the corridor."

"You didn't—"

"No, just gave him a knock. He'll recover."

She seemed relieved at the idea. She had enjoyed their coupling as he had, but it was purely a physical thing. Maybe, she too, had dreamed and fantasized about what it would be like again. Now they both knew.

She gathered herself together best she could. "You've ruined my dress," she said and seemed to find amusement in this.

"You can afford another."

"What will you do now?"

He thought about it and it didn't take him long. "I can't stay here. I can't stay anywhere. I'll have to go somewhere. Maybe Mexico. Maybe Central America. I've heard it's warm there and you can pick bananas straight off the trees." He paused and zipped himself up. "I suppose it would be pretty damn foolish of me to ask you to sell this off and come with me?"

Her silence answered that one.

"Where's my money, Anna?"

"I have it."

"You said that. Where is it?"

"That man who was here—Lord Johnny Max—I'm partners with him in a silver mining camp up in the Superstitions."

He gave her a menacing look. "What else are you two partners in?"

"That's not fair." She looked like she'd been slapped, but recovered quick enough. "The mining camp is called the Durant. It's easy to find. The road up there is marked, ore wagons come and go all day from there to the mills here in Dead Creek. The money is in the safe of the mining office. It's in a black valise, all of it. I'll send word that a man will be coming for it and they'll give it to you."

"You won't ride up there with me?"

She shook her head and her auburn hair swam at her golden shoulders. "No. I can't be seen with you."

Partridge pulled himself together and donned his hat. "Don't try and screw me on this, Anna Marie. I get up there and find a posse waiting for me, I'll come back for you." He helped himself to another one of her cigarettes. "I grew hard in incarceration. Hard and mean and I think that way of life bled all the good and decency I might have once had right out of me. I have nothing to lose any longer. But tell me…for whatever heart I have left…tell me the truth. Back then, did you love me? Did you really love me?"

Her face was lit by a strange glow. "Yes," she said. "I loved you very much."

It was the truth and he knew it. It was enough for him.

"Send word tonight that I'm riding up there."

"I will."

He turned to leave and had his hand on the doorknob. "I loved you, too, Anna Marie, and part of me still does."

There were tears in her eyes when she said, "Get your money, Nathan, and when you have it…please don't come here again."

53

Partridge went back to his room at the boarding house.

He didn't bother checking on Gibbons to see if he was around. With any luck that crazy old man was reliving his youth with a tubful of women. Partridge did not want to see him. He did not want to see anyone. He wandered the streets and went to the livery, saw that his horse was being well-cared for and was satisfied with that. He stopped at a saloon and had a whiskey and then back to his room. He ordered a bath from the landlady and went up the creaking, narrow stairs to his berth.

He opened the door and locked it behind him and was not sure what he was feeling. Remorse? Depression? That and too many other things. He'd told himself all along it was the money he wanted, but being with Anna Marie made him realize it was something else entirely.

He leaned against the door and was lost even to himself.

He thought: By God, I really love that woman and now it's too late because it's all over and maybe, if I'm lucky, I'll walk away from all this with a valise of cash and not a helluva lot else.

It seemed a hollow victory.

He tossed his hat on the bed and dumped water from the pitcher into the porcelain bowl and scrubbed his face. He changed the dressing on his arm. There was a positively rancid stink in the room. He figured it was coming from the privies in the alley. He shut the window. Then he fell on the bed and was so complete senseless and defeated over it all, he never even realized he wasn't alone.

Not until the closet door whispered open and a dark shape emerged with a gun in its fist and the voice said, "Nathan Partridge, I presume."

54

John Pepper made into the Superstitions and thought: It's nearly over now and goddamn, but I made it. Somehow I did. I made it here and father and son are nearby. Maybe I'm crazy, maybe I lost what mind I had back on the trail, but I *feel* it. I can almost smell them and I know it ends here.

Although the pain was all over him like fire ants on a man smeared with honey, he was still able to think. And his thoughts were sharp and glaring rays of sunlight in that throbbing hurtful darkness. He supposed if he were an animal, he would've laid down and died a long time before. But he was a man and he had his mind. He had his brain and though it was in a bad way certainly, it still guided him, still reasoned, still pointed the way like a weary finger.

The pain came and went like the seasons. And like the seasons, winter seemed to hang on the longest, the hardest, and the meanest. The laudanum wasn't of much use any longer and he had gone from spoonfuls to swallows now. He'd already emptied half the bottle. It was good with the nagging headaches, that ragged tension behind his eyes, but it was impotent in the face of the real thing, those knife blades of agony that cut through his brain. And the thing was, as the days passed there was less and less of an interval between them. Pepper could envision what was coming soon: a ceaseless, tearing agony that would either kill him or drive him insane. One with no relief. Continual, debilitating.

The trail to Dead Creek and the Superstition Mountains had been something yanked straight out of a nightmare. He could remember little of it save bits and pieces and he was not entirely sure what was reality and what was opiate dream. Only his iron will had gotten him here, up into these hills overlooking Dead Creek.

Steadying himself in the saddle, he rolled and lit a cigarette.

As he smoked, he looked down from the shale slope, astride his blue roan. Buildings and houses clung to wild and rising hills like fungi clinging to tree stumps. He could see the dust rising, hear the noise, smell the hot and busy odor of humanity. A boom town and somewhere within its carcass, Nathan Partridge and maybe even Black Jake.

Sighing, knowing he had little time in which to do what had to be done, he started down the slope and a bullet rang off the rocks just behind him. He could hear the rifle report echoing and echoing.

He thought: Let the games begin.

His mount was nervous and he couldn't seem to steer the whinnying beast to safety. She moved in circles, started, stopped. More bullets screamed past him and he knew it was only a matter of time. He strained with everything he had, pulling at the reigns and giving her the spurs, but she would not come to her senses. And maybe he was weakened by the pain and the torment of surviving it, but he just couldn't get a handle on the situation. Then another rifle cracked and the roan rose up just in time to catch a slug straight through the head. Blood and bone spewed from an exit hole and she folded up beneath him.

Pepper threw himself free and landed on the hard, dusty ground.

The roan was laying on her side. She managed a few raggedy breaths and went still. And it was all bad enough but what was even worse was that his Winchester was in the saddle boot and it was trapped under the dead animal now.

Hatless, his body feeling weary and old and used-up, he crawled through the loose rocks and out of the field of fire. He was threaded with aches and pains and it had nothing to do with what was happening in his skull and everything to do with age. He felt stiff and he was having trouble catching his wind.

He was trapped.

Trapped in a natural bowl scooped from the rock. Below was wide open country and above, the bluff from where the shots were coming. He was seriously screwed and there seemed to be no way out. Except...yes, it was worth a chance. Steeling himself, he crawled quickly over the pitching ground to the foot of the bluff. A few more slugs tore up the real estate around him. Before him was a cave or mine shaft cut into the hillside. The opening was small, but a man could slip in there on his hands and knees. It looked like it had been wider at one time, but had collapsed in a rain of boulders and stones many years ago.

He wondered vaguely what creatures might call it home, but knew he had no real choice.

All he had were pistols. The shooters had rifles. Like that day at the Partridge farm, he would have to draw them in. One way or another.

He slipped into the shaft and saw that it was indeed an abandoned mine. There were ancient splintered timbers supporting the roof. They were badly warped and cracked open in spots. Looked like they couldn't hold up a bag of feed, let alone a mountain of rock. But somehow, they did and Pepper hoped they'd hold it up a little while longer.

It was larger inside, but collapsed again farther back. The floor was littered with rocks and debris, animal droppings, slats of rotted wood, and the broken and battered remains of an old Rochester lamp. The roof was making groaning noises, cracking and shifting. He pulled out his Colts and waited near the entrance, for there was little else he could do.

It wasn't long before he heard muffled voices and the sound of boots moving in his direction. They knew where he was, but not if he was alive or dead. He had that on them.

The voices grew clearer and when they did, something cold settled over his skin.

"Did you hit him or not is what I'm asking," a velvet-smooth Southern voice asked. "Did you do our friend a serious hurt or do you suppose he's lying in wait, filled with a burning vengeance?"

"Can't say," a rough, raw voice answered.

"Either way, dear brother, I suspect he's in something of a precarious position. Would you agree with that Lyle?"

"Yessum, I would."

Dear Christ in heaven, Pepper was thinking. Those two. Those goddamn two.

He had suspicions about them from the first, but after what he'd found in the hills above Chimney Flats, those suspicions had fermented into a dire and grisly certainty. He knew what they were and knew he'd rather die than fall into their hands. His head was throbbing, but not bad. Not Yet. His body was hurting him some from the fall from his horse and his hands were cut up from clawing through the rocks.

"In there, can you hear me?" Coy Farren said. "If'n you can, are you injured? Have no fear, we're here to help you, to render any service possible. We've chased off them despicable bushwhackers who sought to do you a harm. Are you able to speak? Pray, call out to us, friend. No sense in hiding in there like some vermin in a hole. Never know what sort of unspeakable things can happen to a man in such a place."

Damn. That sonofabitch must've figured he was pretty damn stupid. Did he really think he was going to fall for that?

The voices faded and maybe that was worse than anything.

He knew these two and he knew they wouldn't just leave him. They were up to something.

So Pepper waited and his head started to hurt.

He thought: Not now, Lord, not now. If I go out now…I'll wake up on a spit. Don't let me go this way, Lord. Please not this way…

It began with a slight headache that nagged just behind his eyes and gradually sent out fingers of pain until his brain felt like it was clutched in the paws of some beast, slowly and painfully being squeezed out. His fingers began to tingle and his hands went numb and he couldn't be certain if he was even holding his pistols. His vision blurred and everything seemed to be in motion and waves of nausea rolled through him and he vomited and maybe he even cried out. There was no way to be sure. It was a bad one and he couldn't control his limbs, they jerked spasmodically and his guns fell away and his teeth sank through his lower lip.

From what seemed miles distant, he could hear Coy Farren's voice drifting like a dream fog: "Throw out your guns, sir, and I will come to your aid in a most accelerated manner. You have my word as a Virginia gentleman—"

There was more but Pepper could not hear it.

He was curled up on the floor, drool running from his mouth, one eye open and fixed, the other closed, the lid trembling. His face was colorless, pinched in a tormented mask. Gagging sounds came from his throat and that awful raging dizziness continued to roll through him with a terrible motion. The earth and the sky were one and neither, spinning and spinning.

He heard voices and something in his brain told him it was the worse possible thing. Then hands had him—huge, callused hands—and he was reminded of a giant from a storybook. Then he felt the sun on him and the dizziness dissipated and he was lying there, just staring at those evil, desperate faces. But he could not remember who they were or how he came to be with him.

The smaller one said, "Well, well, well, if isn't Marshal Pepper in the flesh." He made a clucking sound with his tongue. "And just look at the poor, pathetic man, Lyle! I do believe in complete earnestness that he is ill, struck down just in the prime of his productive years…"

And then the big one picked him up and was carrying him off somewhere while the smaller one droned on and on in that sing-song voice.

Pepper lost consciousness.

55

Partridge said: "You no good dirty bushwhacking sonofabitch! I oughta spit lead into your fucking belly for this! You about scared my shit green!"

"Ah, but ye won't," the stranger from the closet said. "Least ways, not yet."

Partridge sat on his bed in shirtsleeves, his guns near, but not near enough to have mattered if the stranger had been an enemy and not a friend. He sat there staring at the weathered face, those gray and greasy eyes like cold gravy. The long hair that tumbled to the shoulders and gathered there, snakes mating. The way it was touched by gray like a kiss of frost on charred earth. And that scraggly beard which looked as if it could house a family of squirrels.

Kid Kirby. Dear Christ.

Partridge dug around in his coat pocket for something to smoke and didn't have a thing. Kirby handed him a cigarette, a flask of whiskey. Partridge swallowed and then smoked. He felt a smile breaking out across his face like a spring thaw working at months of black winter ice. It came and he allowed it. It was getting easier by the day.

He blew smoke rings into the air. "What the hell are you doing alive?"

Kirby laughed, sat beside him. "Now, how's that to greet an old friend, hillbilly? Why, ye ain't got the common decency the Lord gave a Gila Monster."

Partridge just shook his head. "If you're a ghost, make quick and disappear like a bad smell. If not...Jesus Christ in a skirt, you can't be alive."

"Alive and randy as a heated hound with two dicks, hillbilly."

"How'd you find me?"

"Same as any trigger-happy, mother-humping bounty hunter will—I saw ye walking through the streets. By the time I squeezed the piss out of me shorts, ye was already gone. But I found ye, all right."

"Why are you here?"

"I came to find ye, hillbilly. Word has it ye were heading in this direction."

Christ, that was bad. If Kirby heard about it then probably just about everyone else had as well. The fact that he'd stayed alive and free this long was just another testament to his luck.

He said, "Last I saw of you was an empty horse."

Kirby ran grubby fingers through his beard and by the smell of him, Partridge figured he'd come out with a fist full of lice. "It's a long and strange story, me friend. Some day, maybe we'll have us the time for stroking our dicks and exchanging pleasantries, but that wouldn't be now. Though I must say, ye goddamn peckerwood sumbitch, ye are certainly a sight fer sore eyes. Why, I'm so happy to see that cruel, murdering face of yers, I could just about fill me pants." He bent his head towards his crotch and sniffed exaggeratedly. "Hell, maybe I already did. Ye feel up to washing me backdoor for me, hillbilly? I swear it's just about as dirty as the devil's shitter and don't smell much better neither."

He was rank; there was no getting around that. It smelled like he'd been relieving other men of their odors, collecting them in a central stench.

"Tell you something, Kid, you smell just plain awful. You never were real friendly with soap and water, but I got a tip for you," Partridge said. "While you were away, romancing sheep up in the hills, they came out with a new invention. It's called a bath."

"No shit? What's it fer?"

Partridge just laughed and God, how good that felt. Laughs were few and far between these days.

"No need fer ye to be poking fun at me, ye inbred sumbitch. Times has been tough. I ain't seen no soap in months and I ain't too proud to admit it." He took a swallow of whiskey. "But, when we has ourselves the time, I'm gonna tell ye about me marriage."

"You? You were married?" It was unthinkable. "To a woman?"

"No, to me favorite knothole in the fence, ye low-life dumb shit Yankee sumbitch. *Yes,* a woman. And, believe this or not, I bathed near every day. At night…yes, sir, that bed was a-squeaking and rocking and dancing and talking. Course, I was alone in it, but I sure did smell pretty." Kirby sighed, patted Partridge on the shoulder. "Yer so dang cute I could kiss ye with me tongue. But, tell me, how in Christ did ye survive that Charleston hog-fuck, anyway? Last I see, ye was near surrounded by all the King's men."

Partridge sketched it out quickly for him.

How everyone was killed and how they did a good spot of returning the favor. How only Reese Webb and he rode out of there with Kirby's horse in tow. How Reese died and how he hid the money and was arrested.

"They called it the Charleston Massacre," he said by way of finishing.

"Yes, I know, hillbilly. I can read well as ye."

Partridge looked surprised. "I never suspected. Didn't think they taught you Alabamy rebs to read. Thought you just rooted in the dirt and such."

"Shows ye what happens when stupid Yankee Kansas-born trash like you attempts thinking. I can read a damn sight better than ye, I reckon. Didn't think I had to tell ye about it is all. I can jerk meself off just fine, too, ye need to hear about that as well?"

Partridge said, "Well, I'm sure your daddy taught you all kinds of things."

Kirby thought that was funny and laughed until his face was red as a Wisconsin cherry and he was near to bursting. "Oh, hillbilly, ye are one miserable piece of work." He passed the whiskey. "But we ain't got time fer this shit. I mean, fer chrissake, ye peckerwood ass-fucker, half the Arizona Territories is sweet on bringing ye in. This town is crawling with bounty hunters and ye name it. Ye got to get gone before ye spend yer nights squinting through bars again."

So Partridge laid it all out for him.

He had a right to know: half of that money was rightfully his. He told him about Anna Marie being dead and then being very much alive as the owner and madam of a highly profitable whorehouse. How she claimed the money was in a safe up at the Durant Mine. How he was going up there this very night to get what was his...and what was Kirby's to boot.

"It's a trap, hillbilly," Kirby said. "I feel it deep inside like a finger up me ass a-stirring me innards. Ye know that don't ye?"

"I have my suspicions."

Kirby shrugged. "Well, it's somewhere to start, I reckon. If yer game, then so am I. She's got herself a house like that, ye can bet she plans on staying. If things go wrong...well, we come back after her. That's what."

"I told her as much."

"We'd best make some plans, hillbilly. But first, I wanna try out that bath-contraption. Why don't ye see to it, ye ornery sumbitch." Kirby got up and stretched, started for the door.

"Where you going?" Partridge asked.

"To church to say me a prayer," he said and went downstairs and to the shitter out back where he could commune with his lord.

56

When Partridge closed his eyes, what he saw was Yuma Territorial Prison.

And what he saw particularly was himself dying a day at a time behind those high gray walls. It was a good place to lose your soul and maybe your identity, too, but if you wanted to survive, you had to shut down your humanity. That was the first thing.

You rode up a hill to get to the prison, which looked, at first glance, pretty much like a great and soundless pile of adobe and granite and despair. The main gate was a huge double door of latticed iron set in an oval hewn from pale stone. First thing you saw when they mustered you into that hard-packed yard were a series of two- and three-story structures with sharp-peaked roofs and at night they looked like the jagged spines of some prehistoric beasts lounging in the dry heat, just waiting for it to cool some so they could chomp you down and pick their teeth with your bones. It was all here, everything the Territory decided was needed to maintain and control criminal scum—mess hall, recreation hall, stable, storehouses, even a hospital over the main cell block. There were prison industries: mattress factory, wagon works, tailor shop, and smithy shed.

The gates were continually watched by guards with Winchesters up in the towers on the wall. The main cellblock sat opposite. A massive and long windowless adobe. You went through an iron door that looked like it had been pulled off a tiger cage and down a stone passageway with cell doors to either side. In the cells, there were two tiers of bunks, three-high, clinging to the walls. The cells were clammy and cool even in the summer. Six men crammed into a space eight feet by nine. The walls seemed to sweat moisture and insects. You slept on a thin mattress in an iron bunk and that mattress felt like it was stuffed with stones. Those first few weeks your body ached from it. But after a time, you callused up and didn't know any better. The latrine was a slop bucket in the corner and if you were the new guy, it was your job to empty it...particularly if you weren't white.

Partridge found out about that his first morning there.

The guards came around in their gray uniforms and banged on the cell doors with crowbars and shouted: "WAKE UP! WAKE UP! WAKE UP, YOU GODDAMN FUCKING SHITBAGS! GIT YER SHOES ON! FOLD YER BLANKETS! USE THE TOILET! LET'S GO FER THE LIFE OF JESUS!"

One by one the men did as they were told and took their turn pissing or shitting into the slop bucket. In Partridge's cell, there were three Mexicans serving time for robbery, a Mescalero Apache who was serving life for killing a county sheriff with a knife, and two white men—Caruso and Chambers. Chambers was a confused idiot with the mind of a seven-year old. He'd raped and murdered a schoolteacher in Globe and didn't seem to understand why he was there. He was doing life. Caruso considered himself something of a shootist and bank robber. He claimed to have rode with the James-Younger gang, but Partridge decided right away that was sheer bullshit. The only facts about Caruso was that he had murdered two unarmed miners with a shotgun and stole their horses (though, to hear him tell it, it was the greatest single gun battle in the Territories). Beyond that, he was big and mean and dangerous. He took an instant dislike to Partridge because Partridge had been a real outlaw, a member of the Gila River Gang. Unlike Caruso who was just a wanna-be.

In most of the cells, the convicts took turns emptying the slop bucket, but not in cell #14, Caruso's cell. Usually it was the Mexicans and sometimes Chambers. The Mescalero volunteered from time to time, but nobody made him, not even Caruso, because he was dirt-mean and had eyes like ball bearings simmering in a blast furnace.

That first morning, Caruso said, "Partridge, you empty the shit bucket."

"All right," Partridge said. "Me today. You tomorrow."

Caruso thought that was funny. "No, see that's not how it works. You tomorrow and you for the next month. Now get to it."

Partridge didn't argue.

He picked up the slop bucket and threw it at the big man, washing him down with feces and urine. Caruso went wild, looked like a big, fat grizzly charging from its den with a copperhead hanging off its balls. He started swinging. Partridge avoided the first two blows and hammered Caruso twice in his pig-ugly face. Caruso caught him in the side of the head and then dropped him with one shit-smeared fist. Partridge came up before Caruso could stomp him, drew the big bastard in, and kicked him in the stomach. When he went down, he punted his head nearly from his shoulders.

What that got him was ten days in the hole or "snake den" as it was more commonly referred to.

The hole was an awful place with a bare dirt floor where you spend your time in leg irons that were chained to ring bolts. No mattress or blankets. No slop bucket. You subsisted on a diet of hardtack and water and lived in your own filth. The only light Partridge ever saw was from the air shaft above and that was only at midday. The hole was full of insects that were attracted by decaying fecal matter and he spent a good deal of his time swatting at biting ants and beetles the size of his thumb.

When he got out, he was moved to a different cell where the prisoners shared the labor of latrine duty.

The years passed and he grew lean and hard from pounding rocks into gravel and clearing brush along the river. He worked on the adobe brick crews. He cleaned the TB cells. He worked the stone-quarry gang. He built walls and roads and kept to himself. He trusted no one and had no friends. The other convicts learned he was exactly what he claimed to be—just a man who wanted to do his time and get out. He got in a few fights and one time as he was busting rocks, he split open a convict's head with his sledgehammer when that sonofabitch suggested relations between them. Back to the hole again, thirty days this time.

The years trickled by slowly, but they did pass. Anna Marie visited him a few times and he was never sure if that was a good thing or not. It interrupted the flow of things, it gave him thoughts that a man might have, a real man, not a prisoner. An animal in a cage. And he was no longer a man and could not think those things.

After five years of hard labor and deprivation, he figured he was scarcely human. His only pastime seemed to be pushing himself to the limit and creating new ones. He would make games of it all—how long could he go without water, how many times could he swing a sledge without a break, how many days could he spend without talking. How long could he hold his breath. How long could he hold a fifty-pound stone above his head in that broiling desert heat. And it went on like that until one day he discovered he could withstand punishment and pain that would've killed lesser men.

His only real pleasure was watching the freight wagons going in and out. A dozen opportunities for escape occurred to him, but he wouldn't allow himself to think such things. It would only make his time that much harder.

Then Anna Marie died (or so he thought).

And he started to think about his money. So after five years, he decided to leave. They were down river busting rocks for a road and the guards were sweating and miserable and it was just too damn hot for work. On days like that, even the guards didn't pay much attention. In that heat, no one had the energy to run for it and where would they go anyway with leg irons on?

It was Caruso that effected his escape.

At a prearranged moment, Caruso and half dozen other assorted convicts turned on the guards and smashed them down with sledgehammers. They took their guns. They hammered their leg irons off and made a run for it. It was exactly what Partridge had been waiting for. He picked up his sledge and followed suit. So did five or six others. He took off alone. The first group, led by Caruso, headed south, planning on a run to Mexico. The second group crossed the river and into the flat wastelands of California. Partridge saw them disappear amongst the dirty scrub and shimmering furnace heat. He figured that when the escape was finally noticed (probably not for hours), the posses would track the two large groups and, with a little luck, he'd slip through the cracks.

He ran down into the mud flats and submerged himself in the Colorado. Clinging to the shadowy bank best as he could and its heavy, tangled brush, he allowed the current to drag him into Yuma. By sunset that night, half the Territory, it seemed, was mobilized to bring them in. Waterlogged and chaffed from his prison uniform, he stayed in the water nonetheless. A few times actually submerging himself in the mud and sucking air through a reed when the search parties passed by.

Once in Yuma, under the cover of darkness, he slipped into the Southern Pacific Railroad yards. He had to get well away from the area and a train seemed a likely bet. Just after dawn the next morning, a locomotive pulled out towing two baggage cars, three coaches, an express mail car, and a series of freight cars. It also carried something else: Nathan Partridge. Flattened out like a spider sucking up sunlight on a wall, he clung to the top of a freight car. The sun rose higher in the sky and baked him red against that iron roof that was hot enough to fry sausages on. Somewhere near Sentinel, sunburned, parched, and near heat-stroked, he climbed off the car and leaped out into the desert, rolling down a hill into a dry wash. He didn't dare move until the train was long gone.

Then he hiked up into the Crater Mountains.

He found a spring and drank and bathed, wishing he had something other to wear than his faded gray-and-white striped convict clothes. He had no food. No weapons. Not a goddamn thing. But he was free. That was the thing. As he climbed higher and higher into the mountains, he figured the longer he eluded capture, the better his chances were. By now, the other two groups had probably been run to ground. Regardless, he was in a hell of a spot, free man or not.

And that's when providence shined down on him.

He was following a stream through a hollow at the base of a ragged slope. Night was beginning to set in and he had no provisions and he was hungry, exhausted. The stream kept going and he found a flat, marshy area it cut through where the mosquitoes were so thick you could've knitted a sweater from them. But just beyond, at the foot of a rocky hillside he saw a horse, a dappled mare. It nickered when he came near and then returned to chewing grass, unconcerned. There was a small encampment with a bedroll and a blackened coffee pot sitting on a stone by a firepit.

A man was sprawled a few feet away like a wet dishrag.

He was swollen up and discolored, banded with black and blue welts like some exotic reptile. He was dead, but hadn't been dead too long. Partridge figured he had been bitten by rattlers and judging by the marks on his arms and neck, quite a few of them. He had the tools of a prospector. Probably looking for gold or silver, he wedged his body into a likely spot and found himself in a nest of diamondbacks. Probably made it back to camp and died.

Partridge buried him and helped himself to his supplies.

He had a meal of canned tomatoes, tinned beef, and army biscuits. He also helped himself to the man's cigars, his weapons, his horse. There were clothes in the saddlebag and with a little needle-and-thread work learned in the prison tailor shop, he had a set of duds that fit just fine. He buried his prison garb in the trees and packed up his provisions on the mare and got on his way.

He made for Chimney Flats.

57

"It's the craziest damn story ye ever did hear," Kid Kirby was saying as they followed the rutted, dusty road up into the Superstitions to the Durant Mine. "Not sure if I even believe it meself."

After he was shot out of the saddle in Charleston—he took a round through his shoulder and another creased his hairline—he flew out of the saddle like a baby bird tossed from the nest. But as was Kirby's way, he just didn't fall down hurt into the street, no sir. He flew from leather and tumbled over a few bales of hay outside a livery. As luck would have it, a rain of loose hay fell over him only he didn't know about it because he was blown out like a candle. Next thing he remembered, he was lying in a soft bed and a woman with eyes blue as a summer sky and lips full and sweet as Georgia peaches was changing the dressing on his shoulder, cleaning the furrow at his head.

"I tell ye, hillbilly, I thought maybe I was in Heaven or Dodge City or one of them places. This woman—hair the color of wheat chaff and tits like ripe melons—was named Sadie Crossner and she was a widow. Too bad for her old man, I thought. Sadie poured out her life story in some detail, said she'd look after me until I was feeling better. Didn't seem to cotton to the fact that I was some common outlaw. She owned the livery and made a pretty good living at it. Had a big house out back, too, and rented rooms out of it. All she lacked was a man. She fed me, dressed me, and then she asked me to marry her."

Just like that, Kirby said. She had a set of triplet boys and they were a handsome lot, all blond and blue-eyed with China white skin. Like living dolls. Only they gave Kirby the creeps. They had an unpleasant habit of saying everything in unison as if the exact same thought occurred in each of their brains at the same time. They would walk around shoulder to shoulder, sneezing at the same time, scratching their noses at the same time, even yawning together. Crazy thing was, they even ate in tandem. Anyway, Sadie asked him to marry her and Kirby weighed his options and said yes. It was a quick affair with a preacher friend of hers.

Kirby pulled out a bar of tobacco and cut himself a chew with his Bowie knife. "Yes, sir, hillbilly, damnedest woman. She was cool, quiet, reminded me of a snake hibernating in a hole. The boys were the same—Peter, Paul, and Prescott, never could tell 'em apart. But that first night in bed, hoo-whee, she came alive like a boar hog with a hot blade upside its balls. Fucked me until I was a rag doll and then wanted it again. She was hungry for a dick like a dog hungering for a bone. If ye follow me meaning. Hell, I was happier than a woodtick on a testicle. Thing was, shit started smelling strange..."

Kirby figured he was set and maybe he was. He spent his time like a Republican, laying about and being waited on. The boys took to calling him father and he wasn't at all opposed to that. Thing was, those boys weren't getting any better—the lot of them were still strange. Kirby discovered just how strange when he noticed they had a thing about collecting up dead animals. And that was bad enough until he learned not only did they collect them, but they boiled the flesh and fur off them in a big pot and glued the bones back together in the shed out back.

"Hillybilly, ye had to see this to appreciate it. The walls of that old shed all decorated up with those skeletons they put back together—cats and rabbits and lizards, dogs and mice and snakes and even a big old bobcat. I went in one night with an old oil lamp and saw for my ownself. About made me piss out tacks. All dark and shadowy like a spookshow and them bones and skulls a-leering out at you. Damn. I told Sadie, but claimed she already knew. Didn't see anything wrong with it. But I did."

Those kids maybe needed something, Kirby said. Confinement or a boarding school where the headmaster told them where to squat and shit and how often and how long the turds had to be. Something. They were as fucked as five-dollar whores and Kirby was gravely concerned. They weren't normal. They didn't catch frogs or keep snakes in their pockets (less they planned on de-boning them, that was) or go fishing or tease girls or play ball or play with themselves for that matter. They went around in matching velvet suits and short pants like English brats and they were always clean—hair combed right and pretty, no snotty noses, no dirty knees. Kirby began to speculate that Sadie kept them in matching boxes and wound them up with a key each morning.

"Goddamn, hillbilly, I started to get concerned. The whole thing was eating me, burning at me innards like rock salt up me ass." He shook his head and spat a stream of coffee-colored tobacco juice to the ground. "Sadie was still stropping me pecker nightly, demanding it stand up, salute, and whistle Dixie. As I said, that woman spread faster than the common cold. Thing was, she weren't no better'n those brats of hers. She was getting strange, too. Where before she hopped my meat and mewed like a cat and sang like a parrot, now she was just a-laying there. Like fucking a piece of breathing meat. Made me think all that orgasming business of before was just an act. I could've fucked my own hand and made it come quicker."

It was about that time that Kirby's guns turned up missing. He wasn't too concerned because he'd pretty much reckoned on hanging them up for good. Still, he didn't like it and Sadie and the kids claimed ignorance of the matter. And with what was going on, well, he didn't push it. One night after Sadie had duly screwed him into never-never land and he lay there snoring like a buzzsaw with a broken spindle, he came awake. No reason. Just snapped awake like he knew something was wrong. He tip-toed to the door and opened it a crack. What did he see?

"Jesus John H. Christ, hillbilly, there they was, the four of 'em, walking up that hallway naked as newborns and carrying candles. Was I disturbed? Why, hell yes. If me dick had sprouted feet and ran off one night, I couldn't have been more disturbed. So being the nosy sumbitch I am, I followed 'em down into the cellar and into the coal bin. I'd never been in there—Sadie claimed she'd lost the key. Well, guess what I saw?"

They had a little altar set-up and the four them were on their knees before it. Candles were glowing and flickering and throwing shadows like living tarps all over the place. And that was bad enough, what with the smell in there like something mopped off the floor of a dissection room. Their little altar was decorated up with bones like the shed out back, except these were human ones. Skulls and leg bones and arm bones and you name it. Stacked and heaped like kindling. The centerpiece was a set that had been decorated with beads and feathers and paint.

"I about shit me long underwear, hillbilly. Thing was, they heard me and next thing I knew, old Sadie had a shotgun and she forced me up into the loft and into a bed where the boys roped me down like kicking steer."

It was getting weirder all the time.

But Kirby had it pretty much figured out. They had lodgers coming and going all the time—cowhands and miners and tramps and soldiers and you name it. Sadie was always selling off horses and packing away boxes of used clothes to the church. Well, shit, it all added up. He figured her and the boys were killing guests from time to time, ones that no one would miss. Taking their cash money, selling off their horses and what not. And the bones? Well, who in Christ knew?

But Sadie filled him in. Yes, they were killing people, dregs of society. Doing them a favor in her crazy way of thinking. But the boys needed a father and she intended that to be Kirby. Hell, those boys needed direction, male influence, she said, and they couldn't spend their time talking with their father on the altar (he being the one that was all decorated like a Christmas tree). In time, she told Kirby, he'd come to accept their way of life and want to join in.

"I told this same story to a smart fellah I met up in the Dakotas, hillbilly. Fellah was poking around up there looking for the bones of big lizards he said swam in a sea there back yonder before biblical times," Kirby said. "He told me what they were doing was called 'ancestor worship'. Savages do it all the time— let the meat bake off the bones of their dearly departed and put them up in their huts or what not, worship 'em like a statue of Jesus or the saints. It was just damn weird for white folks to be indulging in it."

The next two weeks, buck naked, Kirby was locked in that room. Then one night Sadie and the boys went off to a church supper and Kirby chewed through his rope like a beaver through bark and got the hell out of there.

"Charleston? It's a goddamn wicked town and I plan on never going back, hillbilly. But...ye ever need a room there, ye let me know. I can fix ye right up."

58

The story was amusing but Partridge had other thoughts buzzing through his head and what he was thinking was this: Do I really believe for one second I'm gonna just ride right up there and some fellow I never laid eyes on before is gonna hand me eighty thousand? Do I really believe that?

But he wanted to, God yes.

Anna Marie said she'd loved him once and maybe she really had. He believed it despite himself and he needed to believe it.

They were in the tall timber country now, following that snaking, uneven road up through the juniper-pinon slopes and staring up at the bald summits above. Towers and shelves of craggy rock thrust from the ground and there were huge red boulders marking the perimeter of the road.

"We should agree on a few basics here, hillbilly," Kirby finally said, his face masked with shadow beneath his wide-brimmed hat. "Ye loved that gal and maybe she loved ye back. But that was some time back. Well, things is different now. It's only you and me and Christ knows what's waiting for us up there."

Partridge's eyes glinted like chips of flint in his drawn face. He said, "If you got a plan, Kid, then now would be the time to tell it."

But Kirby didn't, not just then.

They followed the road another twenty minutes and the trees and scrub began to thin and they could see daylight through the brush. They were close now and they knew it. It had to be just ahead. They edged in closer and sure enough, they started to see the rusting traces of machinery reflecting bits of sunlight—derricks and headframes.

"Now we can either ride right down there," Kirby said, "or we can play it smart and slip off into the bush and have ourselves a look see."

They led their horses over the rocks and into the timberline until they found a shadowy protected cove where they could tether them and know they would still be there when they got back.

They moved off through the undergrowth on foot, dangerously aware that it would be dark in a hour or so and that the shadows were beginning to swim up like coiling tentacles. They moved as quiet as possible, but both men hadn't stalked game in some time and they were much louder than they wanted to be, leaves and dry sticks crunching under foot. Kirby almost stepped on a big timber rattler stretched at the base of a grassy mound and when it rattled its shaker and pulled back its lethal shovel-shaped head, he spat tobacco juice in its eyes and it slid away through the pine needles and twigs.

They came out on the lip of a little wooded ridge and the sun was again bright and warm. They were looking down into a small boat-shaped valley thick with timber, not just pines now but abundant hardwoods, leaves gone red and orange and gold from the cool nights in the high country.

The Durant Mine was just below them, a sprawl of shacks and ramps, outbuildings and corrugated roofs, headframes and hoist sheds. There were corrals with big draught horses and wagons lined up. Thing was, it was dead quiet down there. Nothing moved, stirred, nor breathed. The breeze rustled leaves, a hawk cried in the distance. That was it. There were huge and ugly piles of slag rising up at the perimeters and a sullen stink of smoke and ash and chemicals and grease.

Like a graveyard, Partridge thought.

A working mine lying silent like that when there was still daylight left. When money was coming out of the ground, places like this did not idle silent. He had butterflies the size of rooks fluttering and flapping in his belly.

"Don't like it one bit," Kirby said.

And they soon saw why.

The angle of the sun started reflecting off things down there and not just chips of mica and quartz, iron and glass, but the barrels of rifles. Rifles held by men hiding amongst the buildings and corrals and rocks, waiting, just waiting.

"It's a set-up, all right," Kirby said. "Well, we might as well let 'em know we're here."

And maybe it was a crazy thing to do, but Partridge was just pissed-off enough to follow suit.

Kirby brought up his Henry rifle and dropped two of them before they knew if it was raining bullets or shit. They all started firing down there wildly, shooting in all possible directions and, in their excitement, revealing their positions. Some of them stood up and started shooting towards the road, others sprayed the hills. Partridge figured there were at least twenty, maybe more. But within two or three minutes, Kirby with his Henry and Partridge with his Winchester had thinned the herds by nearly a dozen. They kept taking up new positions and adding to the confusion. Eventually they broke it off and just watched the confusion down there. Finally, some big, mean-looking sonofabitch stood up and started yelling.

"Looks like time to leave, " Kirby said.

And at that precise moment they heard riders coming up the road. A posse? It was hard to say. Four of them came into view and Partridge saw that three of them were decked out like Apache warriors and the fourth was dressed in a black Stetson and a khaki duster that flapped around him like a flag on a high pole. He had stringy white hair that blew over his shoulders like whipping vines.

Partridge kept staring at that man while worms crawled in his belly.

There was something about him, something...

59

"Stop shooting!"

Glen McCall, ramrod of the Durant and certified hardcase, cried out. Of course, no one did. They were pumping out rounds fast as their respective weapons would allow. Ejected shells were spinning through the air, winking back bits of late afternoon sunlight. Fresh ones were chambered, spent, ejected again. McCall, on his knees behind a table of rock, kept calling out for them to stop, but they didn't. Maybe they couldn't hear him with the sounds of those rifles cracking and booming and maybe they were just scared. These men were miners, they were day laborers, they were not professionals. Most of them carried guns, but very few had ever used them against another man. Seeing the bodies of their friends sprawled in the grass—gutshot, headshot, dropped with perfect accuracy by those bastards on the ridge—it had done something to them. Locked them down hard with fear and paranoia.

McCall finally stood up, exposing himself to fire, but not giving a good goddamn by that point. "STOP FUCKING SHOOTING, YOU GODDAMN IGNORANT PISSWADS!" he screamed, pulling the rifles from more than one man and tossing them to earth.

It took hold finally and they did.

Johnny Max Silver told McCall that a desperate fugitive was on his way up to the mine to rob the paymaster's office. That's all he was told. How he stopped the man was up to him, long as he did. It left McCall with precious little time to put together a decent militia. What he got instead were all the workers he could muster and where had that gotten him?

Jesus Lovely Christ.

There were a dozen dead men out here, three or four others severely wounded. There was blood and brains and skull fragments sprayed everywhere. Men moaning. Men whimpering. Men vomiting at the sight of the carnage.

McCall looked up at the treeline, knowing whoever had been up there had withdrawn now. "All right," he said. "Those of you can ride, mount up! We're going after those bastards." He looked at two men who were shaken badly. They would be of no use to him. "You two! Get these wounded in a wagon and get 'em down to Dead Creek. The rest of you, let's go!"

It was about that time that four riders came down the road into the valley.

"Jesus," one of the men said. "Goddamn injuns!"

McCall looked and couldn't believe it.

Renegade Apaches led by a white man.

The shooting started again.

60

It was nearly dark when John Pepper came around.

His head throbbing, he came awake in a panic, realizing he was securely bound and, for the life of him, he just couldn't remember how he'd come to be here. He remembered riding up into the Superstitions, circling above Dead Creek and then, and then—

What in the Christ had happened then?

He thought: See, you dumb sonofabitch, this is what it got you. You were thinking you had this last run in you, but you were dead wrong. You didn't have nothing left and look where it got you, look—

And then he did and it wasn't easy because his vision was blurred in his left eye and his right didn't want to stop watering. It seemed it might be a permanent condition now. The entire left side of his body was tingling madly like ants had gotten just below the skin and were scurrying about madly. In fact, it not only tingled, but he couldn't even feel his left hand and his left leg felt like a wooden limb someone had stitched onto him as a joke. Even had he not been tied, he knew he would not be able to stand. His face felt numb and as he tried to work some blood into it, he realized it was slack and cold.

He was in a state this time.

Jesus, what's that smell?

His right eye stopped tearing and he was able to focus, but only with great concentration. The sun was dipping low and the shadows were thick on the ground. He was in a little meadow, trees to all sides. He saw that old medicine wagon and his brain still worked well enough to remind him, with a jolt of fear, exactly who it belonged to and who held him captive. A fire was burning. He saw other things, things strung up and dressed out and he had to force himself to look away.

"Glad you could join us, Marshal," Coy Farren said, readjusting the worn bowler hat atop his narrow head. "It seems to me you're in a bad way and in desperate need of immediate medical attention. And, believe me, sir, my Christian heart does go out to your apparent suffering. But, I feel, you are beyond hope. Would you agree with me on this, Lyle?"

John Lyle was standing near the wagon, a mountain of flesh and evil intent. He gnashed his teeth and his eyes glowed hot and savage and hungry. He was sharpening a fighting knife against a stone. "Yes, I would agree with that. He is beyond hope, yes."

Pepper had to swallow down the fear that writhed in his belly like worms. It left an ugly, metallic taste on his tongue. He tried to speak, but it was as if he simply didn't know how. His lips felt rubbery, his tongue like a wet piece of cloth. He remembered that doc in Chimney Flats...could see his face, but not recall his name…telling him he could probably expect either a stroke or a massive hemorrhage.

Pepper knew what had occurred, wished he were dead.

He had wanted, his entire life, simply to die, if not quickly, then at least as a man. With some dignity and some pride. And now…Christ, pissing himself like a little boy. No chance at self-respect.

"Course," Coy Farren said, "you're probably wondering if we're merely going to let you die slow and ugly or if we're going to speed things along. Is that what you're thinking, sir? Of course it is. Truth be told, I haven't honestly made up my mind. But even as we speak, the wheels of my brain do turn, do revolve. Maybe I should just let Lyle slit your throat. You'd like that, wouldn't you, Lyle?"

John Lyle made an almost bovine grunting sound. "Yessum, I would like it fine."

There was someone in the wagon. Pepper could hear that much. Another prisoner? Another victim? Maybe. He could remember with a certain clarity his first meeting with these degenerates. Hadn't Coy said something about his mother and father being in the wagon or was that just more bullshit from a man who spouted it like a fountain spouts water?

Coy scratched his scraggly beard. "Hmm, hmm, hmm. What to do, what to do."

Pepper hated the smell that came off the man—not only body odor that was raw and rank, but a worse cloying odor of blood and old meat. A hideous odor. But then the entire camp smelled like that—like a slaughterhouse…or a morgue.

"I could toy with you like a cat to a mouse, make it gradual and most hurtful. I've been known to engage in such practices, yes, sir." Farren pulled a blackened corncob pipe from inside his coat and packed it leisurely with rough-cut tobacco. He gave it flame and blew smoke from his mouth and nostrils. "But should I do it slow? That is the question. You're in despicable shape, Marshal, but you're still a desperate and dangerous lawman. The thought of turning my back on you chills me to the bone and all. It chill you, Lyle?"

"Chills me straight through, yes," John Lyle managed.

Pepper had been concentrating everything he had left into speaking. At this point, he wanted nothing more. His lips were still stiff, but they were workable. His tongue felt clumsy, but he figured he could work it. He opened his mouth and what came out was a dry, cracking sound.

Coy Farren took his pipe out of his mouth. He angled his head so his ear was a few inches closer to Pepper. "What say, Mr. Pepper?"

Pepper drew it up from his guts, pulled it out of his bones and marrow, everything that was left. Any residual bit of strength and coordination he had left.

"Fuck...you...you...peckerwood...cocksucker..."

Coy Farren darted back as if he'd been slapped, feigned shock. He laid the dirty fingers of one hand to his lips. "My, my, my," he said. "Dear Lord in Heaven. My goodness! Such obscenities these ears have never heard. Shame on you, Marshal. Shame, shame, shame. Profanity being a mechanism of a weak mind."

John Lyle took a few steps forward, his knife ready to bisect flesh, but Coy stilled him with the wave of one hand.

Coy smoked his pipe, considered his prisoner. "Back in Virginia in the good days, Marshal, before them damn Yankees tore up the real estate and what not, I had me a slave name of Jim Henry. Good nigger, he was. Big and powerful, just a-rippling with muscle and skinned a delicious chocolate brown. Beautiful creature. But proud, free-thinking." He shook his head and clucked his tongue. "I told him I couldn't allow him to address me in that uppity tone of voice. I ordered, I begged, I cajoled him. I even punished him via the whip and by bedding his woman and forcing her into the most *dis*-gusting acts. Still, Jim Henry would not relent. Well, what was an honest white man to do with a niggra like that? You tell me, kind sir."

Pepper didn't even attempt to. This man was nothing but human filth. Thinking of some sort of revenge against this monster was pointless. You couldn't punish a rattler for being a snake or a grizzly for being a bear or a spider for sucking its prey dry no more than could you hope to punish Coy Farren for being the monster he was. Born or schooled, it no longer mattered, for monster he indeed was. All you could do was put him down like a rabid dog and be done with it. Pepper dearly wished he was able to be the one.

Coy re-lit his pipe. "As I said, old Jim Henry didn't understand gentle persuasion nor rigid discipline. Now, back then, there was a *lovely* plantation owned and operated by a wonderful, cultured gentleman name of Pearle, Horace Pearle. Perhaps you are familiar with his family and their vast, grandiose holdings? No? Well, no matter. Now, Mr. Pearle was a gracious and cultivated man, spoke several languages and even held several degrees from prestigious Yankee universities. His hospitality was legendary. He also had veritable army of niggers working his cotton." Coy was grinning now, reveling in the old days. "Well, sir, Mr. Pearle had traveled extensively, particularly in the orient where his family had holdings. And, while there, he had been exposed to certain, shall we say, *exotic* practices. So, at my veritable wits end with Jim Henry, I sent him over to Mr. Pearle for an unspecified duration. Now, Mr. Pearle was something of a libertine, as I said, and he indulged in certain vices that the Good Book strictly forbids. He had a particular taste for strapping, powerful Negroes, set his mouth just a-watering, they did. So dear Mr. Pearle plied his unmentionable and vile attentions to Jim Henry. Point being, Jim Henry returned a changed nigger. He was cowed and cowering and kissed my feet when I took him back in. I understood he didn't exactly enjoy Mr. Pearle's somewhat unspeakable nocturnal encounters, found them profane and blasphemous."

The sun was setting, painting the western horizon red with its blood and orange with its promise. Coy Farren's face was maze of shifting shadow, making him look positively skullish and abnormal.

He knocked out his pipe against his knee. "Course, you are wondering, kind sir, the point of this somewhat debased narrative. Pray, I will tell you. For even the proudest and orneriest of individuals there lies a punishment which will bring them to their knees, reduce them to sobbing babes. Such a punishment exists for you, Marshal."

Pepper didn't want to know what it was; he only hoped he'd die soon. For death would be a blessing now. Not only in light of his physical condition but for whatever vulgar plan was even now boiling in the cauldron of Coy Farren's brain.

"Marshal, did I ever tell you of Mother Farren? Her peculiarities? Her abnormalities? How the war certainly amplified them. No? Hmm."

He paced back and forth, then tapped a finger to his nose while Pepper watched him with all the hatred he could muster.

"Yes, sir," Coy said, "I do believe that tonight, I will introduce you to Mother Farren. A capital idea. Yes, you won't be quite the same after she's finished…"

61

"I think we better get off this road," Kirby said and meant it.

But Partridge was thinking the same thing. He could hear, in the distance, the sound of approaching hoofs and quite a few of them by the sound. The shooters at the mine had no doubt reorganized themselves for a final counterattack. Partridge didn't relish the idea of a running gun battle in the darkness with a vastly superior force.

"All right," he said and led his mount into the treeline where the undergrowth was thick and tangled and the moving was very slow going.

The shadows were thick and black. After a time, Kirby and Partridge dismounted and led their horses on foot. Around trees, through gullies, up brush-covered slopes. In the darkness, the forest was all but impassible with sudden hollows and jutting spines of rock. It grew cold and the stars began to show themselves above the latticework of branches. No insects buzzed or sounded, no animals scurried in the distance. After a time, they stopped and stood there, smoking in the darkness. About that time, below on the road, they heard a lone rider go charging down the road to Dead Creek and just a few minutes behind him a score of horsebackers that apparently hunted him.

"Must be after what's left of those injuns," Kirby said. "Chances are, hillbilly, they don't even know it was us."

Partridge figured that made sense.

Except that it didn't much matter to him now. He had wanted badly to trust Anna Marie. Maybe wanted and needed it more than just about anything and now that had gone to ash. She had sent him into an ambush and nothing in the world would make him believe it hadn't been for the very purpose of getting rid of him.

All right, bitch, he thought. All right. I gave you a chance. I trusted and you fucked me just fine and right. Well, it's coming back at you now. Goddamn, yes, it is.

They didn't have any real plan as yet, but Partridge figured they would lay low for a time and then later, they would ride into town and hit the Egyptian Hotel. And whatever stood between them and Anna Marie would die a violent death. There was no other way now. It had to end like this.

"Look at that there," Kirby said. "Ye see it?"

Partridge did. A fire burning off in the distance, lower down towards the town. It could either be a good thing or a bad thing.

"What ye say we go have ourselves a look?" Kirby said. "If'n it looks all right, we could warm ourselves at that fire, friendly-like, and think on what we do next."

They led the horses down there and picketed them a good distance away. Then they made their way down a scrub-tangled hillside and to the edge of the forest. There was an old medicine wagon pulled up and a fire blazing away. They could see two men standing about and a third who was obviously bound.

"Hot damn," Kirby said. "Will ye fucking look at that?"

Partridge was and not liking it a bit. "You smell it?" he said.

"I do." The stink of death. They both knew it all too well.

But the smell or the men themselves weren't the worse thing, for they saw what was strung up down there and it was something out of a nightmare.

"Dear God," Partridge uttered under his breath.

"Looks like they got themselves a hostage," Kirby said. "Poor bastard. You up to a good deed, hillbilly?"

He was.

62

"I suppose you got a good explanation for this," Partridge said when he came around the wagon, loathing thick on his voice as if he'd just bitten into a dead mouse. He had his Winchester .44 in his hands and he had a bead drawn on the skinny drifter by the fire. A thin, skeletal fellow with a rodent's face and too many long yellow teeth in his mouth, he wore a ragged broadcloth coat and an Army .44 in a homemade sheath. "No? Didn't suspect so. There ain't much either of you murdering cowards can say about it, is there?" He glared at the skinny one. "You'd best tell your big friend there by the wagon that if he doesn't stop playing with his knife, I'm gonna have to blow that shit-ugly mess he calls a head clean off his fucking shoulders."

The big man did not drop the knife.

He stood there, huge and hulking. He wore a sleeveless beaverskin coat that was just as greasy and dirty as he was. His bare arms were huge like pythons. The muscles bulged and rippled in them. He was grinning behind a shaggy beard and his teeth had been filed sharp as knife blades. Looked like a savage from a dime novel. He took a step forward.

"Lyle," the thin one said, "we'd best—"

But Partridge didn't wait for it. He busted a round right over the savage's head. He didn't even bat an eye, but he stopped. Partridge wanted to kill him. Something in him demanded it. Because this...this was abominable, it was criminal, good Christ, it was a travesty of anything even remotely human or decent.

Something had gone cold and black in him. Things like mercy and compassion and decency had gone to ruin. Because what he was seeing here, it demanded action. It demanded to be erased, to be blotted out, crushed. It took every fiber of will he had not to kill these shit-eaters dead.

Jesus, that smell.

It was within him and without.

Yes, he was disgusted and appalled on every imaginable level. He couldn't believe what it was he was seeing. The words to properly convey his horror, his anger, his absolute revulsion at this nightmare simply didn't exist. The guy roped-up by the fire was bad enough. These two depraved, deranged freaks were even worse. But the camp itself...Christ in heaven, such a thing should not be.

The bodies of two women were strung up, one heavy, the other thin as death. Their heads had been cut off. They had been slit from crotch to throat, eviscerated, and hung up like cattle at a slaughterhouse. There were two crude, cruciform structures like of the sort you might hang cornfield scarecrows from. The women had been mounted to them, upside down. Ankles tied to the crossbar with rope, wrists tied and pulled tight to the same. Just husks now, their flesh clown-white, bloodless. You could see right into the hollows of their body cavities and they looked as thoroughly washed as those of a chicken ready for the roaster.

Kirby was behind them now. He had his Henry rifle out and he looked disgusted. "What in the name of fuck is this?" he said and his voice was empty, dry-sounding.

"Butcher shop," Partridge said and for the first time in too many years, he wanted to cry. It was just too much. "Kid…those barrels…what's in 'em?"

Kirby swallowed down hard, tried to wet his lips but it took oceans. There were three pickle barrels near the end of the wagon. Using the barrel of his rifle, he flipped the lids off one by one. He struck a stick match off the brass receiver of his Henry. His lower lip trembling, he examined the contents, then turned away quickly, letting the match drop from his fingers and trained his rifle on the big man. "They's…they's *innards,* Nate…and in that one there…they's…Jesus…*they's women's heads.*" He got control of himself best he could. "Ye boys et people, is that it? Ye sick motherfuckers."

Partridge was looking at the thin one and his acid leer couldn't melted pig iron. "Guess the party's over, because you're going to your maker now, the both of you."

Kirby said, "When I was a boy in Alabama had me a grand nanny liked to tell us younguns scary stories of things that lived in the mountains. Things that looked like people but weren't. And those things, they liked to et other folks. Goddamn, I never did think I'd meet any of em."

Coy Farren couldn't wipe that lecherous smile from his face. "Gentlemen, there is a very logical explanation for this. I swear that to you. What we have is a predicament easily explained, if only you give me the proper time for doing so."

"Shut the fuck up," Partridge told him.

"Please, sir, I implore you. My name is Coy Farren and this is my dear brother—"

Partridge snarled at him, "I told you to shut your fucking whole and, goddammit, I meant it."

The bound man moved against his restraints. He grunted and moaned and tried to speak, but only made a gurgling sound.

Partridge could just imagine what was simmering in that big, flame-blackened pot suspended on a tripod over the fire. It smelled sweet and spicy and unwholesome, filled his belly with sludge.

He was trembling with rage when he said, "Was he next into the pot?" Indicating the bound man. "Is that what?"

"Why that's insane, completely insane," Coy Farren said and, quick as you please, pulled the .44 from his holster. Only he never got it past his hip because Partridge shot him in the chest, levered, and blew a hole in his belly. Farren swung in a wild circle, spilling blood and shrieking and snapping his teeth. Partridge levered a final time and drilled him in the back of the head. His face blew off the shattered skull beneath, meat and bone spraying into the foliage. He dropped spread-eagle right into the fire, disturbing the big pot and spilling its foul contents into the flames where they sizzled and steamed, much as he did, dead face right in the coals.

The big man charged, knife flashing stolen moonlight. Before Partridge could fire or even think of doing so, Kirby started popping rounds from his Henry. Four of them went into that big sonofabitch and they barely even slowed him. He dove on Partridge and sank the knife into his side. Bleeding and howling like an animal, he pulled the knife free for another thrust and the back of his head blew into bloody confetti as a .44 caliber round from Kirby's Henry ended it then and there for him.

Partridge shoved his cooling bulk away.

The blade would've gutted him easily, such was its sharpness. But by the grace of God the blade had scraped along his ribs and been deflected. But the wound still bled profusely and hurt like a mother. Partridge pulled himself up, gasping and swearing under his breath, splayed fingers pressed to his side.

"Shit, hillbilly," Kirby said. "Oh shit and Christ and goddamn. Ye all—"

But he never finished that.

Partridge could never be truly sure what exactly happened at that moment. About the time the big wild man dove on him he heard a sound in the wagon...a shifting, a dragging, something. Then the lunatic was on him. Then he was dead and Partridge had pulled himself up and Kirby has started to speak and then—and then the door at the back of the wagon exploded open, mere feet from where Kirby stood. There was motion...a shape, a shadow, a wraith...and moonlight winking off lethal razored steel and then that steel had sunk into Kirby's neck, nearly decapitating him. Still gagging on a mouthful of words, he folded up and dropped into the grass. By the time Partridge got there, he was writhing like a worm in direct sunlight, blood bubbling from his lips and he died. Just that quick.

Partridge cried out and shouted and nearly went out of his mind.

Then he grabbed up his Winchester, ignoring the pain that cut into his side like the business end of a barbed lance, and pulled a flaming log from the firepit. Behind him, the bound man was making awful whimpering sounds. But Partridge couldn't think about that, not now. He wheeled around the back of the wagon and tossed the log right through the door. It lit up things just fine. The wagon was packed with gunny sacs and wooden crates and more barrels. From the ceiling, suspended by wires were slabs of meat and human limbs curing and salted, mummified and shriveled, dangling like sausages in a butcher shop window. All of them slightly swaying and turning with a gentle tenebrous motion. Dozens and dozens of them. And just beyond those horrors, a motheaten red velvet curtain, discolored and moldering. He brought the Winchester up and was about to start busting lead when—

When a shape that was more skeleton than flesh leaped out with a meat cleaver in one leathery, sinewy fist. Its face was a death mask like tanned hide, a mutiny of wrinkles and bony eruptions, lips drawn back from sharpened yellow teeth and blackened gums. The head was capped by a wild and stringy fright mask of white hair and those eyes...just as yellow and glowing and full of animal rage as those of a rabid wolf.

It was a woman.

Or something like a woman.

She was naked, save for the rotting remnants of a dress. A set of withered, drooping breasts swung from side to side with pendulous strokes as she clambered forward, moving with an obscene deadly intensity that told Partridge he was nothing but meat to her.

He shot her in the chest and when she snapped back, screeching with a high, piercing wail, he kept shooting until the Winchester was empty. She fell dead over the crates and slid forward, dropping from the back of the wagon in a jackstraw tumble of broomstick limbs and mottled flesh.

The log was still burning, creating a ghastly shadow show of lurching shapes. A few of the gunny sacks had caught now, tongues of flame tasting the ragged curtain. And beyond it, in that black and evil envelope of charnel stink, was another figure. A man. Seated in a chair up against the wall in the very front, he wore the full uniform of a Confederate major…decaying and patched with mold. In the flickering firelight, Partridge saw him and saw he was of no threat.

He'd been dead a long time.

Just a mummy that had been embalmed badly some years before, the skin like fine and crumbling parchment paper, the skull jutting from innumerable holes in the face. The flames continued to rise and the patriarch of the Farren clan accepted the oblivion they offered.

Partridge stumbled back towards the fire. Drained. Shivering. Hopeless. He pulled himself over to where the bound man was. With what seemed great exertion, he cut the ropes and the man nearly fell right on top of him. He wore a sheepskin coat and leather chaps. He lay sprawled over Partridge's lap.

"You're gonna be okay," Partridge told him and his voice was dead, hopeless. A monotone and nothing more. "Okay now."

He pulled him over so he could see his face in the firelight, get a look at him. He didn't look good. His color was sallow, the bearded face slack almost on one side like wax that had melted and cooled. He ran a tongue over his lips and his hand came up and clutched Partridge's shoulder.

That face. That seamed, weathered face.

And those crystal blue eyes.

Jesus, Partridge found himself thinking, I know this man. It's, it's—

"John Pepper," he said.

Anna Marie's Uncle. And a deputy U.S. Marshal. But at that particular moment, Partridge didn't care. He was grateful for company. Any company. Even that of a man who had never liked him and had never liked him marrying his niece.

"Nathan..." Pepper said slowly with a great deal of effort. His speech was slurred, difficult to understand. "...not much time left...you gotta..."

He began to shiver and Partridge held him best he could. He knew that there might have been a lot of reasons the Marshal's Service had sent him to Dead Creek, but only one occurred to him at that moment: He had come to bring in an escaped convict.

Pepper's breathing was shallow. There was blood in his mouth. Partridge figured it probably had little to do with what his captors had done and everything to do with the fact that he appeared to have suffered a stroke.

"Take your time, John. Just take your time," he said. "I figure you came to hunt me down."

Pepper nodded.

"But they got you. You had a stroke. Is that it?'

Pepper nodded vigorously.

Damn. Of all things. Partridge did not relish the idea of facing this man at any time, but he would've rather taken his chances with a healthy and strapping John Pepper than the wretch before him. He deserved a better death than this, a man who had lived like he had. It was terrible. Anna Marie had never liked him and from where Partridge was sitting, this was a good thing. The highest recommendation. Pepper had never cared for him either, true, but Partridge had always felt it was because he understood him. Knew who and what he was. But that was ages ago now, another life.

He propped Pepper up against a tree near the fire. Made him comfortable as he could. He kicked Coy Farren's body out of the fire because it was beginning to stink. Then he cut down the two women. He gave Pepper a pull of whiskey from a flask that fell from Coy Farren's pocket. He rolled cigarettes for the both of them and lit them, placing one between Pepper's lips. Pepper seemed grateful. His right hand worked fine and he was able to smoke.

They sat staring at each other, maybe knowing at last that they had a lot in common. Partridge started talking. Started telling Pepper of everything that had happened to him since he escaped from Yuma. It was the quick version, but it covered all the important parts.

"...me and Kirby saw you and decided...well, we thought we'd better help."

Pepper appreciated it. You could see that. Controlling his breathing, he said. "Be...careful...be careful...Black Jake...he ain't dead..." Then the cigarette dropped from his fingers and he fell right over, eyes still staring, though sightless now. Partridge went to him. Blood was coming from his ears. A brain hemorrhage...something. He was dead all the same.

Partridge closed his eyes and thought about Pepper's dying words.

Fifteen minutes later, he was still thinking about them.

63

When he was able, when he could clear the shit from his brain long enough to think straight, Partridge bandaged himself up the best he could by firelight. Just strips cut from a blanket. It wasn't the best, but it would do. Steeling himself against the pain, he brought his and Kirby's horses back to the campsite. He loaded Kirby over the saddle and brought him out into the woods. In a soft hillside, he buried him despite the pain that chewed at his side.

But it was something he had to do.

Chances were, Kirby would never be recognized for who he really was. But on the off-chance that crazy, improbable things do indeed happen, Partridge wanted his old friend well away from that slaughter yard. When it was cleaned up (and it would be, for he decided he would somehow get word to whatever law there was in these parts), he didn't want Kirby tied in with it.

Pepper was a different matter.

He sat the dead lawman up against the tree again and pressed Kirby's Henry rifle into the Marshal's stiffening fists. There. That would work. Now folks would figure Pepper had killed the two Farrens in the line of duty and died shortly thereafter himself. It was how a man like him had a right to be remembered.

And he was.

Though the truth of what was found at the campsite was considered unpalatable at best for public consumption as it were, John Pepper went into the history books as having died while apprehending two nameless outlaws.

64

Two hours later, Partridge tethered his horse in the alley behind the Egyptian Hotel. He strapped on the Colt .38 Lightning in the cross-draw scabbard on his left hip. He strapped the .45 Schofield to his right. He left the Winchester in the saddle boot and took up the Greener sawed-off shotgun instead. He filled the pockets of his coat with extra shells for it, then went around front. The wound at his side was raw and hurting and every time he moved the wrong way, he could feel it begin to bleed again. But he figured he had enough blood left for this.

He thought: Lookit me now. After all the shit I've swallowed and waded through, here I am. Going to my death. But that's okay because I sure as fuck won't go alone.

He came around front and there was no one plying the darkened streets and no one out front the Egyptian but the doorman. It had to be past one in the morning and still they had a doorman. The place was lit up and Partridge could hear music.

He came up on the doorman quietly. "Evening," he said.

The doorman made to return the salutation, then a shadow crossed his face. "Friend, it's house policy to check your firearms at the—"

But he never completed that, for Partridge spun the Greener in his fist and gave the doorman the butt of it square in the face. He wheeled back, struck the railing and flipped right over it. He lay below in the grass, unmoving. There was blood on the white-washed steps and a few pearly-looking things that might have been teeth.

Partridge opened the doors and blew right in like a fierce wind.

There was a man with a gun waiting for him, of course, in the entryway.

He looked up when the door opened and shock fell over him like a blanket. He knew who Partridge was and he went for the Navy Colt at his belt. Got it out with a speed that was admirable and even got off a shot. But it was low and fired out of fear and with no real attempt at accuracy. The bullet punched into the door behind Partridge and by that time he opened up and did not miss. The chamber explosion of the scattergun was like thunder in the enclosed entry. The buckshot blew the gunman's chest to rags and threw him back four feet, his heart and lungs vaporizing and a good section of spine blowing out an exit wound the circumference of a dinner plate. He collapsed into a bleeding, loose-limbed mass, fingers of smoke trailing from the entry wound from contact burns. He lay dead in a spreading sea of blood, the fancy wallpaper behind him sprayed with gobs of pink and gray tissue.

That's one, Partridge thought and started up the stairs.

65

Patrons inside the Egyptian heard the gunfire and were, of course, immediately concerned. Quite a few made to investigate, but were soothed by the soiled doves, bartenders, and assorted managerial staff. They were told the shooting was out in the street and why bother themselves with it. The patrons accepted the free drinks and the attentions of their ladies, easily diverted. And that was a good thing. For the word had been passed to the staff that there would be some shooting tonight and not to let it alarm the customers. It would be handled.

66

Partridge moved up the carpeted stairway at a leisurely pace, knowing there was no hurry now because he was certain he would not survive this night. The enclosed staircase wound up through the Egyptian in such a way that there was always a blind spot just ahead. But it was well-lit by oil lamps on the walls and what more could you ask for?

The pain in his side felt like there were razors tearing in there.

He sucked in shallow breaths and steeled his nerves. He came around another corner and there was a big man with a huge black mustache like the pelt of an ermine drooping beneath his nose. He saw Partridge, expected him. He did not look frightened. Looked like a hard man who had done his share of killing. He brought his gun up—a Colt Peacemaker—and carefully shot Partridge through the left shoulder. And at the same time took a load of buckshot in the belly. Partridge went to his knees, barely managing to stop himself from falling down the stairs.

The impact of the buckshot threw the gunman up and against the wall where he slid down leaving a bloody trail. His gun fell from his fingers and massive amounts of blood flowed from the blackened crater in his belly. His viscera, ruptured and fragmented, dropped out like mutilated snakes. His eyes were wide and staring, glassy as barroom mirrors. He sprawled there against the wall, dying slowly and painfully.

Partridge pulled himself to his feet.

He broke open the Greener and ejected the spent shells, loaded fresh ones, snapped the breech close. He made it another five or six steps, his coat and gray army shirt red and glistening now. He moved with agony, each muscular contraction needed to keep moving, to pull himself up to the next step threading him with knife-blades of pain.

Another gunman jumped out as he neared the top. A thin and frightened man, he was wet with sweat, his white cotton shirt plastered to his thin body. He had matching Remington pistols, single-action. He jumped out and opened up. One slug kicked Partridge's hat from his head, the other struck one of the oil lamps which exploded and vomited fire down the steps.

Partridge shot him in the throat.

His head nearly came right off, connected only by a few blasted strands of tissue. He dropped right past Partridge, tumbling right into the flames. Then his head did come off, thudding down the stairwell like a child's ball.

Partridge kept going.

67

In the corridor above a man was waiting.

But he had no guns.

In fact, the pistols he had been carrying were set out on the floor before him. He was shaking and his eyes were like the yolks of fried eggs bulging from their sockets. He went down on his knees before the guns, held his hands up.

"God in heaven, Mr. Partridge, I don't want none of this," he said in a dry, squeaky voice. "Just let me go. Swear to God I'll run right out the front door and I won't stop until I'm in bed with my wife."

Partridge just stood there, ghastly in the backlighting of the fire. The shadows crept along the hollows and bony protrusions of his pale, set face like tar. His eyes were wide and staring, fixed like those of a timber rattler ready to strike. Blood dropped to his boots. "You won't, eh?" he said, deciding whether he should just kill this sonofabitch for kicks. Decided against it.

The man was trembling and it smelled like maybe he'd pissed his pants. "I...I got three little ones, Mr. Partridge...if you could just think of them...oh please, dear God..."

Partridge chewed his lip, forced away the pain that darkened his thoughts. "All right, friend," he said, his lips quivering in something almost like a smile. "Straight on home with you then. No sheriff. No trouble. Go home and see them kids of yours. Raise 'em right and maybe they won't turn out like me."

The man thanked Partridge, looked for a moment like he might start kissing his boots, then found his feet and ran through the flames, the entire time rattling on about how Nathan Partridge was some kind of Christian saint.

If he hadn't been hurting so much, Partridge might have laughed.

68

Outside the door to Anna Marie's suite, he stepped out of harm's way and knocked. A series of slugs blew through the panels in answer. He could hear Anna Marie berating someone as only she could for being such a goddamn whining coward and a man's frantic voice telling her to shut up, shut up as his weapon clicked on empty chambers.

Partridge stepped in front of the door and gave it both barrels.

Two huge holes appeared in it, the first taking the doorknob with it and the second nearly blowing it from its hinges. It swung inward. Anna Marie screamed and someone else started shooting. But Partridge expected that. He stepped away and took one of the oil lamps and tossed it in there. It hit something and shattered and flames erupted in there, filling the room with orange, flickering light.

He set aside the Greener and pulled his Colt .38 and threw himself through the door, landing flat on his belly with a spasm of agony. He nearly blacked out. He saw Anna Marie cowering behind the sofa and the man he knew as Lord Johnny Max Silver, pimp extraordinaire, holding out a six-shooter in his shaking hand. He was in his shirt sleeves and tuxedo pants, dandy gear stored somewhere else.

He dropped the gun or it shook loose from his fingers. One way or the other it fell. "Mr. Nathan Partridge," he said. "Damn, I've wanted to meet you for some time."

Partridge kept the Colt on him. "You'd be the one that's been fucking my wife," he said. "The one that no doubt organized that little ambush for me."

Silver's face, which could have been sculpted from ivory such was its pale perfection, seemed to fall somewhat. "Oh, no I assure you that—"

"Assure me only that you'll die without a fuss."

Silver, a man used to talking his way in and out of situations, a man many thought had severe diarrhea of the mouth, found that there were no words to talk him out of this one. His lips trembled open in an easy and (he thought) reassuring smile as his brain tried to feed his tongue, tried to figure out what could be said that would still the gun of this quite common murdering outlaw.

But there were none.

"Please, Nathan..." Anna Marie started to say, but her heart was not in it.

"Keep that mouth zipped, Anna, or I'll punch hole in your pretty head."

He wasn't sure why he waited that long.

Maybe he wanted the hatred to heat a bit, to get truly molten and seething. When it reached that point, he brought up the Colt and shot Silver in the face. The bullet destroyed his right eyeball, splashing it from its socket and shattering the orbit it swam in. Deflected somewhat by the orbit, it spun through his head like a drill bit, macerating the gray matter in its path, and then blowing out the side of his head just above the ear, taking hair and brains and skull splinters with it. He hit the floor with a meaty thud, lifeless, his once handsome face frozen in a look of utter amazement.

Anna Marie was screaming.

Partridge went over to her and slapped her across the face three or four times until his callused knuckles tore flesh and her pretty, porcelain-painted face was spattered with blood. Then she shut up. But her teeth were set and her eyes blazing like funeral pyres.

Partridge thought: There. That's her. The true Anna Marie. Crouched and hateful and ready to kill. That's the beast I married. The one that likes to fuck and scheme. That's her in all her primal fuck you-glory.

"My money," he said. "I want my money."

"I don't have—"

He kicked her in the belly and she folded in half, gagging and gasping. He grabbed her by the back of the hair and pulled her to her feet and tossed across the floor.

"I want my fucking money," he said again. "If I have to, I'll mark up that face of yours so no man will ever want you. They'll puke at the sight of you. Get my money and get it now, you miserable cunt."

She crawled on her hands and knees across the floor, her hair a crow's nest and her red velveteen dress mussed. There was blood running from her nose. Sobbing, she wiped it away with the back of her hand. She reached up and pulled a tapestry from the wall.

A safe.

Shaking and crying, she started to work the tumblers. It was all a big act, of course, the tears. First chance she got, she'd stick a knife in him and he knew it.

"Pull anything but greenbacks out of there and I'll put the first bullet in your ass," he promised her. "And shitcan that sobbing."

"Bastard," she said.

There was a lot of money in there. She took a flowered valise and filled it until it would barely close. "That's all I have, you sonofabitch," she said and there was rage in her words. "It's more than you had. Take it and get out of my sight." She slid the valise over to him.

He reached down to grab it and knew he was getting slow, for he never heard someone enter the room.

"Well, goddamn," the voice said, hard and sharp as metal shavings, "if it all ain't like old home week."

69

Partridge turned and found himself looking down the long metallic barrel of a Colt Dragoon pistol. The sort of weapon that could've blown a hole in him the size of a saucer.

But it wasn't so much the weapon that froze him up like a December creek.

It was the voice.

That smooth and mean voice that haunted his childhood memories. The man who'd rode into the Durant Mine in the company of the Apaches was standing there. He wore a khaki duster and a black Stetson. The left side of his face was horribly scarred, drawing the corner of his lips into a gruesome grin that exposed teeth and gums. But the right side was surely that of his father, Black Jake Partridge. Older. Weathered and worn like an old campaign blanket, but his father, all right. His hair was long and white as November's first snow.

"Hello, son," he said. "Anna Marie."

"Who the hell are you?" she wanted to know.

"I'm your father-in-law, missy." He stared at her and his eyes were just as cold and gray as steel. "Glad to finally meet me?"

Anna Marie looked like she was going to faint. "But you're—"

"Dead? Not hardly. Less you believe in haunts."

His eyes locked with those of his son. They looked at each other long and hard and if there was any warmth that passed between them, you wouldn't have known it.

Black Jake finally said, "Come with me, Nathan. Plenty of money there for the both of us. What we don't have, we'll steal."

Partridge found it very hard to speak.

He wasn't sure what he was feeling. Rage, betrayal, hatred. But not love, not relief that his father was alive. Surely not that. He had hoped against hope that John Pepper had been delirious and didn't know what it was he spoke of. Black Jake had been hanged at Wickenburg. Or so he had always thought. And wasn't it just like that greasy, slick, slithering sonofabitch to slide out of the noose or ooze his way out of the grave?

"Go to hell," he said finally and the words were liberating.

"No way to speak to your father."

"You ain't no father of mine," Partridge said and meant it. "Not now, not ever."

Black Jake ran a strip of tongue over his flaking lips. A darkness settled over his face which belonged in a crypt or a jar, floating in murky liquid. "You were always a disappointment to me. You and my entire brood." He brought the Colt up and Partridge knew he was a dead man. You did not live through a blast from a .44 at close range and Black Jake was not a man who ever missed.

Partridge waited for it.

There was a gunshot, but it did not come from the Dragoon pistol. It came from behind Black Jake. It tore a hole through his belly and sprayed Partridge and Anna Marie with bits of his anatomy and a spray of blood. Black Jake looked into his son's eyes one last time and there was nothing in them but an unflinching, raw hatred. No sorrow. No love. No nothing. Flat and empty as the eyes of cottonmouth snake as it made to bite you. Another round blew his chest open and ripped his heart into shrapnel. He fell over, face-first at Partridge's feet.

Gibbons stood in the doorway, a .45 Peacemaker in one hand. "Well, pilgrim, being a guardian angel ain't quite what they say it is. Never did think us saints had to walk about strapping on shooting irons. But hell and high water, you learn something every day."

70

It was two days later when Partridge woke up.

He came awake in a bed in a dusty prospector's shack tucked away up in the hills. He came awake with a start, immediately going for his guns but they were gone. The dull ache in his shoulder and the not-so dull ache in his side put him right back down. It was night and Gibbons was feeding kindling into a pot-bellied stove in the corner. The valise full of money was at the end of his cot.

"Well, goddamn, Lazarus awakes," he said. He came over, eyes sparkling and mouth grinning with all those worn teeth. "Stay still now for the love of Jesus and his old lady or you'll tear all that fine stitching I laid into you. Yes, sir, pilgrim, I think I might have made a fair sawbones." He lifted the bandages at Partridge's shoulder. "Healing up just as cool and easy as a belt mark on the backside of a whore. Yes, sir. You were lucky, too, pilgrim. The bullet you ate passed clean through and didn't take too much meat with it. You'll mend, I figure, given time."

It all slowly came back to Partridge.

Black Jake. Gibbons gunning him down and doing the world a favor it could never hope to repay. Weak from the loss of blood, Gibbons helped him down the back stairway and into leather. The Egyptian Hotel was burning like a candle by then and the bucket brigades were hard at it. Anna Marie refused to leave. So they left her.

Partridge did not know if she got out and cared even less.

"Yup, you lost a good sight of the red stuff, but you'll pull through."

Partridge managed to swallow some beef broth and then he was out until the next day. He spent most of it laying in his cot, smoking and thinking and waiting for Gibbons to return. He finally did, late.

"Well, pilgrim, we're all provisioned up and ready."

Partridge just looked at him. "Where we going?"

"Well, we sure as hell can't stay here. That's for sure. Those man hunters are still crawling around like worms up a dog's ass. Nope, off we go. Tomorrow late, I think."

"Where to?"

"Ever been to Mexico?" Gibbons seemed excited at the idea. He sat on the bed and patted Partridge's arm. "I'm talking Sierra Madres, pilgrim. I hear tell when you get a dust storm up there you can shake a thousand in gold out of your curtains when it's done. You drink from those streams up there and you can piss straight gold into a cup. No shit, pilgrim, it's the truth."

Partridge touched his arm, gave it a squeeze. "You been awful good to me."

"Told you, I'm your goddamn guardian angel, didn't I? Now I know a village in the Madres, sits at the foot of an old Spanish mission, river running through it. Fruit trees and flowered fields. No one'll ever find you there. Yes, sir. I'll set you up with a big fat seniorita I know and make off for the hills. Time I get back you'll be married to one of her daughters—luscious as sweet grapes, too, I tell you—and you'll be fattening up like a king. They'll love you to death. And you know what, pilgrim?"

Partridge, awed by this man and his kinetic energy level, just stared.

"You might even learn how to smile decent down there, how to laugh and enjoy yourself."

Partridge figured it just might happen.

The next day they started for Mexico. They didn't make that little village for nearly three weeks. But it was just as Gibbons said, like maybe a piece of heaven had fallen to earth. And although Partridge lived a long life, he never once came back to the Territories. Nor wanted to.

--The End—

www.severedpress.com

www.ingramcontent.com/pod-product-compliance
Lightning Source LLC
Chambersburg PA
CBHW031328170626
46807CB00002B/609